# REECE

## A STUD RANCH STANDALONE NOVEL

## STASIA BLACK

# NEWSLETTER SIGN-UP

# 1

———————

MY HUSBAND SAT ACROSS FROM ME EATING THE DENVER OMELET I'D prepared for him while scrolling through his email on his phone with his thumb. Two slices of bacon crisped to perfection sat on a side plate, along with a piece of wheat bread, toasted to a light brown, one pat of butter right in the center. One glass of orange juice, one glass of water. His cup of coffee was in a to-go insulated mug. I'd warmed the cream in a water bath to make it the correct temperature so it didn't cool down the coffee—*not* microwaved. Jeff hated the taste of coffee with microwaved cream.

It all had to be done *just so.*

I'd taken extra care this morning to get everything perfect. All the while knowing that perfection didn't always mean safety.

If Jeff got an email he didn't like, or read something on the news that annoyed him... Well, there were a thousand variables I couldn't control.

A sick part of me sat in anticipation for his mood to turn. For that twitch in his eyes, the flare of his nostrils that meant the placid silence of the morning would turn on a dime to chaos and violence.

Jeff looked up at me sharply and frowned. "Why aren't you eating?"

Crap. I smiled, careful to keep my expression neutrally pleasant. "Just thinking about the day, darling. I need to take the dry-cleaning in today. I look forward to getting some sunshine. The rain's supposed to clear up later."

He frowned before glancing down at his phone. "No."

I blinked and swallowed, my fingers tightening in their grip on my fork and knife as I sliced into one of my two boiled eggs. All I was allowed for breakfast. "Oh? Would you prefer I went tomorrow?"

"I don't want my wife gallivanting all over town in a rainstorm, is that too much to ask? It's supposed to rain all week."

I demurely put the bite of tasteless boiled egg in my mouth. It would be pointless to mention that there was going to be a break in the weather this afternoon. Or that a little rain had never hurt anyone.

Jeff shoveled the rest of his breakfast in his mouth, standing up and grabbing his half-finished toast. Then he glared down at me. "You haven't taken your pills."

"Oh. Forgive me."

I grabbed the handful of pills from the little bowl he'd put them in beside my plate setting. Five pills. Three were anti-depressants. One was an anti-psychotic. The last was a tranquilizer.

I tossed them in my mouth, then took a swallow of water.

"Open," Jeff demanded.

I opened my mouth wide.

"Tongue."

I lifted my tongue to show there weren't any pills squirreled away underneath.

"Good girl." He picked up his briefcase from beside the door to the garage, then his coffee. He stood there waiting, and I scurried to do the expected.

I hurried to his side and kissed his cheek. He patted me on the backside, then looked at me meaningfully. "I expect dinner on the table at six sharp. I might be late, but I might not be. Either way, I expect the food to be hot, so keep it warm in case I'm late. But don't let it get rubbery. I hate that."

"Of course." I smiled. Pleasantly. Vacantly.

"Good girl."

"Have a good day at work, darling."

He ignored me, attention back on his phone as he pushed through the door to the garage and let it slam behind him.

I stayed still, my back ramrod straight, until I heard the garage door open and then shut again.

And then I ran to the bathroom and stuck my finger down my throat until I was choking up the pills. I counted, only breathing out in relief when I saw all five of them floating in the toilet.

I sat back on the cool tile as I flushed. Not for long, though. I got up and brushed my teeth. I was sure the enamel on my teeth was getting worn by this morning routine, but I didn't see any other way. Besides, it was a short-term fix. I'd only been doing it for eight months.

The withdrawal was a bitch, that was for damn sure.

I looked at myself in the mirror. Slim. Long blonde hair. Under thirty. The trophiest of trophy wives.

As long as you didn't look too closely at my wrists and the scars from the deep slashes there. Bruises could be hidden with concealer, but scars were more difficult. I wondered if any of our so-called "friends" ever wondered why I always wore long sleeves or else a watch and heavy bangles on my wrists, no matter the occasion. Then again, they didn't need to wonder. Jeff told anyone who would listen that I'd tried to kill myself. It fit well into the narrative he painted of me as mentally unstable and "fragile."

I'd been on the cocktail of pills ever since I'd made the attempt to exit this shit life six years ago. During the withdrawals last fall, I couldn't say I wasn't tempted to take the shortcut again. Jeff had finally allowed me to be around sharps again after year two out from The Incident. So I had access. I could have done it.

I wasn't sure exactly what I'd been planning the first day I threw up the pills after drinking just enough water to swallow them past my uvula and get them lodged in my throat. Well, the first time had been accident, but the day after it had been on purpose.

Before that, I hadn't felt much of anything at all for... years. I mean I still felt the pain when Jeff hit me. A slap was a slap and a broken bone was a broken bone, and it hurt. He never let me get numb enough not to feel the pain. What fun would that have been?

But the pills let me drift, pull apart from my body. It let the weeks drift into one another, and then become months, and then years were passing.

I was the broken, cowed thing Jeff had wanted from the beginning, and he reigned over me as Lord of the Manor.

And then one day, I stood at the kitchen doing dishes from breakfast and looking out the window, and there was a hummingbird buzzing around the tree that had just flowered outside.

I stopped, hands in the soapy water, and I watched it. It was beautiful, glorious, with wings flapping so fast I couldn't see anything but a blur as it moved from flower to flower. It had this amazing, iridescent breast of feathers. I was absolutely mesmerized.

I don't know how long I watched it... Before, all of the sudden, it zoomed straight into the window I was watching through with a loud *thump.*

I jumped and let out a little screech, horrified. And then I ran outside when I didn't see it fly back off again.

Only to find the back end of the bird sticking out the mouth of a neighborhood cat at the foot of my kitchen window.

"No!" I'd cried uselessly as the cat ran away with its catch.

I'd felt sick, and hurried back into the house, and I'd thrown up my breakfast.

And seen the pills I'd swallowed not fifteen minutes before. Some were half-digested, others were still in their bright capsule casings.

And it all felt so horrifying. What had happened to the bright bird. How quickly it went from flying free and glorious to becoming prey.

Jeff liked to talk about prey. He had a theory he liked to espouse that the world was full of predators and prey. He was a lawyer, a defense attorney, and he liked to think of himself as a predator who conquered the foolish and weak.

That he considered me one of the foolish and weak prey was a fact we both took for granted in this metaphor. He often talked about women as the weaker sex. When he was in a generous mood, he'd tell me patronizingly that it was good I had someone like him on my side, or else the world would eat me alive.

As if he hadn't been that cat waiting to devour me whole the moment I was vulnerable and stumbled across his path all those years ago.

The next morning, I'd shoved my fingers down my throat the moment he'd left for work, and every morning since.

Hurrying from the bathroom into the bedroom, I donned my gardening clothes and then I went into the backyard, grabbing my best hoe from the shed as I went.

It was raining and I was quickly soaked but I didn't care. I was operating on autopilot. If I thought too much about what I was doing, I might not have the nerve. And nerve was the only thing that was going to get me through this.

I'd almost gone twice last week. It had been sunny. There was no reason I shouldn't have done it then.

Except for the fact that I wimped out. Jeff had been in a good mood and I... I don't know what the hell I thought. But then one day, he came home and found me scrubbing the floorboards.

No wife of his should ever be on her knees. Except when he put me there, apparently, because the next thing he'd done was give me a swift kick in the back of my ribs.

Like I was a dog.

It hadn't escalated.

But I'd decided that was the last time he would ever kick me.

I was done.

So I dug into the wet, loamy soil. I dug and dug, one foot down, then another several inches. Until I came to the hard metal cash box. I pulled it up by its handle.

The rain continued to fall, making a mess of the mud and dirt. The box was waterproof, and everything inside double-bagged in ziplock bags, so I ran over to the hose off the side of the house and washed it clean of the clinging wet dirt.

My clothes and shoes were a mess by the time I ran to the back porch and rather than trying to clean them, I just kicked off my shoes and disrobed down to my underwear before stepping back into the house.

I moved fast now. If Jeff came home... The thought stopped my breath. There was almost a thousand dollars in the box, squirreled away bit by bit in varyingly daring bids to build a war chest. Plus other items that couldn't be easily explained away. Wigs, hair dye...

There was no reason for him to come home, though. I tried to breathe and think rationally.

Still, I got quickly ready, blowing out my hair again. I'd already had makeup on for breakfast—Jeff said he wanted to look at something pretty in the morning, that was how he put it, "something pretty," so I always woke up two hours before he did to get ready and make breakfast.

I pulled on a dress, the only sort of thing I really owned besides the gardening clothes.

Plus, putting on a show was important for this leg of the journey. I slid my feet into high heels. Then I shoved the bags from the cash box into some of Jeff's luggage, called for a taxi, and waited with bated breath in the foyer until the cab pulled up ten minutes later.

## 2

I HAD THE CABBIE DROP ME OFF AT A MOTEL HALF AN HOUR SOUTH. I waited for him to drive off before hurrying down to the nearest bus stop. Two local bus exchanges later, I was finally at the central Greyhound terminal in San Jose. Buses going all over the country departed from here.

My heartbeat thrummed a hundred miles a minute. Was Jeff onto me yet? Was he... *here*?

I swallowed hard as I waited in line and finally got to the front of the ticketing window. I was still wearing my Penelope Chambers disguise and the guy behind the counter perked up.

Penelope Chambers always turned heads. Jeff had crafted me into the perfect wife, after all. At least from afar. But I'd felt less and less connected to the caricature he'd crafted me into. Big blonde hair, tight dresses, high heels. I'm sure he would have had me get implants if I hadn't had C cups to start with.

I hadn't felt connected to this shell in a long time and now less so than ever. But it was useful. This one last time I had to be her. Perform her.

I didn't smile though.

There were cameras and this was a performance. Penelope Chambers was beautiful, but she was not brave. She was scared. Furtive.

Jeff would absolutely, one hundred percent be watching this video from their cameras at some point. This performance was all for him. As much as I hated it, this was who I want him to think he'd made me.

Cowering. Terrified.

Someone acting on fear and impulse who would be sloppy and not make it very far.

"C-could I please get a ticket to Chicago?" I asked. My voice was so quiet and tentative that the clerk had to ask me to repeat myself.

"Chicago. I- I'd like a ticket to Chicago please. Cash." I flattened a bunch of crumpled bills onto the counter, along with my ID.

Jeff liked to call me *mouse*. It fit well into his predator/prey worldview.

I was the food you fed to snakes, in his mind.

Who would I be after today? I had no freaking clue. Surviving this was all I could think about first.

The attendant handed me the ticket. "You have a nice day, Miss."

I dropped my head, hiding my face from him and any cameras pointed my way. And only then, curtained by my hair did I allow a small, secretly thrilled smile.

First part down. Holy shit, I was actually doing this. I erased the smile from my face and lifted my head back up. Okay, one last walk for the cameras.

My heartbeat, already ringing in my ears, got even louder and more frantic.

I moved with stately elegance toward the bathrooms. I swung my hips and held my head high. I walked like Penelope fucking Chambers.

Because although he made me weak and meek, he also demanded exacting standards when we were out in public, a wife who wouldn't 'embarrass him.' Mouse in the house but queen on the scene.

He wanted me to be more beautiful, more perfect and elegant and witty than any of his friend's or business partner's wives. Oh, he'd undermine me to those self-same wives to ensure I was always isolated, but he wanted their husbands to be envious of him.

And I paid an exacting punishment when I failed.

So I knew how to own a room. And when I walked, heads turned.

It was one last runway for Penelope Chambers.

May she rest in fucking peace.

And then I got to the bathroom and headed for the handicap stall. I was quick about it. Time was of the essence. I felt it counting down, a giant ticking clock hanging over my head like a proverbial sword.

I couldn't help feeling like I'd wasted too much time as it was. Frustrating, since I'd tried to plan everything to a T. I couldn't have the cab driver bring me directly here. Or maybe it was foolish, Jeff was going to find out where I was going eventually, but taking every last precaution to throw him off the scent seemed smart at the time. Even though I knew he'd always end up following every bread crumb. I just prayed time was on my side.

There was no point in second-guessing myself now, I could only march full steam ahead. He should still be at work, without even a clue I'd left the house. Everything had been normal. Yes, he'd had me followed for a couple of years after my last escape attempt, and again after the suicide attempt, but I hadn't noticed anyone tailing me for the last couple of years.

Everything was fine.

It was *fine*.

Still, I hurried as I shimmied out of the bandage dress one final time and pulled on a ratty pair of jeans. I smoothed my hair down as flat as it would go and nimbly braided the length of it, that I then pinned in a crown around my head. I'd watched this in a YouTube video at the library and practiced in the library bathroom, not daring to try at home.

Once it was pinned as flat as I could get it, I tucked a bit of panty-hose over top to keep it all down, then pulled on a brown chin-length hairpiece that helped change the shape of my face in appearance.

I'd practiced enough times to be able to do all this within five minutes, and a quick glance at my mp3 player showed I was keeping up with my best times. I'd left my phone at home and had picked up the mp3 player at a thrift store. I was so paranoid, I never even hooked it up to our wifi at home. I only charged it at coffeeshops or the library and hid it so Jeff never knew I had it.

I pulled on big, chunky glasses with fake lenses and used a wet wipe to scrub all the makeup off my face. Last, I slipped on what looked like a septum piercing in my nose. A big, baggy flannel shirt completed the look.

My old clothing and blonde wig all went back into a plastic bag, and finally, I pulled a wadded-up denim backpack out of the bottom of my purse. Last but not least were the Converse instead of the high heels. Then I shoved the purse, plastic bag, and all the rest into the backpack and slung it over my shoulders, hopefully completely transformed from the woman who'd walked into the bathroom.

I checked my watch. Okay. The eleven forty-five leaving for Seattle departed in fifteen minutes. I needed to move my ass.

I glanced under the stalls to check that no one was there, then hurried out.

As I came out of the bathroom, I made sure to alter my posture. No more Penelope Chambers, arm candy to the rich and powerful.

I kept my head down, hair swinging in my face, as I slouched out of the bathroom and pretended to be engrossed in a phone that was really just the cheap mp3 player.

Right now I wasn't listening to anything, it was just a prop. I never saw young people these days without their hands on their devices, and it was all about blending in.

I headed to a different ticketing kiosk.

"Where to?"

"Seattle," I say, head still down.

The attended looked bored, barely paying attention to me as he rattled off the amount and asked for ID.

Right. Here we go. This was where it could all go into the shitter.

I volunteered at a soup kitchen once a month—one of my few Jeff-approved outings. Charity work looked good for the little wife to be up to and all that.

And there was a girl who came in sometimes, especially towards the end of the month when her paycheck was running out.

She had short cropped brown hair with heavy bangs. Chunky glasses. A septum piercing. She was small in stature.

Our faces didn't look anything alike.

I paid her a hundred bucks for her ID anyway.

I pulled it out and laid it on the counter along with the money. Then I held my breath. Milliseconds stretch into eons. The sweat on my brow slipped down my forehead behind the bangs of the wig.

The ticketer took the money and barely even glanced at the ID before pushing it and the ticket back across the counter to me.

*Don't show your relief, don't show your relief.*

I mumbled something like, "Cool," before grabbing both and turning back into the crowd.

Right at the same time I heard a familiar voice call out, "Have you seen this woman?"

Shit! Shit shit *shit.*

It was Buchanan, Jeff's overly involved lead attorney and best friend. He who famously covered up, shut up, and otherwise took care of all of Jeff's dirty underhanded dealings that never saw the light of day.

Including *me* several times in the past, when Jeff went too far, and I was left bloody and broken enough to need a hospital.

Broken left orbital bone. Shattered ulna from the time Jeff hit my forearm with a baseball bat. The... *other time* that led to me slashing my wrists. Which he of course also cleaned up, seeing to my in-patient treatment, locking me away, and having them put me on suicide watch so I couldn't escape, even by death. He also made sure I was immediately put on the numbing drug cocktail so no one would believe anything I said, and yes, I did try.

I was diagnosed as being bipolar with schizoid episodes. And suicidal ideation, obviously.

I heaved for a breath that didn't come and turned away from where Buchanan was pushing through the crowd, showing his phone around, no doubt with my picture on it.

*He hasn't got you yet. You can still get out of this.* I stumbled through the crowd, clutching my ticket in my hand.

Away. I just had to get *away*.

I fought back the tears that threatened and bit the inside of my cheek as hard as I could. Fuck Buchanan, fuck Jeff.

I was here. I'd come this far.

Just get to the bus. Get to the *bus*.

I nodded to myself and then reminded myself to shuffle. I was a woman without a care in the world. I was just a normal millennial, barely out of college. Off to visit my sick aunt.

Even though it killed me, I slowed down instead of hurrying. I took my time and though every instinct in my body screamed for me to look over my shoulder to see how close the hunter that was stalking me was—

No.

That was the logic of a person who got themselves caught.

Not this time. Not this fucking time.

So I kept cruising forwards. It took me a panicked second, but I finally found the bus for Seattle. I didn't look over my shoulder as I climbed on. I didn't freeze up even though my feet felt like lead blocks. I kept myself fluid. Just like any other person. Visiting a sick aunt, visiting a sick aunt.

A couple peopled glanced up as I moved down the aisle and took a seat at the back, but only a couple. I wasn't Penelope Chambers, turning heads. I didn't sit by the window even though I preferred the window seat. Any barrier from Buchanan was good right now.

And I'd timed it well. It was only five minutes until we left.

Five horrifying, terrifying minutes where every muscle was rigid and me about sweat out my entire body weight, clutching my back-pack like it was a life preserver, but then—

The blessed noise of the door closing.

I collapsed, boneless, back against the seat in thanks as the bus pulled out of the depot, taking me away from Penelope Chambers, Jeff Chambers, and the prison I prayed I'd never, *ever* see again.

## 3

I WAS EXHAUSTED AFTER THREE DAYS ON THE ROAD.

From Seattle I'd headed across country to New York. I disappeared into the city for an afternoon, then got a cab down to New Jersey. At a gas station, I pulled out the electric clippers that were the last goody in my bag, slapped on an inch and a half guard, and cut off all my hair. Talk about liberating. I'd colored it a neutral brown and was happy to leave all the scratchy wigs behind forever.

Then I got back on the Greyhound and went down to Georgia.

Then to Missouri where I saw the big arch in St. Louis for the first time. I pressed my hand to the window glass as I passed, feeling like an alien passenger in my own body.

Every hour, every minute I was free felt...*impossible*.

I'd dreamed of this for so long, so single-mindedly. But now that I was finally doing it...well, it was beyond surreal.

I didn't know how to feel.

How to *be*.

I'd defined myself for a decade in terms of that prison, and of nursing whatever pain he'd most recently inflicted on me, and to keeping up the façade and trying *so* hard not to wake the beast inside him.

But now I was free to be just...*me* again.

Except I didn't remember how to be her. If I'd ever known her.

Who the *hell* was Not-Penelope-Chambers?

Over the endless hours as I watched the rolling scenery, I tried to remember the me I'd been before her. But when I tried to, it was a shock to think... maybe I'd never really known her—I mean, *myself*. I'd never really had the time to *find myself*, as it were.

But... not to know who you were, at your core... I mean, I *knew* crazy and that just felt plain crazy.

Before my marriage, I'd just gone from my mother's house to college. There had been a brief flare of phoenix-like color when I got to college as I'd begun the process of discovering myself. I *might* have gotten there.

Except that within a month, I'd met Jeff and he swallowed me whole before I ever had the chance to even think of flying.

And now?

It didn't feel like flying. More like I was one of those crippled birds with a sad, broken wing. How was I supposed to fly? I could barely crawl.

But—I sucked in a deep breath—I'd made it this far, right? I was here. And there. And everywhere. All at the same time. Living in the present and the past and still dreaming of a better future.

Except I just felt as unsettled as my roaming body.

The sun was long set as we pulled into a station in Oklahoma.

It was time for me to get off. This bus was headed back to California and that was one place I'd never go back to. No way, no how. Jeff had too much influence and he always would. My most impassioned prayer was that he'd look for me for a while, maybe six months? And then move on.

I bit my lip even as I wished it, gathering my backpack and pulling it on over my shoulders. Because I knew Jeff better than anyone else. I had no illusions that he loved me.

But he hated to lose. More than anything. An insult to his pride galled him like nothing else.

The thought of me of all people besting him, his prey, his *mouse*...

that would gall him until the end of his days. And that made me very afraid of what it might make him do. The extremes it might drive him to in order to find me.

I pulled my hoody up over my head to block my face from any cameras as I stepped down off the bus and made my way into the bus station.

It was cold and mostly empty inside. I pulled out the burner phone I'd bought in New York to check the time. It was eight at night.

I hadn't really checked ahead, and when I got inside, was dismayed to see there weren't any buses heading south until six a.m.

Looked like a night of sleeping in the *super* comfortable bus station chairs was ahead for me. Oh goody.

At least I was tired. I hadn't done much sleeping today in spite of the soothing rumble of the bus tires on the highway pavement.

A chatty woman had sat herself beside me, hellbent on telling me her whole life story. She talked for three hours straight without ever asking me a single question. Not that I minded, I didn't plan on answering any questions. Not honestly, anyway, but still. And her perfume was overly strong.

Thankfully, she'd gotten off in St. Louis but I hadn't been able to fall asleep since.

I found a spot by a plug and plugged in my burner phone that doubled as an mp3 player and FM radio, and settled in.

It charged fairly quickly while I people watched, and then I put my earbuds back in and listened to a couple of podcasts, settling my backpack in my lap and tucking my arms through the straps in case anyone tried to mess with it if I fell asleep.

Then I let my eyes finally settle shut.

The podcaster's voice droned soothingly and I drifted, and drifted, and *drifted*...

"Penelope, can you stay after class?"

I blinked and looked up from my paper. There was a bright C-scribbled on the top of it. My nose stung, which was stupid. It was stupid to feel so wounded over a grade. So what if I'd always gotten all A's in high school.

This was college, and of course I wouldn't ace every paper. It was just... I'd worked *really* hard on this one and thought I had done a good job.

The C- glaring at me said otherwise. C- was almost a *D*.

I nodded at the TA, Jeff Chambers, and my heartbeat started racing for entirely different reasons. He was beloved in the English department, and there'd been much ado about how this was the last class he'd be TA'ing for before switching to his law degree full time. He was already taking classes for it and there was hubbub about how everyone in *that* department expected great things from him too.

*This* was the person who'd graded *my* paper. And now he wanted to see me after class. It couldn't be for anything good, and yet being singled out by him still made me feel special and brought a flush to my cheeks. Which was even more ridiculous. He was going to chew me out for how bad my paper was and here I was blushing because he was so handsome and all the freshman girls had a crush on him, a graduate student.

I hurried down the row of desks to where he sat typing away on his laptop by the lectern.

"Just a moment," he said, not looking up from his task as everyone else filed out of the room. I was the only one he'd asked to stay behind. I stood, nervous, trying not to shuffle back and forth from one foot to the other.

Five minutes of waiting, after everyone else was gone, he finally closed the lid of his laptop and looked up at me.

"Have a seat," he said, gesturing toward the front row of chairs.

I did. "What's this about?" I asked.

He frowned and brought his hands together, one rubbing the fist of the other. "I'm not sure how to put this delicately," he said slowly. "Your paper was..."

I found myself leaning forward on the edge of my seat waiting for what he was going to say.

"It was not well-argued. And frankly, doing a feminist reading of Hemingway is far from original."

His words felt like a blow. I thought I'd put forth a considered and well-supported case for a feminist reading of Hemingway's short stories. But I didn't know how to articulate that without sounding stupid in front of this intellectual giant. "So... I take it that it isn't?"

He smiled at me like I was especially amusing. "No." He reached forward and took the paper I was still so sweatily grasping and flipped several pages. "While I appreciate your empathy for the girl in Hills Like White Elephants, it's not grounded in textual evidence."

"Oh." I sat there wanting the ground to swallow me up. I'd worked hard on the paper, and it was true, I *had* felt empathy for the girl in that story, faced with the callous American demanding she get an abortion.

"Hey," said Jeff, reaching out and putting a hand on my knee, just the quickest touch before removing it. It was just friendly, nothing more, I told myself. "But if you want, I am offering tutoring sessions. There's a group that meets at my house on Tuesdays. You're welcome to come."

I smiled, feeling lit up from his attention. "Really? That'd be great. I want to get my Master's in Literature so it means so much to me to do well in this class."

He smiled back at me, a really warm smile that made him look even more handsome. "Here, I'll write down the address for you, then." He took my paper from me, flipped it over, and scribbled his address on the back. "Tuesday at seven. Don't be late."

"I won't be," I gushed. "Promise."

"Good girl."

I woke with a start, Jeff's, "*Good girl*" still ringing in my ears, and waves of revulsion shuddering through my body.

Only to sit up with a start because oh shit.

No.

No no no no!

My backpack was gone.

I picked up the straps that were still wound in between my arms and looked in horrified disbelief at the ends that had been shorn clean through.

Someone had cut them while I slept and stolen the backpack right off me.

Son of a bitch!

I jumped to my feet and looked left and right, but whoever had done it was long gone. I'd been dead asleep for who knew how long after the days on the road, even in the uncomfortable bus station plastic chair.

Oh shit.

My hands went uselessly to my head as I looked back and forth from one end of the bus depot to the other.

My backpack had everything in it. My possessions. My *money*. Oh shit, it had my money. I raked my hands through my short hair.

I was so fucked.

I'd thought about getting one of those travel money belts that fit underneath your clothes, but in the end I hadn't done it. I didn't think I'd—

I threw the useless straps to the floor and fought angry tears that flooded my eyes.

To get so far and now to lose everything! What the hell was I going to do?! That backpack had everything. Even my tampons because my period was going to start next week. Shit! Shit shit shit shit!

"Do you have a ticket?" asked a voice from behind me. "You can't be here overnight in the station unless you have a ticket for a morning bus."

I spun around to see a guard eyeing me suspiciously.

"Yes. I mean, yes, I'm going to get on a bus in the morning."

"Can I see your ticket?"

Shit. "It was too late when I got in. The ticket booth was closed. But I'll buy a ticket first thing when it opens again." Ha. With what money? Was I going to panhandle?

The guard frowned. "I'm gonna need to see some ID then."

I blanched and the guard wasn't an idiot. Neither was he moved when I tried to explain what had happened, even as I showed him the cut straps of my backpack.

"You need to exit the station or I'll escort you out."

"Well, you see, it's a funny story. See these straps? I was robbed. Just now!"

The guard stood stoically, not seeming moved by my explanations and I couldn't help getting frustrated. "You're a guard on duty. Where were you when the thieves were stealing all my earthly possessions? Don't you have cameras in this place? It should be caught on camera."

But even as I heard myself say it, I got to my feet. "You know what, never mind. I'm out of here."

Because was I really sitting here drawing so much attention to myself and even demanding we look at taped *footage* of me? Jesus, this was a red flag and the exact *opposite* of everything I'd promised myself I would do on this journey. I was meant to fade into the background, be completely inconspicuous so that no one would remember me or be able to describe me in case any of Jeff's minions came looking.

I threw the stupid backpack straps into the trash and then stalked out of the station and into the cold February air of Oklahoma City.

A bold move considering I had nowhere to go and no idea what the hell I was going to do now.

All I had were the jeans, t-shirt, Converse, and oversized hoody I was wearing. Oh, and my socks, I also had my socks. And some chapstick I'd shoved in my pocket.

I wanted to beat myself over the head. What had I been thinking keeping my little clutch wallet in my *backpack*???

Dear God, it was an amateur mistake and now...

Now I was wandering downtown Oklahoma City with no plan, no money, shivering my ass off while I waited for sunrise.

---

I DID the only thing I could think of.

I couldn't risk staying in Oklahoma City. Not after the run-in with the security guard at the station. Was it paranoid of me? Sure.

But the last time I'd run away, I'd made it to Portland and what had led Jeff to me was a goddamned cab driver whom Jeff's private detective had interviewed—the guy who'd picked me up from the bus station.

I'd only been there a week before Jeff showed up, and dear God had he made me live to regret it.

I hadn't been able to eat solid food for a month. He told all our friends that I was "having some work done."

It fit the narrative he always painted of me as being superfluous, over-concerned with my looks, and dramatic to the point of mentally unstable if I didn't get what I wanted.

Besides, in this case it was true, I did have a nose job. Because he'd broken the damn thing and it would be too conspicuous to leave it that way. He told the plastic surgeon I'd fallen down the stairs. Bastard couldn't even get original. The plastic surgeon just nodded along and told me he could do a procedure to deal with the bags underneath my eyes, too, if I *really* wanted to keep a youthful glow.

I was twenty-four at the time.

I did not kick the man's balls in, but I'd dearly wanted to.

So no, I couldn't stay here, but I didn't have any money to get to a more final landing place. I'd been hoping to make my way to Austin. It might still be in the South, but it was supposed to be liberal there, and it had a great music scene.

I had this dream of myself where I was the modern version of a hippie. I'd get some tattoos. Go to concerts. Maybe I'd work at a coffee shop. I'd finally reclaim my body as *mine*, and just enjoy some easy living, drifting along.

Drifting along sounded *lovely*. Maybe get some friends who were the genuine kind, and read books, and watch bad reality tv—the kind that Jeff hated—and I'd learn how to just *be*.

Not exactly a grandiose dream, but one that was mine.

Except that I was stuck in freaking Oklahoma City with no funds and not even a change of clothes! Not exactly an ideal place to start this theoretical new life from.

So I did the only thing I could think of. I started walking. I popped in a gas station that was open 24 hours and asked where the big highway was—I 35—and I walked towards it. Turned out I was in luck. It was just a thirty-minute walk away since the Greyhound station was so centrally located.

Then I found another gas station that serviced big rigs, and I did what I figured was either really stupid or really smart.

I asked around for anyone headed south.

"Girl, you stupid or somethin'?" asked a Latina woman of indeterminate age. Well, I guess that clarified the stupid question.

The woman was maybe in her fifties...or maybe a decade older or younger, it was hard to tell. She was wide set, wearing a flannel shirt, with long braided hair coming out the hole in the back of a trucker's hat.

I squared my shoulders and looked her in the eye. "No ma'am. Not stupid, just desperate. All my stuff got stolen but I've got to get to Austin."

She shook her head at me. "Kids these days."

I didn't correct her that I was hardly a kid at twenty-nine, especially since it seemed like she was considering giving me a ride.

"Well, come on, then," she said. "I'm only going as far as Dallas, but you're welcome along. I could do with some company to keep me awake."

I grinned. "I'm great company."

She huffed a noise of disbelief and checked out with her giant cup of coffee and donuts.

I couldn't believe hitchhiking actually worked! But we had a great morning driving south. Mostly me asking her for stories about her life, and her telling me long spiels.

It was a gift I had. I could usually get people talking. I was a good listener, and was usually interested in what people had to say.

It was also one of my downfalls. Because, say with someone like Jeff who loved to hear the sound of his own voice, a person like me was catnip to him.

At that first Tuesday tutoring session, he'd gone on and on about Hemingway's genius and I'd soaked it up along with all the other students he'd invited. I never once questioned or considered the fact that he'd only invited the type who didn't challenge him and were more likely to think him a god.

And that most of us were women. It was five women and only two guys at that first Tuesday study group. As I became more a part of what I would later realize was a cult of personality Jeff fostered around himself, well yes, it was impossible to *not* notice they were mostly women.

But I told myself we all just flocked to him because he was good looking and charismatic. And smart and gregarious and amazing. I waxed just as poetic as any of them about how wondrous he was.

And it made me feel even more important when, after the first few tutoring nights, it was *me* he chose to talk to long after the sessions had ended. *Me* who he asked on a date. *Me* who he said understood him more deeply than anyone ever had before. *Me*, who, three weeks after meeting, he declared was his soulmate.

I bought it all hook, line, and sinker, because it was everything I'd always wanted to ever hear.

But a man like Jeff knew that. And so he said the words meant to entice me into his trap like a hunter laying out crumbs to entice prey. And like a foolish, foolish little lamb, I walked right into the maw of the wolf.

I thanked Ana and got off at another gas station in Dallas.

"Don't go getting in just anyone's rig now," she warned me. "You seem like a decent girl. Good luck to you. And don't go telling folks you're desperate."

I nodded. "Thanks again. You were a lifesaver."

She waved me off, then I climbed out of the cab and watched as she drove off.

Leaving me once again, all alone. And hungry. Ana had shared her donuts with me, but that was hours ago.

I held my hand over my eyes and squinted up at the sky. It was warmer here in Dallas than in Oklahoma, and I hoped the further I headed south, the warmer it would get still.

As much as I liked the idea of snow—it seemed picturesque to be sipping cocoa or coffee while it drifted down outside, I was a sunshine-worshipper at heart. Texas sounded just right to me if I couldn't have California.

The last few years, I asked Jeff if we could move somewhere where it snowed. I bought snow globes. I took up painting for a few months and painted wintry landscapes. They weren't good, but I was just learning. Jeff made fun of them ruthlessly and threw them out one day after we'd gotten into an 'argument'—his word for when he would hit me. When I woke up the next morning, all the supplies were gone.

Everything I did over the last half decade was so I could escape again, and escape for good, somewhere he'd never find me.

Austin seemed as good a place as any.

So in spite of Ana's advice, I figured I'd continue hitchhiking.

I stood outside the gas station where all the big rigs were gassing up and asked around if anyone was headed south.

One big-bellied guy leered at me. "Yeah, baby, I'll take you as far as you wanna go."

"No thanks," I said and hurried back inside. I hid for half an hour and when I went back out, he was thankfully gone.

I tried again for a few hours and finally found an older man who was rail thin and had the kind of leathery, age-spotted skin of someone who didn't take SPF seriously. If worst came to worst, I figured I could take him.

Unbeknownst to Jeff, I'd taken a self-defense class. Instead of going to Pilates like I was supposed to, I'd snuck away and attended the self-defense class down the hall that met at the same time. I hadn't really thought I'd ever be able to use the moves against Jeff.

If I fought back, he took it as an affront against God and nature and would punish me twice as hard.

Taking the class was just one of my small rebellions. One of the ways I tried to fight back, to begin to feel strong. That if I ever did manage to escape Jeff, maybe one day I could stand on my own two feet again.

Either way, it was enough to climb up into Rick's rig, who'd nodded when I'd asked a group of truckers smoking outside the travel gas station.

"I'm goin' south. I'm Rick. I'll take ya," he'd said, then thrown his cigarette on the pavement and stomped it out with his boot.

He was old, wiry, and also wearing flannel, though he had the arms cut off at the shoulders, exposing thin, sinewed arms.

I took one look at the rest of the truckers who were looking me up and down, shivered, and scurried after Rick.

The smell of body odor and cigarette smoke competed for dominance in the cab of his rig, but I decided beggars couldn't be choosers. I put on my seatbelt and was glad when he reached out with a gnarled hand and cranked up the radio station. Country, naturally.

He seemed to have no interest in talking and that was absolutely *fine* by me.

The next few hours passed in silence as we drove south. He'd occasionally open the window, light a cigarette, and smoke several in a row, taking in long, slow draws of smoke as he drove lazily with one hand.

It didn't seem the safest way to be hauling what was I'm sure several tons of weight, but considering his age, I supposed he knew what he was doing?

He'd only occasionally bang on his horn and cuss other drivers out. Never once looking my direction or even acknowledging I was in the cab with him.

It was certainly strange, but not altogether the worst thing I'd ever experienced, and I was just happy to see the mile markers passing indicating that we were, indeed, getting closer to Austin.

We hit some traffic and it was slow going for a few hours. The sun passed overhead and started on its way toward the horizon. Rick's cussing at traffic increased in direct proportion the slower traffic crawled. As did his cigarette consumption.

Since we were all but stopped in traffic several times, the smoke built up in the cab and I couldn't help coughing, but other than glancing my way a couple times—the most Rick had acknowledged me since I'd climbed aboard, he didn't say a thing to me.

Then, about sixty miles from Austin, he got off of I35 and took a smaller highway. I frowned and looked behind us at the much larger highway we were leaving behind.

"Where are we going?" I asked, a little twinge of anxiety lighting in my stomach. More than a twinge.

Rich waved a hand, lit cigarette between two fingers. "Short cut with no traffic."

He didn't seem interested in saying more and I didn't ask. If he knew a shortcut around traffic, I wasn't going to complain. Especially since we were so close to my destination. Whenever he next stopped, I'd get the hell out of this cab and rethink this whole idea.

Except the signs no longer mentioned Austin, and I kept my eyes peeled for every one of them.

Instead of getting to Austin an hour later, we'd arrived in a town called Burnet. And it was definitely a *town*, not a city. The road we'd been on had officially been *labeled* a state highway, but at times gone down to a single lane and the scenery, while pretty, was far more secluded than I was comfortable with.

As the small town of Burnett passed by, I spoke up nervously. "Could we stop? I need to use the restroom."

"Shoulda thoughta that back in Dallas," was all Rick said.

We'd turned onto another highway as we cruised through the town and that was when I finally saw another sign for Austin. Which said it was 55 miles away.

We'd taken a huge detour *out* of our way, *not* a shortcut. What the hell? This was not good. Very not good.

I thought about opening up the door and jumping out but we'd passed the town and Rick was speeding the truck back up to fifty miles an hour again.

Shit.

*No, stop it.* I was overreacting. Rick was not Jeff. Not every man in the world was out to get me, or wanted to hurt women. Sure Rick was an anti-social dude, but that didn't make him bad.

Still, I swallowed hard. Because the sun was setting now. It made for a lovely sunset. The Texas sky was splashed with color, neon oranges and pinks, with deeper blues and purples at the edges.

But all I could think was that meant it would soon be dark and I was in a truck with a strange man taking me God knew where.

*He's just anti-social. Not every man is Jeff.* Over and over again, that was what I told myself, for the next fifteen minutes anyway.

Until it was full dark and the big rig started slowing down on an especially lonely stretch of highway.

Rick pulled off on an even smaller road and I managed to get words out through my incredibly dry throat. "Um. Where are we going?"

He didn't answer, just kept on driving.

Okay, screw this. Screw being polite. I was freaked the hell out. I'd had enough.

"Look, I really appreciate you driving me this far. You're a life-saver. But if you can just stop, I'll get out here. Thanks again, so much."

I started undoing my seatbelt and that's when his hand suddenly came flashing out of nowhere through the dark cab, slamming into my torso and keeping me in place.

"Where do you think you're going? You gotta pay up for the ride. It's cash, gas, or ass, and we both knew it when you climbed in my rig."

# 4

For a second I was just shocked. I couldn't believe this was actually happening.

Then his hand holding me down started groping me and I *absolutely* could believe it.

And then I wanted to laugh at myself for being shocked. Of course this was happening to me right now. Didn't I know better? Did I actually think it was just Jeff who was the scum of the earth? Why didn't I think that all men, given the chance, would turn into animals?

Rick undid his seatbelt and I could tell he was about to lunge for me.

For a second I froze.

It was just like when I knew I was about to get it from Jeff. I had that trapped animal feeling of knowing there was no escape. The horror of knowing a beating was coming, of knowing this time he might take it too far, *this* time I might die.

But the instant I heard the click of the seatbelt undoing, I shook my head and shouted at the top of my lungs, just like we did at the self-defense class, "NOOOOO!"

I shouted it so loudly and so suddenly that Jeff— No, Rick, *Rick,* jumped back from me, and I took that moment to shove against the door with all my weight and throw it open.

I all but fell out of the big rig cab as I scrambled down to the ground. I dangled by one hand, bearing my weight on the door while I got my footing.

"You fucking bitch, get back here," Rich shouted, and that was enough to have me dropping to the ground.

I landed on my knees but I was scrambling back to my feet quick enough. And then I did what they told us constantly to do in the class if we ever got in a situation like this.

I *ran*.

I didn't even consciously pick a direction. It was dark, I ran. I took off in the direction I was facing as soon as I'd gotten to my feet.

I didn't even look behind me to see if he was chasing. I just freaking ran with every ounce of energy I had. I came to a metal gate in the darkness. I climbed it like a ladder, hiked a leg over the top of it, then jumped down on the other side and kept running.

Past the gate was a dirt road, not paved anymore, but I still just kept running.

Thank God for the stupid treadmill Jeff bought me years ago. He wanted his wife to be perfectly toned, so any time I wasn't suffering from a Jeff-inflicted injury that interfered, he had a strict 'training schedule.' That was what he called it. In reality, it was just another mechanism for control, but goddammit, I was glad for it now, because it meant I had stamina.

When I finally looked behind me after running for a good fifteen minutes, there was no one there.

Just a full moon that provided *just* enough light to make out a dirt road and wilderness prairie grass on all sides. And me. That was it.

Which was when it hit me. Maybe running into the wild wasn't exactly the brightest idea if Rick had a sadistic penchant for hunting down girls.

Just the thought sent chills down my spine and I took off again in the direction I'd been running. If there was a road, surely it had to lead somewhere, right? Someplace I could hide out for the night and wait out Texas Chainsaw Massacre truck driver?

I tried to take in calming breaths. It was much more likely he was the more mundane type of monster who wanted to avoid cardio as much as the next guy. He was likely already back on the highway. I could only pray.

But I wasn't a girl to take chances. I was all done doing this risky shit. I'd used up my lifetime's allotment, I decided right here and now. Getting the hell away from Jeff and getting here, wherever here was.

Embracing paranoia was going to be my new plan from here on out. Paranoia and low-risk living.

So I ran. Run, rabbit, run. Run, little mouse. I ran and then ran more. When I developed a crick in my side, I just held it with one hand and kept going.

And then, finally, like a lighthouse in the fog, I saw a break in the darkness up ahead. Light meant people, right? I laughed and staggered towards it. I looked over my shoulder and it still seemed clear. I couldn't imagine that Deliverance truck driver could have run as fast or for as long as I had, but I decided it would be stupid to slow down right at the end. Paranoia was my new best friend. So I kept up my giddyup until I'd made it to the driveway of a big, two-story ranch house with a wraparound porch. Light poured from a couple of rooms downstairs and I stumbled as I headed towards the porch stairs.

Which was when I heard a male voice call out, "Ruth, is that you?"

I froze. Shit, was that Rick? But when I looked, instead I saw a man with a ten-gallon hat walking with a flashlight up to a fence on the far side of the house. I doubted Rick could have circled around in front of me. Or found a cowboy hat out of the blue.

And as the man approached, I could hear tinny music coming from what I assumed was his phone, blaring out country music. I immediately stiffened, considering I'd been subjected to similar music all damn day.

But it wasn't Rick, that was clear. For one thing, this guy was big.

He had massive shoulders. This was not a point in his favor, whoever he was.

"Thank God, Ruth," he said. "This heifer's having trouble. I've been waiting for you or Jer to get back."

I immediately started backing away as he approached the fence. A few wooden posts between us did not a solid barrier make.

"She's been in labor for two hours and oh—" He stopped mid-sentence, holding up his lantern flashlight and squinting, I assumed to get a better look at me. "You're not Ruth."

I shook my head. No, I wasn't, but I was very interested to know where this mysterious Ruth was. I'd feel much, much better with a woman around, that was for damn sure.

Behind the giant came the noise of cows mooing and what sounded like a fence rattling or the metal of a gate.

The giant looked over his shoulder.

"Son of a bitch," he said, head swinging back to the dark pasture. "She's not happy. I wouldn't be either if I had a breech calf half sticking out of me. Dammit, Jeremiah's gonna kill me if I screw up the first calving of the season."

He looked back my way. "Don't suppose you're good with grouchy heifers having breech calves?"

I held up my hands. "I'm more of a city girl. Look, my ride... uh, broke down. I'm just looking for a..." What could I say? I needed more than just a phone call.

"Oh," he said, his eyes going wide. "Oh. Sorry. I just figured you maybe lived here with Ruth. Jer and I, I mean Jeremiah. He's my brother. We just got here today, too, to work the ranch. I mean to manage it. We're the new managers. But we're getting here right at the start of calving season and you know how crazy that can be."

I lifted my shoulders, along with my eyebrows. "It's a... big deal?"

He huffed out a laugh, then dragged a hand down the back of his neck. "Yeah, you could say that. And my brother's gonna kill me if I don't do right by this heifer."

"Say," he looked back into the darkness and then to me again. "I know this is a big ask, but I gotta get this lady in the chute and pull this calf or it's not gonna have any chance at all. Could you help me? My brother and Ruth are out wrangling a bunch of cattle that got out 'cause of some downed fencing. Basically we got here and everything was less in order than we'd been led to believe. It's all been kinds of a huge mess."

His words immediately set me on edge. Was he really inviting me into the dark pasture with him while no one else was around?

And I'd stupidly gone and admitted I was all alone and didn't have a ride.

I backed away a step and the expression on his open, friendly face changed to one of chagrin.

"Shit," he said, "I don't know what I was thinking. You don't know me."

He pulled off his hat, ran his hand through his hair, then stuffed his hat back on his head. "Look, why don't you go wait inside? There's a phone in there you can feel free to use. Or if you want to wait on the porch—if that feels more comfortable... Again, feel free. I know it's freezing out here, but hopefully Ruth will be back in soon. She'll be happy to help you out, I'm sure."

He took a step backwards, then cocked his head to the side. "Well, actually I don't know her that well, but my brother and I can make sure you're looked after and Ruth will at least be there to hopefully make you feel more at ease. Officially she still owns the house but we run the rest of the ranch so I'm sure we can make arrangements for you—"

He broke off and waved a hand with a short laugh. "Sorry, you don't need a novel. If you'll excuse me, I've gotta go deal with this grouchy heifer and see if I can't help her get her baby born. Good to meet you. I'm Reece, by the way."

He nodded to me, reached up and tipped his hat just the tiniest bit, then turned around and headed back into the pasture. The light from his flashlight bounced through the darkness as he went.

During his entire monologue I'd stood stiff as a statue, unsure what to say or do.

As he retreated, I stayed put, then after a few seconds, walked closer to the fence line. And then watched from a distance as he approached a cow that did indeed look agitated.

I couldn't hear everything he was saying since he was half a pasture away, just the occasional, "Come on now, mama."

The cow would buck or rear and Reece would scramble backwards, hands out. Obviously, he was trying to urge her in some particular direction, but she'd break and jog back and forth, so he'd back up and start all over again.

My mouth dropped open when during one of these lumbering jaunts, I caught a glimpse of small hooves sticking out the back end of the cow in the light of the flashlight.

Oh my God, he wasn't joking! That cow was literally mid-labor.

Now that I knew he wasn't pulling some sort of creepy redneck Ted Bundy come-help-my-injured-cow act to lure me into the dark, I scrambled into action. I had no clue if it was ill-advised or not, but I'd always had a soft spot for animals. I ignored the voice that was screaming that my whole new paranoia-approach-to-life oath had lasted all of five minutes. This was the *one* exemption, I decided as I climbed the gate of the fence and lowered myself over the other side. Because God, it had to be true. Not *all* men were Jeffs.

Still, I approached slowly. "How can I help?"

Reece's head swung my way in surprise, then a grateful smile lit his face.

"We gotta get her through that gate over there. Can you go open it and try to keep any of the other heifers from going through? Then I'll try to drive her your direction. Just stay clear when she gets close. Got it? She's upset and probably in plenty of discomfort. We gotta get this calf out of her pronto, but she doesn't understand we're trying to help and she could hurt us in the process."

I nodded. "Got it loud and clear."

I hurried over to the gate he indicated. It took me a second to figure out the latch system in the dark. The full moon helped.

I felt a rush of adrenaline once I got it open and flung it wide. My presence had disturbed the other cows in the pasture but luckily, none of them were too close.

Then Reece got behind the laboring cow and started clapping his hands and making a ruckus. The cow trotted away from him, coming straight my direction.

I got the hell out of the way, backing into the pasture and out of the way of the chute the gate opened into.

I wasn't exactly sure how my day had turned around from fleeing dirty old truck drivers to fleeing from angry cow mothers, but hey, who said life wasn't completely ludicrous sometimes?

"There you go, mama! That's right!" Reece called from behind her.

She ran straight through the open gate and through into the corral lane. Reece followed fearlessly behind her, even though she was not happy to find herself in a narrower, more confined space.

"Keep going, don't stop, mama," Reece said, continuing to clap. "On into the barn we go." Then to me over his shoulder, he called, "Close the gate up behind us, then follow outside the fence to the barn if you still wanna help."

I hurriedly closed the gate the same way I'd opened it. Reece and the cow were already moving down the corral lane towards the big barn that loomed in the distance.

I moved faster than I would have thought possible after the day I'd had and no real sustenance. But somehow the mother cow's drama seemed more pressing than mine.

I climbed the fence and then ran along the short, penned corral to the barn where Reece was trying to coerce the upset cow to go where he wanted her.

"Come on, mama. No, Jesus, don't charge me, dammit! Just go in the—"

By the time I got over the corral fencing again, I saw the cow had Reece cornered in one area of the barn.

Reece scrambled up on top of a tractor right as the cow charged towards him, hat flying off as he went. The cow trampled the spot where he'd just been standing, demolishing his hat. "Well, that was just uncalled for!" he said, flinging out an arm towards the cow. "That was my favorite."

I wasn't sure exactly what a 'chute' was, but a good guess said it was the big contraption with lots of metal bars the size of cow on the opposite side of the barn from where Reece and the cow were tangling.

"How can I help?" I asked.

Reece looked my way. "Oh shit. Get outta here. She's too unstable."

The cow's head swung my way. She took several steps toward me across the barn.

"Hi, pretty mama cow?" I said uncertainly, taking a few steps backwards.

She mooed angrily in my direction and stomped more steps towards me.

Reece took the few moments of distraction to leap down from the tractor. "In you go, Mama," he said, shoving on her backside, then quickly dancing out of the way when she bucked with her back legs. But she did run forward—right into the chute.

Reece again moved quickly, faster than I would have thought possible. He locked in the bar behind her back legs and then closed the front of the chute bars around her neck to hold her in place.

His whole body slumped backwards after he got her locked in. The cow rammed back and forth in the chute, but was finally caught safe.

"Oh my God, are you okay?" I asked, running forwards towards Reece. I didn't know the guy, but that was just— He'd almost been *trampled by a cow.*

Reece just sucked in a big breath and nodded. Then he said, "Okay, now we gotta get the calf out of her."

Whoa, damn. I looked back at the cow in the chute, feeling my eyes go big. I'd been so concerned with catching the angry runaway cow, I'd all but forgotten about the reason we were trying to corral her in the first place.

"Do we call a vet?"

Reece had the flashlight up and was already yanking open cabinets and sorting through stuff on the shelves on the sturdiest of the barn's walls. "Don't I wish," he said.

Then he must have found whatever he was looking for because he rushed back.

My mouth dropped open when I saw that he was holding a small length of *chain*. I backed away. "What are you going to do with *that*?"

"Pull the calf," he said, not looking my direction. He was too intent on his task. "Can you hold this?" He shoved the flashlight at me. "Keep it pointed at the birth canal."

I grabbed it because he was letting it go and moving on whether I was ready or not. I held the heavy flashlight and tried to keep it steady as he wrapped the chain in small loops around the two hooved legs that were extending out the back end of the mother cow.

And then he did exactly what he'd described. He started *pulling* on the chains, literally yanking the calf out of its mother.

"Push, mama," he said, as if the mother could understand any of what he was saying. Whether or not the cow was pushing, Reece was definitely pulling. Pulling so hard his muscles strained against his flannel shirt.

It was cold outside, but after a few minutes of pulling, sweat beaded on his forehead. The calf had slid a few inches out, but if Reece's occasional slipped swear words were any indication, it wasn't going as smoothly as he hoped.

"Dammit, we're gonna need the big calf-puller. Can you hold this so it doesn't slip back inside?"

Oh crap, he was talking to me?

"Uh, okay."

He'd hooked a handle onto the chains and we did the most awkward handoff. "Just keep pulling," he instructed. "Don't let it slip back in."

Great. No pressure. I dug my feet into the dirt that made up the ground of the barn and pulled as hard as I could to keep up the pressure of pulling that Reece had started while he disappeared into the darkness.

The mother cow was no less restless now that we were yanking a calf from her womb, the poor calf straddled half-in, half-out.

"How long can the calf last like this?" I asked. "Isn't this bad for it?"

"Sorry, I should have told you. It's probably already gone. To be breech for that long, there's not much hope. But we've got to get it out to save the mother."

His words hit me like a brick to the face. *It's probably already gone.*

I didn't stop pulling, though. It was just a cow, I tried to remind myself. A commonplace enough tragedy.

Still, there were stupid tears in my eyes by the time Reece got back with a contraption even more medieval than the chains.

It was a long pole with a T shape on the end that he braced against the back end of the cow. Then he attached a crank to the handle of the pull chains. Instead of us pulling, he turned the crank. Braced against the back of the cow's behind and legs, it had far more pulling power than either of us.

And inch by inch, the calf emerged from its mother.

Finally, in one last *whoosh*, the calf came all the way out and fell in one slippery plop onto the floor of the barn enclosure.

Reece immediately tossed the calf-puller pole down and leaned down. Then he let out a little whoop. "It's alive. Holy shit, I can't believe it. Little guy's actually alive!"

"Oh my God, really?"

I couldn't tell, it was lying limp on the ground. I leaned down, aiming the flashlight closer.

But Reece was getting right in there, sticking his fingers in the little calf's mouth, checking its airways were clear, I assumed. And indeed, little eyes blinked open against the light, befuddled.

The animal was wet and slick with blood and afterbirth, and then the wet had gotten dirty and muddy from the floor, but it was also one of the most amazing things I'd ever seen in my entire life.

I'd just witnessed the birth of *life*.

"What now?" I asked excitedly. "Will it nurse?" I looked back up at its mother who was still banging against the chute agitatedly. Maybe she was just trying to get to her new baby?

"First let's get them both out of here into the yard," Reece said. "It's cold out there but maybe if we give them some space Mama will clean..." Reece lifted one of the baby's legs, "*her* off and she can get to nursing like any other calf."

Reece tried to pick the little calf up to see if she would stand on her legs, but she just immediately collapsed right back into the dirt. "Come on, little lady," Reece said.

Then he lifted it into his arms like it was nothing, even though the calf had to weigh at least sixty pounds, probably more, and carried it towards the other end of the barn that opened to another much smaller pasture, more just a small yard.

He set the calf down and tried to get it to stand but it immediately crumpled back to the ground again. "Hmm," he said.

"What? Don't all baby calves take a while to figure out walking?"

He shook his head. "Calves should be able to do it right after birth. Or at least within a few hours. Let's bring Mom out here and see if she'll clean her off and bond with her at least."

Reece made me climb outside of the fence while he let out the mother, which I took to be responsible of him considering that the mother didn't seem any less agitated once she was free again.

She certainly didn't seem to be interested in the new baby we'd just pulled out of her.

Reece kept trying to entice her to take notice of her newborn, but she'd just charge right past the baby, looking for the exit of the yard back out into the bigger pasture.

Finally Reece climbed over the fence where I was. "Maybe it's just cause I'm here. We'll give her twenty minutes to figure it out for herself."

"What happens if she doesn't?"

Reece's mouth flattened into a hard line. "Well, then my brother will be pissed at me and we'll have to bottle feed the calf for a little bit while we keep trying to get her mom to take her in."

"That's terrible. How can she not connect with her? It's her own child!"

Reece looked my way and laughed. "Hey, it's okay. It happens."

I nodded absently. Yeah. Sure. I guess it would be weird to say I had a *thing* about mothers not loving their kids enough to fight for them when it mattered. But that was definitely more a *me* issue than this poor cow's fault.

"You cold?" Reece asked, looking over at me. "Jesus, where are my manners? We could go in and get some coffee and a bite to eat. Shit. If you came in from the main road, that's a long walk. And then I put you to work with the cows."

He wiped his hands on his jeans, but I wasn't sure that made much of a difference, considering what he'd just been handling with all that had been covering the little calf, hugging it to his chest as he carried it into the yard. Both of us were fairly stinky at this point, but at least I wasn't covered in cow birth.

I laughed. "Maybe you shouldn't go in the house but I could get *you* something to eat and drink. I'm pretty good around a kitchen if you just aim me in the right direction."

He looked down at himself and his look of dismay was comical when he looked back up at me. "Shit, this isn't the best first impression, huh?"

I laughed out loud at that. "You're doing just fine. I'm... Charlotte, by the way." *Charlotte?* Where the hell had that come from? I'd always thought it sounded pretty, like a name I might call a daughter if I ever had one. But then I suddenly panicked because what if I didn't answer when people called me it? Not that I'd be here long enough for—

"Charlie for short," I quickly amended. I was used to going by Penny, and Charlie would be a natural shift.

Reece just grinned, a mouthful of straight, white teeth, though one of his front teeth was just ever so slightly crooked. It made him look even more charming than he already did. My mind told me anyone so good looking could only be a heapful of trouble, but again, I wouldn't be here long enough for it to matter.

So I smiled back and basked in the moment. Just a woman, enjoying a man smiling at her. No past, no future. Just here in this moment.

"I'd shake your hand, but well..." He looked down at his dirty hand and we both laughed.

"Yeah, better not."

I had a brief out-of-body experience in that moment. Who the hell had body-snatched my life? Who was this person easily laughing with a stranger on a *ranch* in the middle of nowhere *Texas*?

It certainly wasn't Penelope Chambers, socialite and trophy wife extraordinaire. I blinked and took a step back from the fence. "So, um. The kitchen?"

"Right." Reece nodded and looked down, the smile dropping from his face as if he was embarrassed to have gotten so lost in the moment, too.

Oh God, had we just been having a moment?

I felt like a teenager again. I didn't know how real humans acted in the actual world. I'd grown too used to a plastic world of fake inter-actions, so busy keeping my secret that I didn't even know how genuine people interacted anymore.

I followed Reece across a wide yard to the big, two story house I'd seen when I first walked up the road. "You can head inside," he said. "I'm almost as new here as you are, so feel free to eat and drink what-ever you find. If you could make me a sandwich if there's anything to make a sandwich of, that'd be great. I'll stay out here on the porch to wash up and keep an eye on the mom and calf."

He kept a respectful distance as he said it, and I wasn't sure, but I wondered if it was more than him being dirty that kept him outside while I went in. Was he remembering my first reaction to him? But still, was he really so trusting? I was a stranger and he was just going to let me wander around in his house?

"Are people around here always so trusting?" I asked before I could think better of it.

He barked out a laugh. "You gonna rip us off?"

I was glad it was dark because I could feel my face warm up and knew I was probably blushing. "I don't know. It's just where I come from people lock their doors and don't just let anyone inside."

But Reece just waved a hand. "It's the good part about living in the country. We aren't as paranoid. Also," he grinned, "It's not my house. That's Ruth's shi— I mean stuff, in there. So it'll be her you're robbing blind if you're of a mind to."

"Ha!" I said. "I'll have to tell this Ruth when I meet her you were so free with her belongings."

He rolled his eyes. "Serves her right. She sold this ranch to my boss but had her lawyers write in some crazy loopholes *his* lawyers didn't catch so instead of selling all the land, he only gets to *lease* the land with all the buildings on it from her. And she gets to keep this tiny plot with the house. Don't know why anyone would want to stay and be a landlady when they don't even own the land around them anymore, but that's Ruth for ya."

I felt my eyebrows lift. "Really? Well, was the land in her family for a long time or something?"

"Apparently so. Four generations. Seems stubborn to hang on by a thread when you've sold off everything else, but what do I know? My mama wasn't exactly big on passing down..." he paused, then shrugged, "well, anything, come to think of it."

That perked my interest. I probably had an unhealthy fascination with people's screwed up family dynamics. But getting into it in the middle of the night with a complete stranger was probably far too random, even for this new body-snatched version of myself.

So I punched a thumb over my shoulder. "Well, I better get to the food and coffee."

Reece smirked. "And all that ransacking."

I let out a surprised laugh. "Can't forget the ransacking."

I hurried up the stairs into the house, and so bad wanted to take one last look over my shoulder to see if he was watching me go. I stopped myself at the last second, because, dear God, what would I do if he was? And I didn't want to be disappointed if he wasn't.

Then I shook my head at myself for being ridiculous and went inside to make some damn sandwiches and brew some damn coffee.

By the time I got back outside, it was midnight. I was exhausted, but it wasn't like I'd exactly figured out my sleeping arrangements. Plus, I was starving, and the simple ham sandwiches I'd made had my mouth watering.

I brought out two plates stacked with four sandwiches and another little tray I'd found in the kitchen in my other hand holding two steaming cups of coffee.

Reece met me at the door and took the tray from me.

"Any change with mom and baby?" I asked as he set the tray down on a little outdoor table set up on the porch. He'd switched the flashlight to its lamp setting and put it down in the center of the table. I put the sandwiches down and pulled out the second plate from underneath the first, then portioned out the sandwiches.

Reece had indeed cleaned up, with water and soap from the barn or somewhere else, because while his clothes were still filthy, his hands were clean.

He didn't waste any time biting into the sandwich, shoving almost half of it into his mouth at once.

"No change," he said. At least that's what I think he said. His mouth was so full of sandwich, I could only guess. But when I looked out at the pasture beside the barn, I could see the heifer was still at a distance from where we'd left the calf. She was near the gate, like all she could think about was getting back to the wide open field.

"What's wrong with her? Why won't she go to her baby?" I asked before taking a bite of my own sandwich. I closed my eyes with the bite. They'd had lettuce and tomatoes, and the fresh ingredients tasted like absolute heaven after so many days of road junk food and then today of absolutely nothing. I wanted to do exactly what Reece had and shove the whole damn thing in my mouth. Instead I just chewed quickly so I could get to the next bite, and the next.

I didn't notice Reece was watching me until I realized there'd been silence and he was taking his time answering my question.

When I finally looked up at him, again feeling my cheeks heat, and our eyes met, he looked away and answered.

"She's a first-time mom. That's what makes a heifer different from a cow. Since she's never done it before, it's easier to get confused. Then with the difficult birth... I dunno, I guess she's agitated."

I nodded, trying to eat more slowly...but who was I kidding. I shoved the last few bites of food into my mouth and then started on the next sandwich, occasionally drinking some coffee and then eating more.

I swore a meal had never tasted better in my entire *life*. Not even those stupid high-dollar meals at the restaurants in San Francisco where Jeff liked to parade me around. I could never enjoy those dinners anyway. I was too busy being nervous about how Jeff would critique me later. Did I greet his friends the right way? Was I *overly* friendly with any of his friends? Was I not interested *enough*? Not that it mattered. No matter what I did, I inevitably did *something* that invited his wrath when we got home.

Sometimes he didn't even wait until we got home. Jeff was more than happy to hit me while we were driving home if he was good and riled.

"Sorry, you don't have to answer if you don't want to."

"What?" I looked up at Reece. He was looking at me, and I realized he'd asked a question I hadn't even heard.

"I didn't mean to pry."

"No, sorry, I just spaced out. What did you ask?"

"Oh." He'd finished both of his sandwiches and he rubbed his hand on the back of his neck. "I was just wondering if all your stuff was back in your car? You said you stalled on the road? Did you leave even like, your purse there?"

Oh. Right. Crap.

I reached for my coffee and took a big gulp. Shit. Too hot, too hot. I coughed and slammed the ceramic mug down on the table, waving my hand.

"Oh damn, are you okay?" Reece jumped up from his chair and I was even more embarrassed. "No, I'm fine," I gasped. "Just...*hot.*"

"Here, let me get you some water."

Then, just like that, he disappeared inside the house and came back with some water. So obviously it hadn't been his dirtiness keeping him out earlier.

He returned with a glass of cool water and handed it over. I took it thankfully and took a long drink. "Thanks," I croaked afterwards. Then I looked back out towards the cows. "Do you think it's been twenty minutes yet?"

Reece let my not so smooth change of topic pass graciously, standing up. "Yeah, looks like she's not gonna let the calf nurse. And we gotta get some colostrum into the little buddy."

He did that thing where he rubbed his hand down the back of his neck, looked out at the dark ranch, then back at me.

"It's late, and if you don't have a place to stay for the night, I can't imagine Ruth would mind you crashing here tonight. She pointed out some rooms for me and my brother. I can put you in mine. There's a bunkhouse for ranch hands and I'll stay out there for the night."

"Oh my God, no, I wouldn't want—"

But he held out a hand. "Look, I don't know your circumstances and I don't need to. But no way you're sleeping out in the cold or trying to find anywhere else when there's a perfectly good bed right upstairs. And I want you to feel comfortable, so I'll stay out in the bunkhouse. It's perfectly good for the hands and up until recently, that's what I been. I don't need to go getting fancy all of a sudden. Please. It'd mean a lot to me."

I opened my mouth, then closed it. Then I put my hands on my hips. "How did you just twist those words to make it sound like I'm doing *you* a favor by sleeping in your comfy bed and sending you out to the bunkhouse?"

It was not normal logic and half of me was amused while the other half was trying to search out the trick in it.

He cracked a grin. "Cause I'm just that good?"

I shook my head. "Fine, but I'm coming to help with the calf."

He started to wave his hand, but I butted in. "Surely you aren't going to *rob* me of the chance to see it through with this little baby calf. Plus earn a little bit of my room and board by helping out any way I can to salvage my dignity?"

His left eyebrow popped up. "Did you just twist those words to make it sound like trying to let you off the hook and knock off early would be insulting?"

I started down the porch stairs. "I guess I'm just that good?"

His laugh followed me.

# 5

My eyes were crusty with sleep when I finally blinked them open against the bright morning sun.

And then I shot up in bed, panic spiking through me.

Bed.

I was in a soft bed.

But when I looked around, it wasn't pristine eggshell-white walls and the muted light from the morning San Francisco fog coming in the windows. Nope. It was all yellowing mid-century wallpaper and a window with bright sun shining through instead.

I collapsed back dramatically into the soft mattress and soft pillow.

Jesus Christ. I just hadn't slept anywhere soft since I'd left San Francisco.

Was this what it would be like for the rest of my life? Always terrified that my life now was a dream?

Duh. I was there for almost a decade. Did I think I my past was just *gone* because I'd physically left?

I groaned and covered my face with the pillow. Because um, yeah, part of me had hoped so.

I guess I'd just assumed the leaving was the *end* of the story. It was certainly as far as I got in most of my fantasies. Afterwards was always just this vague happily-ever-after that I tried not to think *too* much about because that felt like torment.

But as I dragged the pillow away from my face and looked around, it dawned on me... holy crap.

The leaving was just the *beginning*.

Now started the rest of my life. What the hell was I supposed to do with that? The conundrum that struck me briefly on the bus hit me all over again. Who even *was* I if I wasn't *her*? The carefully crafted HER that was acceptable to *him*.

But who was *I*?

I swung my legs out of bed and landed heavily when I stood up, stiff and a little sore after last night.

I smiled, remembering going back out to tend to the little calf whose mother wouldn't attend to her.

We'd gotten towels from the barn and cleaned and dried her off. I'd never been that close to a baby cow. It was so... *sweet* was the only word that came to mind. Or maybe that was just my experience of the situation.

But the little cow, once we got her dried off, was so unsteady on her little coltish legs she couldn't even stand, she'd just keep collapsing when Reece tried to help her stand.

He decided to give her some colostrum to help her get the nourishment she needed. He had to use an esophageal feeding tube, but he stayed calm and was so kind and gentle to the animal the entire time.

I was overcome by emotion just watching this big man with the animal in his lap, coaxing the first life-saving liquid into her. The calf seemed to feel it, too, because she kept bumping her head into his chest, almost nuzzling into him.

I was probably anthropomorphizing. She was likely just searching him for more milk, but Reece had explained that cows are herd animals and touch and community and interaction is actually really important to them.

I was so moved, embarrassingly so, but Reece either didn't notice or was thoughtful enough not to make a big deal out of it. Maybe he was just good with creatures of all kinds like that.

There wasn't much left to do after that. We made sure the calf was snuggled up in some hay and Reece said he'd check on her in another few hours, but that we should get some rest. His brother and Ruth weren't back yet from their cow-wrangling, so he lent me some of his clothes to sleep in and said he'd throw mine in the overnight wash with his and have them ready for me in the morning.

I looked down at myself, engulfed in his large, faded Grateful Dead t-shirt that came just a few inches short of my knees and hugged my arms to myself. It was chilly in the room and my feet on the wood floor were cold.

I'd need to go hunt down my own clothes soon. For another second, though, it was nice to just breathe in the cold air of this new life and wonder who I'd be today.

I was stretching my arms high above my head when the door suddenly pushed open and a tired-looking, mud-drenched woman came in the room. She was tall, with thick brown hair that escaped in all directions from a braid that was barely holding together anymore.

It was shocking to see a stranger opening the door. Shocking too, because apparently me trying to jam that chair underneath the doorknob wouldn't have done anything if Reece or anyone else had tried to intrude last night to molest or otherwise harm me. Ruth had pushed the door open and the chair had just bumped free and pushed along the ground with the door. Good Lord. The hairs on my arms raised.

Which was right about when the woman saw me and let out a little screech. Her face went immediately bright red. "Who the hell are *you*? And what the hell are you doing in my bed?"

"Oh, hi," I said, scrambling to my feet, then realizing I was in nothing but a shirt and underwear. She had to be Ruth.

Then I looked around in confusion. "Isn't this Reece's room?"

I waved awkwardly, deciding to start over. "Hi, I'm Charlie. God, I'm so sorry. This is your room? I must have gotten the rooms mixed up last night when he told me where to go. He said second door to the left, but I wasn't sure if he was counting the bathroom, and it was so late. I just saw the bed and kind of face-planted honestly. Reece said—"

If I thought her face was bright with color before, it was nothing to her reaction at my words.

"Get dressed," she snapped at me. "I can't believe he let his whore sleep in my bed."

My mouth dropped open. "Excuse me?"

But she just glared back at me. "Oh my fucking God. Get out of my bed and the fuck out of my room. Take the sheets with you, you can toss them in the washer on your way out."

My mouth dropped open. This woman had gotten the wrong impression, and maybe I couldn't blame her, I didn't know how I'd feel finding a strange woman in my bedroom. But I also did *not* appreciate being called a whore at whatever the hell o'clock it was in the morning.

At the same time, considering it had been her warm bed I'd slept in, the first in over a week, I just zipped my lip and gave her a single nod. "Sure, whatever. I'm outta here, anyway."

She scoffed, then shook her head at me. Then she spun and stormed down the hall, yelling, "Reece Walker! We need to establish some house rules. Right the fuck now."

I shook my head and looked around. I didn't really have any *things* to gather. So I just gritted my teeth and pulled the sheets off the bed and balled them in my arms. I'd handed my dirty clothes through the door last night for Reece to wash, so there was nothing to do but walk downstairs if I was going to retrieve them.

At least I'd seen the washer and dryer on the way in yesterday. Easy, since they were in the mudroom we'd entered through last night. There hadn't been much in the way of a tour—just us tromping into the house, me following behind Reece as he gave me some clothes to sleep in, let me change in the bathroom and directed me on where to go upstairs to sleep. His pajama bottoms swamped me, but they were good enough for decency's sake while I made my way upstairs, basically holding them up the entire way.

I'd considered the fact that he didn't follow me upstairs to "show me the bedroom" really cool of him, as if he knew a woman alone in a house with a man would not appreciate that. Which I wouldn't have.

Now I was back holding up the pajama bottoms and trying not to trip as I made my way back downstairs. Right when I was near the bottom of the staircase, I heard the sound of raised voices.

"—didn't think it had to be stated, but I have a no-whores-allowed-in-my-bed policy. Where did you even find her? You were supposed to be putting in fence posts, not carousing at the local bar picking up chicks. Jesus, who did I just sell my daddy's ranch to?"

"Stop laying into my brother, Ruth. You're just cranky cause you were out all night chasing runaway cows."

"Will both of you just stop?" It sounded like Reece's voice.

I paused at the bottom of the stairs, listening.

"You've got it all wrong, Ruth. She's not— She's not what you called her. She helped me deliver the calf last night. She was good with the heifer. Maybe if you'd give her a chance, you'd see she was—"

"Oh, so you think you can just come in here and have little cowboy bunnies hanging around the place to service you whenever you get tired of bailing hay, is that it? This is exactly what I was afraid of, a bunch of men coming in and taking over the place. Disgusting, absolutely disgusting—"

"Number one," came another masculine voice, I couldn't tell if it was Reece or his brother, they sounded so much alike, "there's no need to be so puritanical. We're not likely to be abstinent while we're working here. We're not monks, and just because you're leasing the place to us doesn't mean you get to dictate our sex lives."

"You're twisting my words. I don't give a shit about your sex lives! You can go fuck the whole county if you want and get every STD known to man. Just keep it the hell *out* of my room, and preferably out my sight."

"Look, could we all just take it down a few notches? If you'd just give me a second to explain—" Okay, that was definitely Reece, but Ruth was not having it.

"Take it *down* a few notches? Oh, I'm sorry, big fella, is my voice too *shrill* for you? Do you have a problem with assertive women?"

"Jesus, Ruth, you need to back down. You are seriously barking up the wrong tree. Maybe get a chance to know my brother before you make such snap decisions about him."

Ruth scoffed. "As far as I'm concerned, I've seen all I need to."

I'd had enough of this woman. I marched straight into the kitchen, since I had to go through to get to the mudroom anyway.

Reece's eyes shot my way, and he looked immediately concerned. Was he worried I'd overheard? Too late, buddy. That train had left the station.

"Thanks for the hospitality, Reece," I said kindly. I wanted him to know I didn't blame him for Ruth's rudeness.

"It was very kind of you to put me up for the night when I didn't have anywhere else to stay after that sleazy trucker kicked me out on the side of the road." I looked at him, really hoping he could see the sincerity in my eyes. After it slipped out of my mouth, I realized I'd just admitted the truth, especially when I saw Reece's eyes widen. Well shit, there went my attempt at a secret. But you know what? It felt liberating to just tell it like it was.

"I really don't know what I would have done if you hadn't offered me a warm place to stay last night."

Then I looked at Ruth. "And I get it that you didn't know I was borrowing your bed, but thanks for it all the same."

I lifted the balled-up sheets in my arms. "I'll make sure and get these in the washer before I go."

Ruth's mouth was dropped open.

I just walked across the now silent kitchen and pushed into the mud room. "Thanks again," I called out to the room at large.

When I got to the laundry machines, I found my own clothes folded neatly on top of the dryer. Reece must have done it.

I tugged the pocket door shut behind me, then tugged on my jeans and socks. Last, I slipped my feet into my trusty Converse. Reece had even gone to the trouble of clearing the mud from them and as clean as they were, he'd likely thrown them in the wash with the rest of the clothes. One of my own favorite tricks for keeping tennis shoes and the like clean. It made my heart squeeze in an unfamiliar way.

No one ever did nice things for me. Ever. It was ridiculous that such little things could have me all but tearing up. I swiped at my face as I slid Reece's shirt off and pulled my own worn flannel back on.

A knock on the door came a couple minutes later, right as I was finishing lacing up my shoes.

"Can I come in?" Reece called. "You decent?"

I smiled, then reached out and slid the door open.

He stood there, all six foot four of him, waiting with an anxious look on his face. "Look, I'm really sorry for her." He jabbed a thumb over his shoulder. "We're new here and she doesn't really know us very well. She's a little jumpy about having anyone on her family ranch, much less a couple of strange men."

My insides softened even more. It was a compassionate and honest assessment of the situation. If it had been Jeff, he would have just called Ruth a bitch.

Not this guy, though. He was willing to try to understand Ruth's side of it, even when he didn't like how she acted.

I reached out on impulse and touched his arm, smiling up at him. "Don't even worry about it. I get it."

It was a mistake to touch him, though. I jerked my hand back almost immediately after making contact with the hard muscle of his forearm. He was warm, and solid, and did I mention warm?

I swallowed and took a step back.

"Well, I guess I'll be getting on my way now." I shoved Ruth's sheets into the washer and filled the top catch with detergent that was on a little shelf above the machines. I looked back at Reece after I'd turned it on. "I really do appreciate you helping me out last night."

He shook his head. "No, you were the one who helped *me*. I needed an extra pair of hands and you showed up out of the blue."

I laughed at that. "Pretty sure all I did was open and close a couple gates."

His eyebrows shot up. "Uh, and you helped distract that angry heifer when I was cornered on top of that tractor. It was both of us that got her in that chute. And if it had been any longer, who knows if she would've had a live birth."

Well damn, now I felt all warm and fuzzy. Jeff only ever tore me down, he never *ever* complimented me or said anything nice. It was ridiculous that even the smallest bit of kindness could make me feel so lovely and lit up inside.

Yep, it was definitely time to make my exit. My emotions were too all over the place around this guy. I was like a little puppy who'd been kicked so many times that I was hungry for any scrap of kindness. I couldn't decide if it was pathetic or refreshing. But it was definitely all far too confusing for whatever time in the morning it was.

Still, when I looked back up at Reece, I was caught in his blue-gray eyes and his gentle smile. He was handsome—in a rugged, genuine way that was completely different from Jeff's suave, over-moisturized face and perfectly coifed hair. Reece's hair flopped this way and that—a little too long, with some bits that stuck out in funny angles that was the result of genuine bed-head and not the artfully arranged city boy version.

Reece was just so *real*. I had the most absurd impulse to throw myself in his arms and hug him. I bet he gave really great hugs. I hadn't been hugged, just *hugged* and reassured that it would be okay, in so long I couldn't even remember when.

It was a ridiculous impulse and instead I swallowed hard again and stepped back.

"Well." I nodded. "Thanks again."

He looked like he wanted to say something, but before he could—

"That goddamned bastard! How dare he show his face here?" Ruth yelled, and then, before either Reece or I could move, she stormed into the mud room. Both Reece and I barely had time to jump back before she barreled between us and out the door.

"What now?" Reece's brother asked, sounding exasperated as he followed her out. Reece went after his brother and well, I was in no hurry so I went out to see too. As long as Ruth was aiming her ire at someone other than me.

It was cold as all get out and I regretted not grabbing a coat, but the humongous truck had pulled to a stop in front of the ranch house, gravel and dust only just now settling. It was no time to go back for my hoodie.

A relatively short man jumped down from the tall cab, giant ten-gallon hat balanced on his head and wranglers about two sizes too tight suckered to his legs. I crossed my arms, glad I at least had my flannel as I settled in to watch the drama.

"Get off my property," Ruth called out. "You aren't welcome here."

"Ain't your property no more, Ruthie," the man called out. "I came by to introduce myself to the new owners."

"That's us," Reece's brother said, stepping forward. "Jeremiah Walker. This here's my brother, Reece. We're part owners and we're working the place now. You are?"

The man stepped forward, hand out.

"A snake in the grass," Ruth said at the same time as the man said, "Trent. Trent Patterson of Patterson Ranch."

Jeremiah shook Trent's hand. Trent had a wide smile. Wide and charming. I shivered. It was a Jeff smile. Fake as a plastic toy from a fast-food joint—it'd make you smile for an hour and then it breaks and you're crying in disappointment.

Trent kept on smiling at Jeremiah, then at Reece. He didn't even look at Ruth. Or at me for that matter.

So he was one of *those*. The kind that only considered other men as worthy of their notice. I'd met plenty of the sort when Jeff paraded me around as his trophy wife. Sometimes they'd look my way—or at least my *body's* way. They'd just never quite get to looking at my face, or bother with learning my name.

I was glad for my oversized flannel and short, boyish haircut.

"I'm your neighbor to the east. Always good to make friends with the new neighbor, don't you think?" He was still shaking hands with Jeremiah.

Jeremiah wasn't smiling. He finally yanked his hand back from Trent. Jeremiah shrugged. "Got enough friends."

I didn't miss the tick in Trent's jaw but his smile never wavered.

My impulse was to take a step back from him. I had a feeling Ruth was right about the snake part. I liked that Reece's brother didn't seem taken in by him either.

Trent laughed, obviously aiming for good-natured. "Don't know where you boys are from, but this here's Texas. You need your friends in Texas. We look out for our own."

"Oh please, Trent," Ruth laughed. "You woulda begged, borrowed, or stole to get this piece of land. God knows you tried. But these boys swooped in and outbid you, thank God. I know your daddy's been trying to get my land since the time I was in pigtails. But it's over. He's not getting it. The HB will never be y'alls. The end."

Anger flashed in Trent's eyes and he pointed his finger at Ruth. "You never did know your place or when to shut that mouth of yours. Your daddy was a loser and a gambler and a nobody, and the fact that you're still trying to hold onto this farm when it was sold out from under you is *pathetic*, everybody thinks so."

Yep, there it was. They never could keep it in for long. Narcissists had the most fragile egos of anyone on earth. You poked them and they lashed out, every time.

"Only one who looks pathetic here is you." The words were outta my mouth before I could really think about what I was doing or saying.

Trent's head swung my way, disbelief all over his features. "What'd you say, dyke?"

I laughed. Laughed in his face. It felt so good. Absolutely liberating, actually. "Bullies like you are all the same, aren't you?" I shook my head at him.

Then I looked over at his truck. "Though guessing by the size of that truck, you're overcompensating for a little something, aren't you?" I let my eyes fall to his waist, just in case his thick head couldn't follow my innuendo all the way through.

"You little bitch!" he snapped. I saw it in his eyes the second he lunged for me. The same way Jeff regularly snapped. It was that instinct for violence that insecure men had when you threatened their oh-so-fragile egos.

So no, I wasn't surprised, but I still froze.

Except, unlike when Jeff came for me, this time there were two large protectors who leapt in front of me.

Reece and Jeremiah grabbed Trent and threw him backwards to the ground. He landed hard on his ass.

And Reece, gentle, calm Reece was suddenly on fire mad. "You think you can lay hands on a woman? Or even *talk* to a woman that way? Get the fuck off our ranch. You ever step foot on it again, we'll call the authorities."

Trent scrambled backwards, furious as he stumbled back to his feet. He pointed his finger at Jeremiah, then Reece. "You just made a mistake. A big mistake."

"I'm quaking in my boots," Jeremiah said, deadpan. "Now get the fuck off my property. This is Texas, right? I hear you can shoot trespassers on sight here."

Trent didn't say another word. He just climbed back in his truck —and I do mean climbed. He was so short, he had to grab onto the rung and heft himself up into the thing, it was so tall.

He spun around and spit dust and dirt our way but we were all already back on the porch and heading back inside.

I wasn't sure what to expect once we got there.

I figured Ruth would be pissed at me again for stepping in when I was a stranger. I'd hoped for a cup of coffee before I hit the road, but I might have to make a quicker exit now.

Sixty miles wasn't really that far. I could walk it. Maybe two or three days and I'd be there.

But as soon as we got in the house, Ruth threw her arms around my neck. "You're a badass," she said, squeezing me tight and giving me that hug I'd been longing for so badly only minutes before.

Startled, I hugged her back. She was wiry but sturdy, and a surprisingly good hugger.

When she pulled back, she was grinning at me. "I always wanted to say that to his face about that stupid truck of his."

Then she linked her arm through mine and pulled me back into the kitchen. "So you were passing through? Hitchhiking? Oh honey, we girls gotta stick together. You're good people. I'm sorry I was such a bitch this morning. I haven't slept. I was up all night chasing cows that had escaped out onto the 284 back onto the property. Then we had to fix the damn fence so they didn't wander right back out again."

"You got a new calf," Reece cut in. "First of the season."

Ruth beamed even bigger. "See. Eat your heart out, motherfucker!" she shouted, giving the finger with both hands at the window in the direction of Trent's retreating truck. "The HB is *back*."

Jeremiah rolled his eyes. "How about we start with some breakfast and then finish fixing the pen to keep the cows we just rounded up, 'cause those two troublemakers were already eyeing the temporary cow pens like they were planning the Great Escape Part Two."

"Sit, sit," Ruth waved us all to sit down. "I'll make my grandma's famous flapjacks and eggs."

Jeremiah just lifted his eyebrows at Reece as if to say, is this the same woman who was just screaming at all of us ten minutes ago? but we all sat as instructed.

Well, Jeremiah sat and half-dozed while Reece insisted on helping with coffee and I volunteered to help with cooking.

# 6

"So shit, girl, you were hitchhiking last night?" Ruth asked almost as soon as I started frying up some bacon. "That's nuts."

Apparently she wasn't one for beating around the bush. Or the bacon, as it were.

I shrugged, noticing how Reece had quieted while his brother talked on about all the chores that needed doing that day. Was he listening?

"Just trying to get where I'm going."

"Where's that?" Ruth asked.

"Austin."

She nodded. "You got family there?"

"Um... No, not really."

"Friends?"

I shook my head as I reached for a fork and flipped the sizzling bacon. "Just looking for a fresh start, I guess."

Ruth let out a low whistle. If the guys hadn't been listening before, I didn't know how they weren't now.

"I don't really like to talk about it," I said hurriedly.

"Oh sure, sure," Ruth said, pausing as she whipped the pancake batter.

But as soon as she'd plugged in a big griddle, after I'd finished the first round of bacon and was starting the second, she continued.

"I respect that. A brand new start. God knows I'm not exactly one for letting go of the past." She let out a humorless laugh, but then gazed out the window.

It was a beautiful view, I had to admit. We were in a part of Texas I didn't even know existed. Instead of being flat like the rest of the state, there were dramatic, rolling hills. Cattle dotted the hills, and it was a bit breath-taking, to be honest.

"Well, some pasts can be hard to let go of," I said quietly.

Ruth still heard me, I knew because her head swung my way. She nodded, before her attention got taken away by the pancakes which needed flipping. "Yeah, I guess that's true," she said a few minutes later, startling me because I didn't imagine she was still thinking about my words.

"So how ya gonna get to Austin? I hope you don't try hitchhiking again. I'm happy to take you, but I gotta hit the hay first after breakfast. I'm swamped and a two-hour roundtrip journey might be a little much at the moment after the all-nighter I just pulled."

"Oh my God," I almost dropped the fork I was flipping bacon with. "Are you serious? That would be amazing! But of course, of course, get all the sleep you need."

"Sure. No problem. We gals gotta stick together, right?"

Again, I was struck by the urge to hug her. To hug *someone*.

And to cry. Because here was the second person in as many days to prove that there *were* actually good people in the world, despite all evidence to the contrary in my previous lived experience.

"Thanks," I said, trying my damnedest to swallow back my emotions. "I would really appreciate that. You have no idea."

She looked over and her eyes softened. "I know what it's like to need someone to just throw you a rope once in a while." Then she huffed out, her mouth hardening into a line. "And how much it bites when there's no one there with any ropes in sight."

I nodded. Yeah. Yeah, that, I knew exactly what she meant.

"So we pick ourselves up by our own bootstraps?"

She huffed out again. "More like crawl out of one hole of doom and hope for a less doomy hole tomorrow."

I laughed out loud at that. "Yup."

Which was also when I saw Reece look my way, as if startled and then pleased to hear me laugh.

Which made me... feel things.

Good Lord, being an unleashed human in the real world was intense and overwhelming, and I'd only been at it for a few days. I felt like unfamiliar emotions kept assaulting me left and right. I barely knew what to do with one before another one hit. Part of me wanted to go back to bed, curl into a ball, and pull the covers over my head for a long, long time.

I decided instead I should just focus on cooking bacon, and then eggs, something I *actually* knew how to do. One foot in front of the other. I'd figure this all out as I went...right?

Meanwhile Ruth turned her attention on Jeremiah, getting into an argument with him about the best way to go about hiring ranch hands.

She thought they should get some hands as soon as possible, as many projects as needed tackling. Jeremiah said he'd rather have the *right* man than the first man to walk through the door.

Ruth countered back, asking why the hell he assumed it needed to be a *man* at all.

Jeremiah rolled his eyes. "I meant man in the universal mankind way."

Ruth just lifted an eyebrow. "Gendered language matters."

I smiled, enjoy them ribbing each other. That was the theme of the entire breakfast. It was nice not being the only odd man out there. None of us besides the twin brothers knew each other. And Ruth was not shy about grilling the brothers on their qualifications to do the job.

Jeremiah especially, grilled her back about the state of the facilities and ranch.

Ruth bristled any time he insinuated her family ranch wasn't up to snuff. But even she admitted that a lot of the equipment *had* been sold off to pay her father's debts. "We sent accurate pictures and representations of the property to the buyer."

Jeremiah scoffed at that. "Please. Those pictures had to be at least ten years old. The stable is all but falling apart and the bunkhouse only has one working toilet."

Ruth shrugged. "Your boss bought the ranch in AS IS condition, all cash. It's why he got the place for such a steal."

"You call five point eight million dollars a *steal*?"

Ruth just shrugged. "America lives on beef. We're a vital part of the economy. It's an exciting venture capital opportunity that a whole new generation is invigorated to be a part of. Reconnecting with the land, discovering a whole different pace of life."

Reece laughed at that. "Great sales pitch, but we're already sold. We love the life. So does our boss. He knows this place is a money sink, but he's a rich bastard and believes enough good people falling in love and reconnecting to the land is the only hope this planet has."

I could only stare at him, a little appalled by the naïve conviction of anyone who stated *anything* with such easy hope. At the same time it was such a beautiful sentiment. Who the hell *were* these people?

Jeremiah did not seem moved by his brother's argument either. "Yes, but what you and our idealistic employer fail to realize is that there's still a very important bottom line we have to think about for *any* of this to be a successful endeavor. There's no point in wasting a ton of exhaustive labor for shockingly thin profit margins. It's time we take this ranch into the twenty-first century or there's no point to any of it."

"And how exactly do you propose we do that?" Ruth asked, shoving the last bite of pancake into her mouth.

I had to give it to her, her grandma's pancake recipe *was* to die for. They almost tasted like *cake*. A thin drizzle of syrup and a thick pat of butter and I was in freaking heaven.

Pancakes were absolutely on the No list from Jeff. He had a hate-hate relationship with any wife of his consuming carbohydrates.

I was busy enjoying the absolute divinity of the pancakes while

Ruth and Jeremiah continued arguing the best ways to take the ranch forward.

Finally Jeremiah threw down. "Obviously, your ideas for the ranch didn't work. Your family drove the place into such overwhelming debt it was about to go into foreclosure if you didn't accept a short sale on the place. I don't even know why I'm arguing with you."

I looked up from my plate, my mouth stuffed full of pancake, eyes wide as Ruth's face turned beet red. She threw down her napkin and stood up so abruptly her chair scraped the linoleum as it went backwards.

"I never had a chance to run anything. My father didn't get the son he wanted so he never listened to a damn thing I had to say. He was the one who ran this place into the ground." Then she looked at me. "Charlie, this might not be my ranch anymore, but it's still *my house*, and you're my guest. You're welcome to stay a few more days or I can take you into Austin later today. Just let me know. But first I'm gonna go upstairs and get some damn sleep after chasing *your* cows all night."

She glared at Jeremiah and then turned and stormed up the stairs.

Reece let out a low whistle.

Jeremiah glared at him. "Don't even start with me, brother. We didn't sign on to deal with that woman or her issues when Xavier bought the place and sent us here. This is our shot and I'm not going to let anyone think they can second-guess my decisions constantly. Xavier trusted me to know what I'm doing." With that he shoved the last bite of eggs in his mouth then stood up and grabbed his coat from the door.

"Jer, you need to sleep too," Reece said.

"I'll sleep after I get the cows fed."

"Jesus, Xavier didn't just send you down here. We're equal partners," Reece said. He stood up, leaving half his breakfast uneaten. It was probably wrong that I eyed the food covetously. I was already stuffed and if I ate anymore, I'd probably feel sick. Jeff had just monitored everything I ate so strictly, it felt ridiculously liberating to eat whatever the hell I wanted for once. No one here gave a damn.

And the thought struck me—no one would give a damn what I ate for the rest of my life. I could have ice cream for *dinner* if I wanted to.

I was startled out of my thoughts by the continuing drama between the brothers.

"You don't know how to work the tractor or the bailer," Jeremiah said. "There's nine hundred cows to feed. This is different than the fifty head back at Mel's."

Reece looked frustrated, but then his tired-looking twin put a hand on his shoulder and looked him in the eye. "Plus, someone needs to keep an eye on the heifers and cows. And there's the calf that needs feeding. This ranch needs the both of us."

Reece nodded. "I'll go feed the calf and check on the ladies to see if there's any progress with them. Then I can make a list of all we'll need to fix up the bunkhouse and stable."

Jeremiah smiled tiredly. "Good man."

"Okay, but after you do the morning feed, then you'll at least take a damn nap?" Reece asked.

Jeremiah shrugged and Reece rolled his eyes.

"It's the first day on the job. I'm not gonna sleep through it."

"All I'm asking for is a power nap somewhere along the way. The place survived whatever the hell piss poor management was happening before we got here. It can last another couple hours while you catch some shut-eye."

Jeremiah cocked an eyebrow. "Since when did you become big brother? I'm the one who looks out for you, remember, little brother?"

"Seven minutes does *not* make you my big brother."

"You lost that argument a hell of a long time ago, little brother." Jeremiah grabbed Reece in a headlock and I could only watch on in a sort of astonished joy at seeing the obvious love and camaraderie between them. Holy crap, was this what real family looked like?

Reece fought his way out of the hold and shoved his brother, but they both had smiles on their faces and then Jeremiah was all serious again. "Okay, okay, back to business." Jeremiah reached for his worn and dirty cowboy hat that was on a peg beside where his coat had been.

He looked my way. "Nice to meet you, Charlotte," he said with a nod. Then he was out the door.

Leaving me and Reece in the kitchen, which felt a lot smaller all of a sudden with me and the big man in it.

Our eyes met and locked for a moment, then I jerked my gaze away as I felt my cheeks heat. I started gathering up dishes, if only for something to do with my hands.

I expected Reece to head out the door after his brother, but instead he surprised me by saying, "Those can wait. Want to come with me to see how Bessie is doing this morning?"

I looked up. "Bessie?"

He grinned, and he looked both rakish and endearingly boyish in the morning light, a mixture that hit me straight in the belly. "That's what I named the baby calf."

I laughed and put down the stack of plates I'd gathered. "Of course I want to see her."

He waved an arm. "Come on, then. Let's get her her morning bottle."

"Um." I looked around at the mess from breakfast. But he was right, it could wait. I wasn't sure why I even thought it was my responsibility to clean it up. Because I'd cooked and they'd given me free room and board for the night? Because cleaning and making things pristine was always what I'd done and it was now my instinctual go to?

"Yeah, that sounds amazing."

"Here, I'm sure Ruth won't mind you borrowing her coat." He pointed towards Ruth's coat.

I raised my eyebrows. "Considering how she reacted to me borrowing her *bed*..."

He waved. "That was just a misunderstanding." He grabbed the coat and held it out to me. "It's cold as a steer's balls out there. Come on."

I smiled, how could I not, and took the coat. It had been cold when we'd gone out earlier.

When we stepped out, I was greeted by the sight of the ranch in its full glory by the light of the morning sun.

I hadn't really had the chance to take it in earlier when we'd all piled out to deal with Trent the Asshole.

But I took it in now. It was cold and quiet, but not still. There was a wind that moved the grass on the surrounding hills that seemed to fold into themselves all around us. There were a few trees on the property and their bare winter branches were alive and dancing in the morning breeze. The same breeze that cut through my thin jeans and had me zipping up Ruth's coat and shoving my hands in the pockets as Reece led the way back to the barn.

It wasn't much warmer in the barn, especially considering it was open to the elements on one side, but the break from the wind did help. But our little calf was nestled underneath the roof in the dry hay, all curled up.

Reece immediately went to the corner of the barn where there was a small counter with a big drop sink. He turned on the water from the spigot and waited for it to run warm before filling up about half of a big four-pint bottle. Then he opened a big plastic bucket and scooped some powder into the bottle. He closed the top and shook it vigorously. He finished by snapping on a big rubber nipple before coming back to me where I stood beside the calf.

"How's she doing?" I asked.

"I got her up on her feet in the middle of the night, so that was encouraging. But we've got to make sure she can get up as much as possible today if we're gonna keep her alive."

My heart lurched at the idea that we could still lose this precious little life.

She looked up at us with big moon-black eyes.

"Here, you feed her." He handed me the oversized bottle. "I'm gonna see if I can get her standing again. Maybe the food will encourage her to try out her legs more."

I looked up at him in alarm, holding the bottle awkwardly. "I don't know how."

He smiled at me. "Just hold it upside down. Don't worry. We used to have the little kids do this back where I worked before. You never want a bottle calf, but the kids always loved them. They become like the family pet."

Okay, well, that did make me feel a little better.

"Come on, Bessie, up you go." He hooked a leg over the calf, then leaned over and grabbed the calf from its middle to help her up onto her legs.

Bessie extended her wobbly legs, collapsing a few times before she got them underneath her. She was still unsteady, and Reece helped keep her up while I held the bottle for her.

She bumped it with her nose a few times curiously. When milk dribbled out onto her lip and her little pink tongue came out to lick it, then she got more interested and started to suckle at the nipple.

"Oh my gosh, she's doing it!" I grinned at Reece, feeling like an absolute superstar, even though all I was doing was barely keeping hold of the bottle while Bessie did all the work.

But Reece smiled just as wide back at me, the smile where he showed all his teeth. "Told you you could do it. You're a natural."

Bessie suckled a little too hard and almost yanked the bottle out of my hands and I yelped and snatched it back before it fell. But I took it as a good sign if she was attacking it so vigorously.

"Look at her go," I couldn't help announcing, still delighted down to my bones as the liquid disappeared from the bottle. "She's amazing!"

"Of course she is. She's Bessie, firstborn of the HB's new heritage."

"The HB?" I asked.

"Harshbarger Ranch. Jer and I didn't see any reason to change the ranch's name. Especially with Ruth staying on, it'll probably mean even more not to change it. Besides, what's Xavier gonna call it? He'd just name it after his wife again and we'd have another Mel's Ranch."

I smiled. "That's sweet."

"He's crazy about her. And the kids. His family's the guy's whole world."

I shook my head, looking down at Bessie as she finished up the bottle. "I can't imagine," I said before thinking better of it, then announced, "All done!"

Bessie was still bumping her nose at the bottle and trying to suckle it.

"Here, trade off," Reece said. "You see if you can help her stand up and walk around while I prepare the second bottle." He let go of Bessie and she actually wobbled forward a few steps uncertainly.

"Way to go, baby!" I cooed.

Then she stumbled backwards and went down again, landing on the soft hay. Reece took the bottle from me. "Keep working with her," he said, walking back to the other side of the barn.

"Uh," I started saying, but he was already turning on the spigot.

So I hauled a leg to straddle the calf like he had, then reached down and picked Bessie up, stabilizing her between my legs. When I let go, she stood for a little bit and took another step furtively forward.

It was amazing. Human babies took months to learn how to walk, but cow babies somehow came out just knowing how to do it? I'd had no idea.

And as if invigorated by the first bottle, she stayed on her feet, awkwardly stumbling forward on her long, coltish legs. By the time Reece got back with the second bottle, she was moving around the pen like a little champ.

"Look!" I said.

Reece grinned. "I leave you ladies alone for two minutes and look at this."

I giggled, delighted even though I knew I hadn't really done anything.

"You want to feed her again?" he asked, holding out the bottle to me.

Was he kidding? Of course I did. I took the bottle and Bessie was getting along with the program at this point. When I went over to where she stood, she latched right on and started suckling.

I thought she might get full and not finish the whole thing, but nope, she sucked down every last ounce of liquid from the bottle, and then trounced with a little more sturdiness with each step.

"Oh my gosh, look at her go."

When I looked over at Reece, expecting him to be watching Bessie like I was, instead his eyes were on me, and they were quizzical.

I immediately felt self-conscious. I'd forgotten myself. For the first time in... well, years, I hadn't been stuck in my head. I'd just been in the moment. In the wonderful moment, present with the animal, and the crisp morning air, and with him, unselfconsciously.

But now I was entirely self-conscious again. I handed him the bottle and hugged my arms around me, suddenly very aware that I was in another woman's coat. Wearing the only pair of clothes that I had. Standing somewhere I didn't belong.

"Well, I should go back and see to the dishes," I said. "Thanks for letting me tag along and see how Bessie is."

I turned to go and was almost at the open edge of the barn when Reece called out, "Wait!"

I paused, looking over my shoulder. He strode forward, his eyebrows drawn.

When he got to me, he had to lift a hand over his eyes to block the bright morning sun that had crested with a vengeance over the hill behind the house.

"Look, I didn't mean to eavesdrop, but I overheard what you said to Ruth. That you were hitch-hiking and heading into Austin without any friends or family there. That doesn't— I mean... Do you even have any money? What are you gonna do when you get there?"

I felt all the blood drain from my face. I suppose it was better than blushing with embarrassment, but the mortification was no less humiliating.

I tried to wave a hand. "I'll be fine. Don't worry about it." I tried to turn to go again but he put out a hand to stop me. Though he stopped short of actually touching my arm or grabbing me.

His hand just paused, hovered in the air. "Wait. Sorry, I'm saying all this badly. I'm not always so good with words. What I'm trying to say is, I've been where you are. Or shit, no. I have no idea what your situation is. Just that me and Jer..."

He huffed out a quick breath like he was frustrated at himself for not being able to get out the words he wanted to. "We haven't always been... *this*. We grew up shit poor, bouncing from foster home to foster home. And when we were seventeen, we split altogether. Lived on the streets for a few years."

I paused, my need to flee the conversation at all costs suddenly withering up.

"You?" I asked incredulously. "But you guys seem so..." I trailed off, looking out towards the horizon where Jeremiah was out with the tractor on a hill, unwinding a bale of hay in a long line behind him, cows trailing after him for their morning meal. I met Reece's eyes. "You guys have your shit so together."

Reece scoffed at that, then rubbed his hand on the back of his neck. "Yeah? That how it seems to you."

He nodded. "Well, that's good, I guess. At least we can pull off looking like we know what we're doing."

That made me laugh and he smiled. The sun caught his blue eyes and made them almost translucent.

The next breath of air I sucked in had nothing to do with my embarrassment at being caught at having nothing and little plan of where the hell to go next—and everything to do with the handsome cowboy standing in front of me.

Which was absolutely ridiculous and the *last* thing I needed right now.

"Well... dishes," I said, hiking a thumb over my shoulder towards the house again.

But Reece took another step forward. "Ruth said you could stay a few days. Why don't you take her up on that? At least rest for a while. Look, I don't know where you been or why you're headed where you're headed, but it couldn't hurt to take a minute and take a breather for a few days, could it?"

I hugged my arms around myself, feeling the chill of the morning for the first time since I'd stepped out of the house. "Why?" I asked, shaking my head. "What's the point? I might as well get on with what's ahead."

"Is there something waiting for you?" he pressed, not letting the point go. "Someone?"

I let out a long exhale, then answered honestly. "No."

"You don't even have a bag. Do you have any money? Forgive me for asking. I know I'm being a jackass. But you show up here, you help out so much last night and I— Look, there were people who helped Jer and me when we were down and out and had no place to go and what kind of man am I if I don't try to pay that forward?"

I made a helpless noise and tossed my hands out. "That's not how the world actually works. People don't just..." I tossed my hands outwards. "Help strangers. I don't know what your angle is, but I'm just trying to get a new start. I left a bad situation and I want a new start."

Reece nodded vigorously, eyes wide. He took a step back and held his hands up. "That's fine. Look, I get it. I probably wouldn't believe me either 'cause I've known my share of users and takers. Just a few days is all I'm saying. Get a few more good meals in you. A few more good nights' rest. Then Ruth can drive you into Austin like she said."

I frowned at him.

"You can help out around here, if that makes you feel better. You cooked this morning. You're earning your keep. It's not charity. God knows we can use all the help we can get. The bunkhouse is a goddamned disaster. If you wanted to do some cleaning in there, it'd be a godsend."

I blinked. Okay, well... Well, maybe that was different. "I guess if I was working for it..."

He immediately brightened. "I can give you a list of chores."

I laughed, still skeptical.

"Look, plus you're helping my karma here."

I rolled my eyes. "You don't believe in karma."

He looked offended. "Are you kidding? My fourth foster family was all hard-core hippies. I still meditate and everything."

"A meditating cowboy?" I smiled, charmed in spite of myself.

"If you hang out for even a few days, you'll see that ranch work is monotonous. Cowboys and Zen monks have more in common than people think, I bet. Long days with no one around, doing the same thing over and over, connecting to the land and living things around you. It's a trip, I'm telling ya."

"Huh," I said, not sure what the hell to make of Reece Walker. "Okay, well, um, I'll think about it. But I might as well put myself to good use while Ruth sleeps. So I'll go clean up the kitchen then I can start on the bunkhouse. Where's it at?"

Reece grinned like he'd just won the lottery. "Epic. Here, I'll show you since that's where I'm headed next."

And he talked my ear off the whole way about his Buddhist hippie foster family and all the things he'd learned from them, like we'd been best friends for years and not strangers who'd met the night before.

How was it that two days ago I'd felt all alone in the world and now I had enough people in my life to fill a breakfast table?

## 7

Doing hard work that day felt good. The bunk house was in a disastrous state. A deep clean was the least of its worries, as Reece and I soon discovered when I joined him after cleaning up breakfast.

I entered the building he'd pointed out and was immediately hit by the smell.

"Oh, dear Lord," I said and Reece grimaced.

"I know," he said, looking around. The building was a doublewide trailer that had been set up on the property, but it was pretty trashed inside.

"You slept here last night?" I asked him, feeling even worse, especially since I'd slept in the wrong room and he might as well have had his own bed last night.

He smirked and waved a hand. "Oh, this is nothing compared to some of the places I've spent the night. Plus, I found a cot that was pretty clean." He pointed to a cot he'd set up near the kitchen. There was a suitcase underneath it and more piled up beside, a reminder that he and his brother were as new here as I was.

I looked around the place, then back at him. He'd slept in worse? Then I remembered—he'd said he and his brother had lived on the streets. What kind of life had this man had? What kinds of things had he seen?

"Still, it would be good to do a deep clean so we can even start to see where the problems are," he said, finally frowning as he looked around.

There was just so much *stuff*, like whoever had last lived here had left in a hurry and almost willingly trashed the place on the way out. Either that or they'd just *lived* in this pigsty. There were beer bottles and stray clothing all over the floor. The kitchen had cups with molded over contents still in them.

"If you don't mind tackling the kitchen," he said, "I'll go wrestle the plumbing in the back." He grimaced. "It's not pretty back there."

"Oh my God, I'll take your word for it."

"Smart woman. Here, I've got some thick rubber gloves if you're gonna dig in here."

"I hope you have some industrial cleaning supplies too."

He laughed at that, but pointed to a bucket on the floor beside the disgusting kitchen counter. There were all sorts of bottles and sprays in the bucket, along with the rubber gloves he'd mentioned.

"Sorry I don't have a gas mask, but we can open the windows to at least get some fresh air in here. Cold, but fresh."

I didn't even wait for him, I just immediately went to the windows and started opening them.

"What kinda tunes you want?" he asked, holding up his phone. "Country or 70's rock?"

I thought of my long truck ride with Rick yesterday and scrunched my nose. "Anything but country."

He grinned. "Lynyrd Skynyrd and Kansas it is." He thumbed through his phone and then "Highway to Hell" started blaring more loudly than I would have expected from the small device.

He left it on a shelf in the living room between the back bathroom and the kitchen where I was. Then I snapped on the rubber gloves and got to work.

It was surprisingly cathartic to clean a really dirty room while rocking out to the classics. By the time "Hotel California" came on, I was swinging my hips and dancing along while I shoved item after item into the first of what would be many big black trash bags.

Song by song, bag by bag, order came from chaos and space began to open up from the disgusting clutter.

Occasionally I'd hear noises or Reece cursing from the back room where he worked on the plumbing.

If I stopped and thought about it, it should be shocking to me that I was in an enclosed space with a man and not freaking the hell out.

I was in the middle of nowhere with a guy who was all but a stranger to me. Ruth was asleep in her bed in another building and Jeremiah was God knows where.

But I... wasn't afraid.

I paused scrubbing the counter in shock when that realization hit me. In fact, dancing along to the music while I cleaned—something I never would have dared at home—was almost *fun*.

And this feeling I was feeling right now... this was what it felt like to *not feel afraid*. Holy crap.

I stumbled back, bumping against the counter at the thought. Sometimes it would happen at home, but only while Jeff was gone at work, and even then, there was always the underlying anxiety knowing he'd be coming home soon and wondering what sort of mood he'd be in.

I could never really... *unclench*.

But here I was, dancing around this strange bunkhouse, cleaning, doing whatever the hell I wanted, about to leave tomorrow and go somewhere completely new still and—

No one had a hold of me or a say on what I did.

I put down the rag I'd been scrubbing so diligently and let my head fall back as Aerosmith hit the high notes in "Dream On." I threw my arms out and then drew them dramatically back to my chest along with the lyrics.

*Dream on, dream on, dream on.*

I spun around, ready to throw my arms out again when I saw Reece standing in the hallway, arm leaned against the doorway, watching me.

"Oh!" I yelped, reaching out and steadying myself against the counter.

He was smiling. "Sorry to interrupt. Just wanted to know if you wanted any lunch? I'm gonna go grab some and feed Bessie her midday bottle."

"Oh!" I picked up the cleaning rag, feeling my cheeks flushed pink. "Oh. Um. Shouldn't it be me getting you the lunch?"

He frowned and laughed, then gestured around at all the bags of trash. "Looks like you're getting more done in here than I am back there wrestling with those pipes. But feel free to take a break for lunch." Then he rubbed the back of his neck with his hand, "Or however long you want, obviously. I had no idea you'd get so much done, frankly."

"Oh, I haven't even really gotten to the kitchen yet," I said. "There's about a decade's worth of grime to get off that stove."

He just paused and smiled a little quizzically at me. "Where on earth did you come from, Charlotte..." He trailed off at the end, like he was waiting for me to fill in my last name, but I didn't.

I just held up my now-brown-formerly-yellow sponge. "Well, I guess I better get back to it. I'll have whatever you're having for lunch if you wanna bring me back a sandwich."

He nodded. "Sure thing," he said, but for another long moment he just stood there, watching me with his head tilted like he was trying to figure me out. It was a little unnerving.

"What?" I finally asked and he blinked like he was embarrassed to have been caught staring.

"Nothing. Sandwiches. Right. Got it. Aye aye, Captain Charlotte."

I laughed at him when he swept up his hand in an over-exaggerated salute before heading out the door.

I didn't miss that he left his music behind for me.

Wow, he was sweet.

*And sexy,* cut in a foreign voice in my head. A voice I'd all but forgotten.

Holy crap, was this what it felt like to be... to be *attracted* to a man? I blinked, and not just from the astringent cleaner I was using to degrease the oven.

I was attracted to this guy. I thought of the way his muscles had bulged when he'd leaned against the wall.

*You're married*, said another appalled voice.

To an abusive asshole. Who I never intended to *ever* see again, in my entire life. Besides, I'd considered myself his wife in name only for most of our nine-year marriage. After he— After he—

Well, some things were unforgivable, and that was that.

Familiar pain lanced through my chest and defiantly, I shoved it away.

No. I wasn't going to sit and wallow in my pain anymore, not here in this new life.

My eyes strayed towards the rickety door Reece had exited through.

"Don't Fear the Reaper" came on, blaring throughout the trailer. Now that I'd cleared it out, the music echoed around the room to greater effect.

And I had a wild hair of an impulse, because dear God, I wanted to fly too, for real.

No more strings holding me down, no take backs. What if I did the one thing that would erase Jeff forever? Exorcise him from my body.

I wanted to claim this future for myself, in a way that would actually make me believe it was real.

Tomorrow I'd take Ruth up on her offer and have her drive me in to Austin. I'd hit the city early in the morning, look for work, find myself a women's shelter to stay at if I had to while I figured things out.

Yes, just one more night here and then I'd be gone.

My eyes flew back to the door as Reece came back in, a friendly smile on his face as he held up two plates, one with a sandwich for each of us.

Tomorrow I'd be gone, but tonight...

Well, tonight was a night to fly.

I worked hard all day on the bunkhouse trailer, fairly nonstop. Reece was in and out throughout the day between working on the plumbing and checking on the pregnant cows to see if any more were "dropping calves," as he put it. By sunset, he'd replaced the entire toilet and carried out several bags of trash from the bathroom and back room—they'd smelled so badly I'd had to hold my nose while he went by.

And apparently the ranch had two new baby calves, born without complications this time. I thought they would put the mother and baby calves up in the barn, but over dinner I was informed differently. They just let the mothers give birth to the calves wherever they happen to be out at pasture. Apparently, it was less stressful and cleaner than having them all penned up where it could get swampy with manure.

They talked about manure a shocking amount over the dining room table, that was something I was coming to find. But then again, it seemed no topic was off limits.

"Well, that's a good start to the season," Ruth said when Reece mentioned the second calf of the day he'd tagged just before coming in for dinner. "Three already. I saw the bottle calf running around outside so it looks like he's gonna make it after all."

"She," I corrected. "Her name's Bessie." Reece and I had both showered—me in the main house and him in the bunkhouse bathroom. Apparently the shower was passable enough to use. I glanced across the table at Reece, wondering if he was even single. Maybe he had a girl back in—where was it he'd said he and his brother had just moved from—Wyoming? Maybe he had a girl back in Wyoming and she just hadn't had a chance to move here yet.

Ruth lifted her eyebrows. "Don't go and start naming them now. They all end up at the beef processing plant sooner or later."

"First of the season always gets a name," Reece countered. "For luck."

Ruth rolled her eyes. "Sentimental."

I glanced across the table at Reece, wondering if he was even single. Reece just grinned and shoved a buttered roll in his mouth. I watched in fascination. How did he even make eating a roll look sexy? Maybe he had a girl back in—where was it he'd said he and his brother had just moved from—Wyoming? Maybe he had a girl back in Wyoming and she just hadn't had a chance to move here yet.

Blinking, I yanked my gaze away from his mouth. His lips in particular. They were full and wide, much fuller than I'd expect for a man.

I licked my own lips and then reached for my lemonade. Was the heat set a little high in here? I took a long drink. I was likely overcompensating. This was all a way to avoid thinking about trauma, right? Getting distracted by a good looking man? Giving in to the feelings he made twist in my stomach.

And then a rebellious streak inside me asked, so what? What if it was?

When I looked back at the table, it was to find Reece watching me. He looked immediately away, like he was the one embarrassed to be caught looking at me.

Which made my cheeks flush and my stomach do a little swoop.

Conversation swirled on around the table. Jeremiah started grilling Ruth about when the cows had last been vaccinated and where was the best place to get equipment they'd need to start reseeding grasses.

I tucked into the food, meatloaf Ruth had made for everyone, and enjoyed the laidback atmosphere of being around *people*. It had been so long since I'd been in a room anything like this. With conversation that was by turns easy, occasionally contentious between Jeremiah and Ruth, but always real. With real people talking about real things.

Was this what it could be like? Wherever I actually landed, when I got friends of my own, anyway. I swigged the overly sweet lemonade, another treat Jeff never would have allowed, and wondered when I'd stop comparing everything to my life with him, if ever.

After dinner everyone went their separate ways and I settled onto the bed in the room Reece had given up for me.

I was tired after the day of cleaning and scrubbing, it was true. But being tired after a day of actually *using* my body was so different from being tired from a day of tense muscles and dread of what might come when Jeff came home.

I felt exhilarated, flushed, and unable to sleep.

And the absurd, ridiculous impulse I'd had earlier in the day while watching Reece flitted back through my mind.

I turned off the light, got in bed, and tried to sleep.

Hours later, I was still trying.

I pulled the pillow over my head. God, no. It was ridiculous! I was Penelope Chambers, I couldn't...

But even thinking that name had me sitting up in revolt.

No.

NO.

I wasn't her anymore.

I'd never be her again, goddammit.

I looked at the clock. Ten at night. And then I yanked on the leggings Ruth had let me borrow, shoved my feet into the slippers— also from Ruth, and ran downstairs before I could think better of it.

---

I KNOCKED on the door of the bunkhouse. No answer.

Crap. I looked over my shoulder at the bigger house and suddenly felt ridiculous. What the hell did I actually think I was doing here? Just showing up like something out of a movie, and what exactly had I planned on saying? *Hi, you're sexy, wanna have sex?*

God, I was such an idiot.

I took a step back from the door, about to turn around, when it suddenly swung open.

And there was Reece, looking disheveled, one hand on the hem of his shirt like he'd just yanked it on to come to the door.

"Charlie." He looked very surprised to see me of all people standing on his doorstep. He moved his body behind the door and it was only then that I realized he wore just his boxers and the under-shirt. Right. He'd probably expected his brother.

I gulped.

"Is something wrong?" he asked, looking behind me to the big house, which I knew was completely dark.

And I was just standing there frozen like an idiotic statue in the middle of the night being a complete freak—

"You're sexy and I wanted to have sex with you."

Oh shit. Did I really just blurt that out? My hand slapped over my mouth like it couldn't believe I'd just said it either.

Reece just stood there, still looking stunned in front of me, one hand on the top of the door, the other on the door frame. Wow, he looked *really* sexy standing like that.

Holy shit, what the hell was I thinking?

Abort! Abort!

I yanked my hand down from my mouth and took a step back. "Shit. I'm so sorry. That was completely inappropriate of me. God." I waved my arm in the air. "Forget I ever said anything. Look I'm leaving tomorrow, so we can just—"

But before I could say another word, Reece had grabbed my flailing hand and pulled me inside the bunk house.

He closed the door behind me and for a second we just stood there inside the dark bunkhouse—there was only a nightstand lamp set up on the kitchen counter beside his cot to illuminate the large space.

I blinked, my breaths short and heavy, feeling goosebumps rise but also a flash of heat making me sweat at the same time.

And then we crashed together. I threw my arms around his thick, corded neck and dug my fingers into that unruly hair of his.

And oh my God, it felt good to have a warm body against me that *wasn't Jeff*.

This was a man I chose.

A man who was safe.

Although thinking that... I completely froze up. Because what if now that he had me alone in his space, I *wasn't* safe? What if I changed my mind and said no? Would he stop? I was nuts to be here. I didn't know anything about this guy, not really.

I yanked back from him.

And waited for hands to follow. I waited for his voice to turn cruel. I waited for fingers at my throat shoving me up against the wall, calling me a fucking tease.

Instead, Reece's hands went limp, then lowered as he looked in my eyes. "Charlie? Is everything okay?"

My heart was racing a mile a minute, a war raging inside me. Fornicate or flight?

I don't think I'd ever wanted a man between my legs more—I was shocked to even have an impulse like this, so raw and needy and... and *dirty*.

But I just needed to know—

"You'll stop if I say stop?" I whispered anxiously, my hands reaching out and clenching reflexively around his shoulders.

His eyes widened, like almost for a second he looked horrified, and his hands dropped off me completely. "Charlie, look, we don't have to do anything. Why don't we slow down? I've got some tea I can make and we can talk—"

"That's sweet," I said as I grabbed his jaw and went to kiss him desperately again.

I paused just a tiny moment before meeting his lips, allowing him the choice too. He chose the second I offered, and our lips met in the most—

It was like being lifted out of my body and coming back into it for the very first time.

I blinked open in shock and looked into his blue-gray chameleon eyes. They changed colors, I realized now, depending on what he was wearing. In his gray nightshirt, they were stone gray.

We kissed again and *wow*. I cemented my body against him, needing to touch as much of him as possible, all at once. Surface area, I needed surface area.

Why were our stupid clothes still on, anyway? What the hell? I wanted to be touching his skin. I wanted *my skin* to be touching *his skin*. I wanted *all the skin* to be rubbing, and sliding against each other, and I wanted to lick all the way down his—

I broke the most glorious kiss on God's green earth to grab for his hem. He met me and together we yanked his shirt up and off over his head. It got caught on his forehead and we both laughed and then kissed, and then laughed through our kiss. And then kissed until there was nothing more to laugh about.

I reached down and pulled my long-sleeved shirt off over my head. I wasn't wearing a bra. I *had* had a plan in mind when coming here. There was a yellowing bruise on my back from where Jeff had kicked me last week, but it was fading. As long as we stayed facing each other, it should be fine.

But all my plans seemed silly now that I was faced with the reality of Reece in the flesh. Dear Lord, I'd had no idea, I'd been a little fool thinking I'd just try to get something out of my system when—

Reece reached down, his hand slipping directly underneath my leggings and my panties all at once. And just like *that,* he found the spot.

I gasped and arched into him at the cool touch of his middle finger against me. It was so intimate for him to touch me there. Reece. Oh God, Reece was touching me *there*. He tickled inside me, pushing in my channel just a tease and then pulling out again and expertly finding my clit.

Holy shit, who *was* this guy??? I thought guys being able to do this, well, were a myth.

At the moment, I didn't fucking care who he was, just that he was here, and he was with *me*.

He circled deep, and I mewled. Yes. Mewled. But now he was *stroking* with his finger, deep in the channel, then circling my lips and landing on my clit, then pulsing with his palm in hard, round rubs right where I'd always ever wanted. Oh shit. Oh God. Holy— Yes, that, holy shit, *that*—

His mouth on my mouth silenced my shouts. I wasn't being quiet because I couldn't, I couldn't, because now he was flicking my clit with that devilish middle finger of his flicking and then circling, flicking and circling—

So I cried my pleasure into his mouth because it— It—

It just felt like I was bursting out in a starburst. My whole body flying upwards, like energy had burst out from my sternum and then resounded back in through my pussy.

And when I landed back in my body, holy shit. Holy shit, it was him and me. He was there, and his mouth was still demanding and in charge of mine.

I met him, aftershocks rolling through my body, pulsing through our kisses.

"Bed," I gasped, glazed tears of pleasure at the edges of my eyes, realizing only now we were still just standing in the doorway, me clutching Reece's body while he played my mine like an instrument.

"Bed. Let's do this." My breaths came out panted and I couldn't say much more than that.

He slid his finger out of me *achingly* slowly; only to grab my waist and tug me over to the cot.

Which was when we both realized that yeah, it was a cot.

I put my hand over my mouth and started giggling. Reece just grinned, kicked off his boxers, and sat down to straddle the thing. He leaned over and reached down in his dusty suitcase that was still under the cot and pulled out a condom.

"Very good boy," I said. I arched an eyebrow, to which he grinned and held out his hands in a ridiculous *ta da* motion. Dear Lord, the fact that I was managing human speech at all after what he'd just done to me... *Somebody give me a damn prize.*

"Ready and waiting, honey."

Then he reached out his arms for me as he lay backwards on the cot, legs still straddling either side like he was bracing for me. He was cocky and confident as hell, but also had a twinkle in his eye that told you he didn't take himself too seriously at the same time. I'd never seen anything more attractive and my sex contracted remembering the orgasm he'd coaxed out of me with just the twitches of his finger.

I went forward, pushing off my leggings and panties and glad for the dim light. I was standing completely naked in front of a man. A man who was not my husband. It was terrifying and exhilarating. For once in my life, I leaned *in* to both emotions instead of running away towards numbness. I wanted to feel everything tonight. I wanted to feel alive.

Reece just grinned and I couldn't help giggling with lightness as he grasped my hips and helped me get situated atop him. His strong hands clutched my hips and helped shift me into place as I lifted and lowered myself onto him. And *hello*, he was very ready for me.

He slid into me slow, meaningfully, and one inch at a time.

For a few moments there during the transition, I'd lost track of the intensity that zinged down through to my bones, it felt like.

But then, within moments, we were back in the thick of *it*—that ridiculous connection and chemistry I hadn't known or even suspected was actually possible in the real world.

A spasm rocked my lower half at the memory, leftover from the earlier high he'd taken me to.

Another inch down. He grasped my hips, hands so large the edges of his fingertips were squeezing my buttocks. I clenched around him, convulsing even as my next orgasm started rising. I'd never been so conscious of my body, inside and out, as I was right in that moment.

And gah, where he took me... It wasn't an orgasm as I'd experienced before in any recognizable form. This was— This was—

It was bright sunlight from inside me and then these pulses started coming, lashing me higher and higher and—

His hand came between our lips to cover my mouth. Because oh, apparently that high-pitched squealing was coming from *me*.

It didn't slow either of us down. He just held my gaze, kept his hand over my mouth, and dragged me down onto him with his other hand.

My whole body shuddered. As the peak hit me, I blinked and looked at him. Unable to look away, to look anywhere but at him, tears leaking from the edges of my eyes.

He yanked his hand away from my mouth and sat up, kissing me hard and pushing up into me at the same time I ground down. I ground down and rode him, shamelessly chasing more pleasure.

He pulled away from my lips and he was just watching me in wonder, almost, in awe—

And then he gently cupped my face and kissed me soft while he began to thrust from beneath me.

He was—

I didn't know this man. He was a complete stranger. But he wasn't at the same time.

I threw my arms around him and clutched him to me. I kissed him more frantically than I even knew I knew how.

He met my lips with his, calm to my frantic, and then frantic to my frantic, and then both of us calm and languorous. All as he made love to me in turns slow and then *hard* and then grinding and then slow and torturously again.

Until I dug my fingernails into his hair and dragged his chest against mine.

He grinned, and kissed me deep, and thrust several more times, long, long and deep. Over and over and over again.

Until finally, in his time, but not too long, I felt the moment he came. And I saw it on his face, that agonized pleasure, his eyes cracked *just the tiniest bit* so he could keep his eyes on me even in that moment. Maybe *most* in that moment.

My thighs shuddered and we were left gasping and clasped in each other's arms.

I dropped my head against his chest, laughing. Oh my *God,* that had felt good. I'd needed that.

I felt his big chest rumble as he started laughing, too.

"What are you laughing at?" he asked.

I giggled harder. "What are *you* laughing at."

"I'm laughing at you, giggling and jiggling up and down on my cock. You keep it up much longer and we're gonna be ready for round two."

At which point he proceeded to flex his cock inside me to remind me that, oh yes, he was still very much inside me.

I giggled so hard I thought my red face was going to explode. I climbed off him. He made a disgruntled noise, but let go of my waist. After I got off, he turned to the side and discreetly disposed of the condom. Ah, yes. This was not his first rodeo.

Well, I supposed not, as good looking as he was. The fact that he *didn't* have a girlfriend or wife was probably the real indicator. Ruth —ever the interrogator-in-chief—had pressed both him and Jeremiah about their relationship statuses.

Of course it was all for the better if he was one of those kinds of guys who might take a number to be polite, but never call it anyway.

I was leaving tomorrow—well, *this* morning, considering it was now likely far past midnight.

I reached down for my shirt, still careful to make sure my back was angled away from him, and started to tug it on over my head when he reached and tugged on the fingers of my hand.

"Hey, what's your hurry?" He hopped off the cot and held out his arms in a gentlemanly gesture, only *slightly* undercut by the fact that he was buck naked. "Look, the mattress is yours even."

I giggled and leaned over, then grabbed his shirt and tossed it in his directions.

"I'd say, 'Another night,' Romeo," I said with a wistfulness I wasn't sure was trying to be funny bravado or genuine, "but unfortunately, I leave in the morning."

Suddenly neither of us was laughing.

And he crossed the distance between us and pulled me into his arms. It didn't feel sexual. He just held me.

I clung to him back, feeling something desperate in my chest at the thought of leaving in the morning.

I broke away as soon as I could, and tried to smile breezily as I turned and hurried towards the door, then out it, and all but raced back to the house and up to my own bed.

Where I would fretfully reimagine everything that happened back down in that bunkhouse in *exquisite* detail, on repeat, torturing myself until morning light broke.

# 8

I FINALLY FELL ASLEEP FOR TWENTY MINUTES BEFORE MY ALARM WENT off, which was *not* conducive to preparing myself for the day I had ahead of me.

I'd only be starting my new life today. No biggie. Not like I might need *all* of my mental and physical capacity at *full* this morning.

I climbed out of bed—the *correct* bed this time, and couldn't help my hand caressing the mattress. What would be Reece's mattress.

Ridiculous, thinking about a man when there were so many bigger things to contend with today. It was probably just a defense mechanism or something. My brain focusing on the hot guy I'd had the incredible sex with last night instead of all the scary things that lay in front of me.

I nodded, deciding that was it as I pulled on my jeans and got dressed.

Ruth was kind and, realizing I didn't have any other clothes except the ones I'd shown up with, had given me some extra shirts and an old pair of her jeans, along with a couple pairs of faded leggings. The jeans were loose and too long, but I just leaned over and rolled them up, grateful I didn't have to go downstairs again in sleep clothes just to change into my own in the laundry room.

I folded the few other items, then wrapped them all up in the largest shirt, using the arm sleeves to tie the bundle shut.

It was a pathetically tiny bundle of belongings, but hey, compared to what I'd had just days ago, it was improvement. I was moving up in the world.

I rolled my eyes and then headed down for breakfast.

Or what I assumed would be breakfast. Instead, I walked into a stand-off between Ruth sitting at the table with her arms crossed over her chest, glaring at Jeremiah who looked like he'd just walked in the door, Reece behind him.

"What?" Ruth asked. "You expect me to just make you breakfast every morning and help around the ranch? Why should I? It's not like you're paying me. And you didn't inherit a wife with the property, buddy."

Jeremiah just glared her down as he yanked off his hat. "Never thought I did. Didn't intend to inherit a landlady with the property either." He jammed his wide-brimmed hat on the hook. "And I can cook myself breakfast just fine, thank you very much."

"Oh, let me!" I said, hurrying into the kitchen.

Ruth swung her head towards me, as if I'd just betrayed all womankind. Shit, I hadn't meant that.

I held up my hands. "Or not. Just trying to be helpful in return for hospitality. Sorry if I'm overstepping."

But Jeremiah's gaze landed on me, and it didn't glance off immediately like it had all yesterday. Instead he paused and seemed like he was assessing something.

"I saw the work you did out on the bunkhouse yesterday," he said. "I can't believe you cleaned up that whole place by yourself."

"Oh." I shrugged, not expecting the compliment. "I don't mind a little hard work. And I'm so grateful you all gave me a safe place to stay when I needed it."

He nodded. "Reece said you were good with the calf, too."

I smiled. "Bessie's a pleasure. Can I see her again before we leave?" I asked Reece, then looked to Ruth. "I know we'll need to get going soon, but maybe I can feed her one last time?"

Ruth opened her mouth to say something, but Jeremiah cut her off. "What if you didn't leave?"

"What?" I choked out right at the same time as Ruth said, "First good idea you've had since I met you."

I looked back and forth between Jeremiah and Ruth, suddenly acutely feeling Reece's presence in the room, but not able to bring myself to look at him. Who was I kidding, the entire time since I'd stepped in the room, he was all I could think about, all I could sense, but I'd refused, *refused* to look his direction. So what if I felt even an iota of the heat I had from last night? God, I'd die of embarrassment of anybody else here sensed any of that.

So I kept my gaze firmly averted.

Until his brother suddenly came out with the ludicrous question about me not leaving.

I met Reece's eyes and they were staring right at me, steely gray to match his dark gray Henley shirt he wore.

"I agree," he said. "You should stay. No need to move on so soon if there's no one waiting for you."

I blinked, then looked back at Jeremiah, if only for my sanity. "But I'm not strong enough to be a ranch hand."

Ruth scoffed. "That's bullshit. You think women haven't been doing this work for centuries? Plus, machines do most of the heavy lifting these days. I kept the ranch afloat almost a whole month and all the cows fed and watered before these two showed up. All by myself." She waved her arms toward the twins.

"No wonder—"

Ruth pointed her finger in Jeremiah's face. "Finish that sentence and I'll put this boot so far up your ass you'll be coughing leather. You try running this place by yourself. I about dropped with exhaustion at the end of every night. And guess what. No one was paying me shit. It was just for love of these stupid animals and this land."

Jeremiah's face gentled, just the slightest bit, but he didn't say a word to her, he just moved his eyes from her, back to me. "See? I've known plenty of women who worked side by side with a man and were more reliable by half. I know you got your own plans and being a ranch hand probably ain't on that list. But the way I see it, we're short-handed at the moment, and you probably need some cash to make an easier start of it. At least stay through calving season. That's two months' pay to set you on your way, and two months for me to find more permanent steady labor."

I blinked and felt stupid that I didn't know what to say at his offer.

It made sense when he explained it like that.

But I'd made plans. I'd had it all mapped out so clearly in my head.

My eyes flicked involuntarily to Reece, and I realized what was really stopping me from accepting.

I never would have been so forward and slept with him like that, been so uninhibited, if I knew I'd be staying on.

But what did I really have in Austin?

The hope of *maybe* finding a women's shelter and hoping they had a spot for me. I'd googled several on Ruth's computer last night and had their addresses. Yeah, I could call ahead, but even if they did have space, what if I couldn't find a job right off?

Jobs required things like social security numbers and IDs. I'd have to find someone willing to pay me under the table and who knew what kind of work that would end up being.

I didn't feel comfortable bringing it up right now, with all three of them staring at me, but something told me that Jeremiah and Reece would understand the need of paying off-the-books. Dear God, not that I ever wanted to explain just what the hell my *situation* was, but I could probably get away with some half-truths.

It was certainly a much better option than trying to befriend a whole new strange employer when I had a good potential one right here in front of me.

So I made a split decision and held out my hand to Jeremiah, focusing all my attention on him and not the searing gaze I could feel from his twin coming from behind him. "When can I start?"

He sat down beside Ruth at the breakfast table and held out a hand. "Right now, if you're rested enough, with breakfast. Reece is good with a quick camp breakfast too, if you want to take the morning off to get your bearings and start later this afternoon."

"Oh, no!" I held up a hand to stop Reece in his tracks. I wasn't sure I could handle any closer proximity to where he stood, still by the door. "I got it. Take a load off with your brother."

And that was how it began.

My first day on the job.

Cooking breakfast and then Jeremiah suggesting after we were all finished that I should go out with Reece for the morning rounds to learn what to look for and how to tag the newborn calves myself so I could take over the job.

He said it so casually. Just ride out with Reece.

Meanwhile, I was freaking out more and more on the inside because when I'd accepted the job, I'd just assumed yesterday was a one off, that I wouldn't be working anywhere *near* Reece on a regular basis.

Only to find myself staring down the business end of a four-wheeler ATV with a single seat, with Reece asking if I wanted to drive or ride behind.

"B-behind," I stuttered, feeling my cheeks go scarlet.

He just grinned.

I glared at him, as a thought struck me. "Did you tell your brother to offer me the job? Because look, last night was just a one-off. Don't go thinking that—"

He held up his hands before I could go any further. "Nothing of the sort. I did tell him he should come by and see how much we'd gotten done on the bunkhouse, but that was all. I swear I didn't say another word. Your work impressed him all on its own."

"Oh." I stood there, feeling a little silly. "Well."

"So last night was just a one-off, huh?"

My head jerked up, just in time to meet his gaze. I nodded firmly. "Yes," I said, before climbing on the back of the long four-wheeler seat. It was like an extended motorcycle seat that forced you to straddle it.

Reece came up and climbed on in front of me, grabbing hold of the handles and revving it to life.

He looked over his shoulder at me. "Hold on to me. It can get bumpy."

"I'm fine, thanks."

He shrugged. "Don't say I didn't warn you."

With that last ominous statement, the four-wheeler jerked forward. My hands flew to the frame of the ATV underneath and behind me. Anything so I didn't have to grab onto *him*.

Though as smooshed together as the rest of our bodies became as the four-wheeler jolted forward, it was all but a moot point. I still clutched onto the back frame, refusing to hold on to him.

He didn't go too fast though, and I had a feeling he was taking it slower than he usually would, for my benefit.

It was chilly out and without any gloves on, my hands and fingers were immediately freezing. But as the crisp February air blasted me in the face and we drove straight out into the pasture, leaving the house in the distance behind us... well, it was surprisingly sort of *exhilarating*.

Riding ATVs was definitely not anything Jeff would have let me do. Certainly not in the cold open air like this.

We crested one small hill and then a whole valley opened up, the winter sun bearing down through the heavy white clouds onto the wheat-colored land. Nothing was green here. It was all spun-honey-brown, as far as the eye could see. Faded grasses shivered and listed as the wind blew through.

And then we finally got to where the cattle were. I gasped when I saw them herded together, munching on both sides at a line of hay that had been unspooled down the field for them. There were so many. I tried to count but quickly gave up.

There had to be hundreds between this pasture and the next hill we crested. We slowed down when we came to the next group all bunched up together.

"Look, see there's one of the calves from yesterday," Reece said, pointing to a cow and a small calf standing in amongst its legs. Let's go check up on him."

Without waiting for my response, the ATV shot forward again. The cows barely turned their heads our direction. The must be used to the four-wheeler. That was good.

Only a few looked disgruntled when we stopped amongst them and Reece sat with his hands loose on the handles, watching on.

The small calf rooted around at his mother's udder, then began to feed. Reece nodded and reached for the handles again. "Sometimes a check-in can be as easy as this. All you need is to see that the calf is on its feet and bonding with its mother. She should be doing most of the work taking care of him."

I nodded, glad he was treating this as instructional and that I hadn't ruined everything by sleeping with him. Some guys could probably turn into real jackasses once you slept with them if you had to work together. Any other time I would have kicked myself for doing what I did last night... But considering how damn good the sex had been, I just couldn't bring myself to. I wasn't sorry, even if it made things a smidge awkward today. Sorry, not sorry, but it had been worth it to feel that way, even if only once.

This was my new life. And I was going to grab it by the balls, goddammit. I'd been terrified of making a move for ten years. Enough was enough. I was making decisions now, for better or worse. Last night I had and that had seemed to work out well for all involved. I bit my lip and tried not to remember exactly *how* well as we left calf #2 in peace and moved on.

We drove on, crested yet another hill and then Reece stopped by a wooden wall that looked like one side of a building that no one had ever finished.

"What's this?" I asked Reece as we slowed down.

"Wind break," he answered. "It gives the cows a good place to stay warm on windy days. And look, here's our newest addition and Mama."

He pulled the ATV to a stop and got out. Again I saw another mother/calf pair, but the calf was lying at the feet of the mother cow. "Alright #3, it's up and at 'em time." All the calves were only known by their tag number, not given names like Bessie since that was only reserved for the first born of every season. Information I'd gathered like a good little sponge at the first stop. Because this was simply instructional. We had a professional relationship now and that was *all*.

He smiled at me and it was harder to remember the professional BS I'd just been trying to convince myself of. I mean, it wasn't like we were in corporate America or anything.

"I swear all the newborns hate me 'cause all I do is come around and disturb their rest during calving time. But you'll have to do this too. In fact, here, come on over." He gestured me to join him.

I climbed off the ATV, my legs feeling a little wobbly once I hit land again after the vibrations of the four-wheeler, but I managed.

"Help him stand up like you did Bess the other day," he instructed. "See if he can walk around. It's important the first few days to make sure they're always able to get up so we can double check that they aren't having any problems."

I nodded and walked over to where the little calf was laying nestled in some hay. The mother snorted and took a step my direction.

"Whoa, Mama," Reece said, voice calm but his hands out low and wide, stepping between me and the mother. "But be careful. Not all the mothers are excited by the idea of you messing with their babies. We just have to remind them that we're here to help them, that's all. We want your baby to thrive just as much as you do, Mama," he said, directly to the cow.

I reached down and grabbed the torso of the big baby calf and hefted him up. He was a heavy fella, maybe seventy-five pounds, so a little more than half my body weight. But he was doing some of the work. At my coaxing, he got right up on his feet and then started walking around his mother like it was no big deal. He started nosing at her utter and nursing.

"It worked!" I looked over at Reece.

He smiled at me. "Of course it did. You're a natural." I couldn't tell if he was just blowing smoke up my ass, but I'd take it.

I went to climb on the back of the ATV again, but then paused. "All right, so I guess if I'm gonna be doing this I should get comfortable driving this thing, huh?"

The sooner I could do this myself, the sooner I could get out of his proximity. Plus, I wanted to be useful, not have a babysitter.

He tossed me the keys. "You're up, Captain."

"Oh," I said, only just managing to catch the keys. A good thing, considering there was a cow pie on the ground right in front of where I stood.

I climbed on the front of the ATV and put the keys in, turning it on. Reece gave me a brief rundown on how to work it. It had a button shifter on the handle, hand and foot brakes. Nothing too hard. Plus, driving it looked... well, *fun*.

The only moment I got a little trepidatious was when Reece climbed on behind me. He didn't put his arms around my waist or anything, but I was suddenly very aware of the inside of his thighs cupping the outside of mine.

"Okay. Where to?" I called over my shoulder.

He reached forward, bringing his face into near contact with mine, so near I could smell the mixture of mint from his toothpaste mixed with his morning coffee. "Up over the ridge. You'll see there's a sort of trail that's been worn down between the grass."

I had the ridiculous thought of how easy it would be to turn my head and kiss him.

Which was one of those absurd, fleeting thoughts that just turned your face red and made you think: what the *hell*?

And simultaneously made me think with a sort of wonder—holy crap, was this what attraction felt like? When being close to a person feels like a torture and a tease both at the same time? It had been so long, I'd forgotten.

"Ready?" he asked.

"Yup!" I said too quickly, in a voice that was a little too squeaky. I cleared my throat. "Just... I mean, I'm ready when you are."

He chuckled, a warm sound in that husky voice of his. "Ready to go, Captain."

I pushed on the gas with the handle and the ATV launched forward with such suddenness that Reece's arms immediately grabbed for my hips. He let go a second later, as if he'd been as surprised by the four-wheeler's quick takeoff as I was. Not that I let up. This was way too much fun.

We couldn't be going faster than ten or fifteen miles an hour but it felt exhilarating to be flying across the pasture with the air rushing against my face and through my short hair. We came up to another group of cows and Reece tapped on my shoulder.

"Slow down," he called out in my ear from behind, his chest pressed up full against my back.

I nodded and down-shifted with the button like he'd shown me, slowing us, still a good distance from the cows. "What is it?" I asked him.

"We want to watch to see if any of them look like they're about to drop a calf."

I pulled the ATV to a stop. "How do you tell? What are the signs?"

He shrugged, eyes still examining the herd. "You start to learn how to tell."

"Not helpful. If I'm supposed to be out here looking for this by myself, I'll need more to go on."

"Okay, well, legs hanging out of a cow are a pretty good sign."

"Gee, thanks, I'd have never figured that part out for myself."

He chuckled again. "But there are some other tried and true ways."

"Such as—" I waved a hand.

"Well, if you see a cow acting weird. Not like herself."

I could feel my eyebrows lift. "How am I supposed to know how cows normally act?"

"You'll learn."

He spoke so confidently. And as if I'd be around long enough to learn the ins and outs of cow behavior.

"I'll still come out twice a day the first week to teach you what to watch for. But it'll be helpful to have you doing all the other trips so I can work with Jer to get the ranch up and running. Your job will be with the newborns, checking on them like we just did, making sure they're up and moving. Plus keeping an eye on the moms who are laboring. Some days it'll be busy and some days we might not have any newborns at all. But since the calves are the most important part of the ranch, we try not to lose a single one."

I nodded, suddenly feeling a little wowed that they were allowing me to be part of such an important task. And then immediately worried. "Wait, don't you think you should give this job to someone who has more experience? Like Ruth?"

Reece just smiled. He had a bad habit of doing that, especially since his smile was particularly lethal to parts of me I'd rather not acknowledge at the current moment. Okay, my nether regions, it was my nether regions. Every time he smiled at me it made me go liquid. Not helpful for my concentration.

Case in point, I blinked, realizing I'd lost track of what he was talking about. "Wait, sorry, sorry," I said, waving my hand. "Can you repeat that last part?"

"I was just saying that whenever we do find a calf, I'll show you how to tag the ear. Ninety percent of the time, there won't be a problem and we'll just find a calf on the ground, mama's taking good care, and all we need to do is tag the baby and log them into our system."

I nodded. Okay, that didn't seem too hard, except for the tagging part. "Does it hurt them?"

That smile again from Reece.

I blinked and looked away, squirming on the seat of the ATV. Not especially helpful, since it was still rumbling between my legs. I'd never, in my whole life, had my body feel so... well, so *awake* on me.

"Oh look, over there," Reece said suddenly. "See that red lady?"

I frowned and held a hand over my eyes in the direction he was pointing. I saw a group of cows. Most of them were brown, a few a lighter brown.

"Her. Look, the one that's separating herself a little from the others."

Okay, I did see one pulling away a little. She was sort of waddling, shuffling back and forth. It was definitely easy to tell the pregnant ones from the non-pregnant ones. They looked like they'd swallowed a barrel.

"I think she's about to pop," Reece said. "You can see she's uncomfortable. A cow about to give birth will separate out from the herd like that, and go between lying down and standing up. It's the first stage of labor, and it ends when the fetal membrane or water bag breaks. It can last from two to six hours."

"Should we go closer?"

"Nope. Just means we should keep an eye on her. And clock the time." He pulled out his phone. "It's ten o clock now. Next time we come around we will go closer and see if her water's broken. Then comes hard labor, which shouldn't take longer than two hours. If it does, we start to get concerned, like we did with Bessie's birth."

"'Cause it can mean something's wrong?"

He nodded. "Exactly."

I shivered. "What do I do if I'm out here alone and run into that?"

"Come get one of us."

"That's the answer I was hoping for."

"Don't worry, we don't expect you to know what you're doing. You're just our eyes on the ground so I don't have to be out here riding around all the time doing the basics. That's all we're asking of you, just the basics. The complicated stuff we'll still handle."

I nodded. Okay, the more he talked, the more I felt I could *probably* handle this.

Until a few hours later when we came back by to check on Red as Reece had taken to calling her, and it seemed, magically, there was now a calf on the ground beside her!

"Oh my gosh!" I cried as we drove up. "Look! Look!"

We'd gotten lunch after Reece had driven me around the rest of the pastures. He'd sketched out a rough map of the land to help me orient myself—it was a bit overwhelming. The ranch was two thou-sand acres large. Two thousand!

Then we'd done a little more work on the bunkhouse. I hadn't quite finished yesterday. And now, here we were again. And there was a new baby cow!

"Excellent," Reece said, hopping off the ATV and then unzipping a bag on the back of it.

He showed me how to load the tagging gun, then held it out to me. "Just grab the ear and push the trigger as quick as you can. You don't always have a lot of time since the moms can be protective of their newborns."

I blanched. "Don't you think I should watch you do one first?"

He smiled his Reece smile. "No better way to learn than by doing. The more you do while I watch and can run interference with Mama cow, the better."

I gulped. "Um. Sure."

I wore a pair of gloves Ruth had lent me and I awkwardly grabbed the gun from him. A tag with #4 stuck out from what was essentially a giant ear-piercing gun.

"Just get the ear in between here," Reece pointed at the little slot in the gun, "and pull the trigger."

I looked around at all the cows milling around us to see where their ear tags were placed and they all seemed to be in the flappy part, but not too near the edge. Okay, okay, I could do this. I could totally do this.

Except, as we got closer and closer to Red and her small baby, still wet from afterbirth, I was pretty sure, nope, no way could I do this!

But Reece was there beside me, talking to the mama calmly and jovially, congratulating her on her baby and then he was all, "Go, do it now. You got this. Go for it before she gets riled."

So I approached as quick as I could and leaned down. The calf scrambled to its feet. Oh my gosh, yay, it could get to its feet all on its own! I was so excited I almost lost the little guy, or girl, crap, that was something else I was supposed to look for.

"Straddle 'em," Reece called, again stepping between me and the mom. Something Mama Red did not seem happy about at all. "And do it quick. Don't know how long mom's gonna be distracted over here."

Shit! I got a leg over the baby cow who started wiggling like it wanted to bolt and grabbed its ear.

Its little head started waving back and forth but somehow I slipped the ear in between the flap on the gun. I slammed my finger on the trigger. I jolted with the impact of the piercer, but the cow didn't flinch at all as the tag went in.

I jumped off and was about to scramble away when Reece called, "See if it's a boy or a girl. Grab a back leg and peek under the skirt."

Good Lord, this was no time for jokes. But I did it. Before the calf could scramble away again, I awkwardly grabbed the wet back leg and peeked underneath.

"Girl!" I called triumphantly. "It's a girl!" I let go and then jumped back and looked at Reece. "I think, anyway. Not sure what a boy would look like."

He laughed. "Pretty sure you'd know when you saw it."

"Will you double check just in case?"

He laughed but did. The mother cow mooed at us, but Reece was able to confirm that it was indeed a female calf. The mother moved in and continued licking at her calf, but not for long before the calf was out of her reach, nuzzling for one of her nipples and sucking earnestly, if ineptly.

"How'd I do?" I asked, watching in pride as the little tag bounced in the calf's ear. I handed the tagging gun back to Reece.

"Just like a pro. Next time, though," he grinned, "the tag does go the other direction."

"What? Oh!" I said, looking back down at the calf. Unlike all the other animals around us, the number wasn't actually visible because I had indeed tagged her backwards.

I rolled my eyes to the sky, but Reece just laughed and patted me on the back. "It was an excellent first tag. Come on, I'll show you how to enter the new calf in the system."

And so I learned.

# 9

A WEEK LATER, I WAS DRIVING THE ATV BY MYSELF WITH CONFIDENCE. Tagging newborn calves still freaked me out, but at least I was putting tags on the right direction.

A couple of days ago, one of the cows who'd given birth had mastitis—I wouldn't have even known what to call it. But her teats were gigantic and swollen. So much so the calf—#9—wasn't able to nurse, and we'd had to take him back into the barn on the back of the ATV.

Nine would have to be a bottle calf. Which was good news for Bessie, because now she had a buddy to play with. They were herd animals, so that was important. But it had been touch and go for a bit making sure Nine would make it. So Reece had stayed on with me another couple days. But they'd gone perfectly smoothly, so today I was on my own. We were now on calf #16 and since calving season was now really cooking, I was busier than ever.

Each day it felt like I gained yet another skill that would have felt completely foreign and alien to the woman I had been only a month ago.

There wasn't a lot of time to stop and think about it, but at the end of another long day, I slowed the ATV to a stop at the top of a hill as the sun dropped behind the western horizon. There'd been another two calves born today and I'd handled tagging and logging them all on my own, no problems.

I'd been completely terrified when I'd seen the mothers in labor earlier. My first instinct had been to drive the ATV back to home base to grab Reece from whatever project he and Jeremiah were working on, and drag him back out to... do what? Watch me tag the animal? Protect me from the mother cow?

I kept my cool and everything went fine. Reece was right, mostly the births went along fine without any help from us.

It felt great to finally be going it alone because I hated keeping Reece from his other duties when I was getting paid to do a job. It made me anxious to think I wasn't carrying my weight. So I'd been cooking and doing anything else I could think of to make up for it while still getting trained.

This meant I dropped into bed absolutely exhausted each night.

But keeping busy meant there wasn't time to think, and that was a plus. I was a big fan of not thinking.

It was harder than I'd imagined. For example, it had been pretty hard not to think about Reece when I was constantly cemented up against him as we drove the ATV all over the thousands of acres of ranch together day in and day out.

We hadn't talked once about *that night* since after the first morning when I'd said it was a one-off.

He'd been completely professional. He'd been kind, patient, and joked with me like he did with Ruth around the kitchen table.

But just because we didn't talk about that night didn't mean I didn't think about it. And trying *not* to think about something was the absolutely surest way *to* think about something, nonstop. That I had discovered this past week.

So I'd expected today to be better.

And it was.

Sort of.

Without Reece here to distract me, his big warm body and those strong thighs of his wrapped around mine from behind... see, there I went again.

I huffed out a laugh at myself as I watched the sunset. God, there was nothing like these Texas sunsets.

I swallowed hard at the same time. Because there was still an instinctive dread that struck every time the sun started to go down. Borne of a decade's worth of fear that the sun going down meant that *he'd* be home soon.

My fingers gripped the handlebars tightly and I closed my eyes, feeling the wind on my face and breathing in the fresh air that was so foreign from the stale, Lysol scent of my house back in California. I was in a pasture with cattle, so there was a slight scent of manure in the air.

Jeff would hate it here.

He hated camping and anything outdoorsy other than jogging. Even that he preferred to do indoors at the 24-hour gym two blocks down.

I looked down at myself—my mud-covered boots, flannel shirt, blue jeans with a rip in the knees. None of it was mine. Ruth had lent me every single item of clothes I was wearing, down to the underwear and socks. I wouldn't have any money to buy my own clothes until my first paycheck.

Jeff hated the idea of charity—though he gave publicly for appearances' sake, I knew in private he despised those who took it. Of course he did. Empathy was as foreign a concept to the man as compassion.

Great. Now that I didn't have Reece to distract me, I was thinking of Jeff.

I sat back in the ATV seat.

Did I always have to define myself in relation to the men in my life? Did that mean I was weak? Or broken, somewhere deep down inside?

I looked up at the sky. Neon pinks bursting through bright oranges, with deep blues and electric purples bleeding on the edges.

It was so beautiful, it didn't look real.

I looked around at the rolling hills, the animals, the brown grass waving in the wind, the clusters of cacti. Land, land as far as the eye could see. No people. No cars. Not even any planes overhead.

Just me and the open space.

I took in a deep breath and held it in my chest.

This, right here, was everything I hadn't even known to dream for. I hadn't known life like this was possible, but I'd suspected it could be, deep down in my soul.

And now here I was. I felt as free and open as the land, stretching outward on all sides and the wide, wide sky splashed with color above me.

My nose stung and I bowed my head as if that could keep the tears from falling, but of course, it couldn't. They fell down my cheeks. Defiantly, I raised my face back to the sky and watched the sunset. The wind hit my tears and made me even more aware of them.

"You're here," I whispered to myself. "You're really here. You made it, honey. You're safe."

I didn't think about anyone else. I didn't think about a man. Or where I would go next. Or where I'd been before.

I wrapped my arms around my torso and held myself, and watched the sunset, and cried.

# 10

I WAS JUST PULLING BISCUITS OUT OF THE OVEN WHILE KEEPING AN EYE on the sausages sizzling on the griddle when Ruth came downstairs a few days later.

It was only eight-thirty in the morning but I'd already been out and done my first round checking on the newborns, as well as feeding Bessie and Nine their morning bottles.

I was dancing to a song on my mp3 player as I turned and smiled at Ruth. "Morning!"

She stared at me, then her eyebrows furrowed. "You realize you haven't had a day off since you came here."

I set the tray of biscuits down and hustled to grab the spatula and move the sausages around. "Oh, it's okay. I don't mind. Plus, isn't that the whole gig? Life on a ranch never stops? The cows don't take a day off, so neither can we?"

Ruth laughed. "Dear God, it's like you were meant for this life. Or you just haven't shoveled enough manure yet. Dealing with the calves is the best part, I will admit."

She sidled up to me by the counter. "But you don't own this place. You just work here. And you get time off. Pretty sure it's the law."

"Oh," I said. I hadn't really thought about it. Frankly, I was glad to have things to do every day. What would I do with time off? Ruminate on things better off forgotten. No, better to keep busy.

"I don't mind," I started to say, but just then, the door off the kitchen opened and Reece and Jeremiah came in, and they came in loudly, mid-conversation, like they often did.

"I'm telling you, we need to move them in," Reece said.

"We can't," his brother answered. "The pastures are a mess. They gave no thought to recovery periods or optimal growth cycles, and the soil! Jesus, the soil!"

Reece just shook his head. "But another fence was downed in the west pasture and I'm telling you, I don't think it was the cows. When I looked closer—"

"Hey," Ruth interrupted. "You ever gonna give your employee a day off?"

They both looked up at us. I started to wave my hand and say it was okay, when Jeremiah took off his hat, putting it on the hook, and said, "Of course. I know it's been busy while we trained you, Charlie, but we can set up a schedule now. Xavier always gave us one day a week off, so if that sounds fair to you—"

"Absolutely," I said, and didn't miss Ruth rolling her eyes.

"How about I take her into town with me today?" Ruth said. "We can even get more cake. I saw you were running low."

"Cake?" I asked, laughing.

"Cottonseed meal, dried grains, maybe sunflower meal," Reece said. "Plus the minerals and protein cows need. It tastes good and they're usually excited to get it."

"You need more and how about I take our girl in town to get it? You set up an account with Mr. Rivera, didn't you?"

Jeremiah nodded. "Apparently, I'll be spending the morning chasing down lost cows again, and we'll need both ATVs anyway."

"Perfect!" Ruth declared, grinning and throwing an arm around my shoulders. "Then I'm sure you won't mind fixing yourselves lunch, too, while I kidnap our girl here for lunch out."

"Oh, I don't have to be away that long," I said hurriedly. "Especially if I'm needed here."

"No, no," Reece said. "Go. You deserve some time for a breather."

I looked up and met his gaze, something I tried not to do most of the time for exactly this reason, this zap of electricity or energy that hit me every time I did. He'd taken a step forward but then stopped, and the way it looked in his eyes, it was as if he was intentionally holding himself back, even though he wanted to come closer. "Enjoy town. You've been working your butt off. We got it and like Jer said, we'll be on both ATVs anyway."

"Okay," I whispered. Then cleared my throat a little and nodded, still not looking away from Reece. "If you guys are sure."

I finally dragged my gaze off Reece and looked at his brother. Who was also looking at Reece, his brows drawn together slightly. Oh crap, had he noticed something? Was there something to notice? Reece was just being friendly. He was a friendly guy.

I smelled something burning and then turned back to the sausages. "Shit!" I yelped, grabbing the pan and yanking them off the stove. One side of the sausages was blackened.

I flinched, freaking out and terror-stricken as I looked down at the ruined sausages. "Oh my God, I'm so sorry. I'll make a fresh batch. And you can take this batch out of my salary, I'm so sorry—"

"Hey," Ruth said, touching my arm. "It's no biggie. It's just packaged meat, honey."

Which was when I looked up and realized they were all looking at me strangely. And not because I'd burned the meat.

I looked from one face to another. "I... um..."

"Don't worry about it," Reece said, stepping forward and grabbing one of the sausages that had to still be way too hot to handle from the plate where I'd flipped them from the pan. He took a big bite off the end and even though I heard the audible *crunch* from the burned side, he just grinned at me. "Tastes great to me."

And I wanted to burst out in tears. Ridiculous, stupid tears. Because of course burning a little pan of sausages wasn't a big deal.

Except it would have gotten me beaten black and blue only weeks ago. And apparently I couldn't switch off a body's instincts that had been honed over a decade. Dear God, would I always be such a mess?

I nodded and turned away from all of them, taking the pan to the kitchen sink. Of course it wasn't necessary to clean it right now, but I couldn't bear for them to see the emotion on my face. I shoved the water lever to hot and started scrubbing the pan, blinking rapidly to try to get rid of the tears that were *still* threatening.

Ridiculous, completely ridiculous. I was furious at myself and at my stupid unwieldy emotions. For ten years I'd been stone cold, the master of control. So what the hell was wrong with me now?

At least the others had begun talking again behind me. I was too overwhelmed to actually hear what they were saying, but the buzz of their voices was calming, knowing attention wasn't on me anymore.

At least I thought so, until I felt a presence and looked over to see Reece's big body looming beside me.

"Hey, you okay?" he asked.

"Fine," I said, turning the water colder as I rinsed the pan, angling my body away from him to put it in the drying rack. I wanted to run away to the bathroom to cry, not be interrogated by anyone, least of all him.

And maybe he sensed that, because he backed off again. "Okay," he said. "Just, if you ever need to talk. I can be a friend. I hope we are friends."

I looked over at him in spite of myself, which I immediately regretted because I didn't know what emotions were still on my face. And I wanted to control myself around this man, desperately, because he made me feel out of control. He made me *feel* things that were out of control. He made me want to *do* things that were out of control.

And when a stupid tear slipped out of my eye and down my cheek and he saw it, I wanted to—

I didn't know what I wanted, honestly.

But then he reached over and swiped it away with his thumb and leaned in and said, "It's okay to cry, you know. You can cry over burned sausages or spilled milk or any damn thing you want."

He said it quiet, and Jeremiah and Ruth were still talking in the background—okay arguing, it seemed they were always arguing. But that meant the moment Reece and I were having was genuinely private, and I appreciated all of them so much in this moment.

"Sometimes it's not," I said back to Reece. "It's not okay to cry."

He shook his head. "Whoever taught you that didn't understand pain. That's bullshit. You let it out, whenever you need. No one here will judge you."

I frowned at him, feeling too many things, and gave a half-nod-half-shrug, and turned away again.

I pasted on a bright smile, something that felt familiar. The familiar felt good right now, so I stuck with it. "Who wants biscuits?"

---

"ALL RIGHT, Jesus, finally it's just us girls," Ruth said as soon as she shoved the truck into drive and jammed her foot on the petal, spitting gravel as we shot forward.

I grabbed the bar overhead, then quickly yanked my seatbelt on.

She looked over at me and grinned. "So tell me everything. God, I can't believe we haven't had a chance to talk since you got here. Sorry, I should have pulled you aside earlier for girl time but I've been dealing with my own shit." She waved a hand. "Dad left a shitstorm when he passed that I've been cleaning up ever since."

"I'm sorry for your loss."

She waved her hand again, but I didn't miss the slight tightening of her mouth. "He was a mean bastard. He certainly never bothered to give a shit about me when he was still around so why should I now that he's gone?"

"Don't let the bastards get you down," I said. I'd always loved the quote.

Ruth looked over at me and grinned like she was surprised. "Fuck yeah."

We drove a little further and then she looked at me. "So. Spill. You just show up out of nowhere. What's your story?"

"Oh." I blinked. I'd been grateful that nobody had pressed me about my past. But I guess I should have known that out of everyone,

Ruth would be the one to eventually ask. She wasn't exactly big on tact. That much was obvious by how much she bickered with Jeremiah all the time, even though they barely knew each other.

"Oh you know, I just needed a change of scenery. So I decided to start over somewhere new."

She made a scoffing noise. "Honey, people do not just decide to start over without any luggage or money and end up hitchhiking on highway 284 in the middle of nowhere Texas. I mean, believe me, I've lived here my whole life, and good looking strangers don't just go showing up out of nowhere."

"Reece and Jeremiah showed up out of nowhere," I countered.

She looked at me and slow-grinned. "So you think they're hot, huh?"

"What? No, I was just—" I waved a hand, flustered. "Shouldn't you be watching the road?"

She finally moved her eyes back to the dirt road, just in time to slow down because we'd come to the gate. "Hold that thought." She pointed at me. "We're going to come right back to this."

Dear God, did we have to? She jammed the truck in park and hopped out to go open the gate. I rolled my eyes and sat back heavily in my seat, looking at the ceiling of the truck. I wouldn't have agreed to come if I knew I'd be in for a game of twenty questions.

Far sooner than I would have liked, Ruth was back in the truck and we were rumbling over the cattle grate.

"I'll close it up," I volunteered before Ruth could lob any other intrusive questions or get out her pointy finger again.

I gulped in a few deep breaths as I closed the gate, and one last deep breath for good measure before I climbed back up into the truck. I hoped that Ruth would have moved on as she pulled back onto the pot-holed road that I thought was generously called a "highway." It was just a two-lane road.

"So, you and Reece. I've caught him looking at you a couple times. He's cute. If you're into that big, dumb cowboy sort of thing."

"He's not dumb," I said, a little outraged on Reece's behalf. "He's really smart. And good with the animals."

She raised an eyebrow like I was just making my point for her. "I knew you liked him."

Well damn, I walked right into that one.

"Let's not talk about them. We work with them for God's sake. That's just..." Immediately scenes of Reece's body beneath mine, hands clenching my hips flashed vividly through my head. I wiped my hands on my jeans. "Awkward," I finished lamely.

"Oh, fine," Ruth said. "Then tell me what it was like where you came from. Let me live vicariously through you."

Her head swung my way, immediately making me nervous that she wasn't watching the road. "Unless you're on the run from something. Did you rob a bank? Commit petty larceny? Breaking and entering? Did you poison a lover?"

"What? Jesus, how long have you been thinking about this?"

She shrugged. "My mom always told me I had an overactive imagination."

"God, well, it's not any of that, okay? I'm just a boring, normal ol' person. I just needed—"

"Needed a change of scenery, blah blah blah." She rolled her eyes. "Yeah, you said." She slit her eyes over in my direction, suspiciously.

I shook my head. "What even *is* petty larceny?"

"The fuck I know," she said, laughing. She punched me on the shoulder. "Lighten up. You wanna be Miss Mysterious, fine. But I'm an open book. You can ask me anything, I'll tell you, no problemo."

"Okay." I shifted on the truck bench to look at her. "What's a strong woman like you doing clinging to this ranch when you're obviously capable and motivated to get what you want when you put your mind to it?"

I still thought it was impressive the way she'd outwitted the twins to keep her small slice of the property—the most important slice, in fact. I just didn't understand *why* she'd done it.

"Oh, you won't dish on your story but then you want me to spill mine?"

I shrugged. "You don't have to, no pressure. I was just curious."

She laughed. "I'm just fucking with you. I'm not good with boundaries, if you can't tell. It's a problem. I used to be really concerned with doing everything right and not stepping on anyone's toes. But then Dad was an asshole who screwed over the entire town and almost everyone I knew turned on me, so I stopped giving a fuck."

I frowned. "So why don't you *leave*?"

She scoffed. "And give them all the satisfaction of driving me out of town? Never." She all but spit out the last word. "This is *my* home. This land has been in my family for four generations. Four *generations*. Then last year my dad goes and gambles what should have been my birthright into the ground because he didn't think a daughter was important enough to save it for."

I could tell she was seething, even just talking about it. And I felt immediately bad for asking. "Look, I'm sorry. I of all people should know I have no business to pry."

But she went on as if she hadn't even heard me. "Yeah, I get it, Mom was the glue holding us together, and when she died it all sort of fell apart. He and I were just going through the motions the past few years. At least I *thought* we were. I kept trying to get him to listen to my ideas about sustainable ranching but he could not give *less* of a shit. *It's been working my way for thirty years, Ruthie, it'll hold out another year just fine*," she intoned, lowering her voice in imitation. "And another. And another. Except it *wasn't*. And he just refused to look at the numbers. The only thing he ever wanted to do was be done by five so he could hit up the gambling halls and try his luck with the desperate bar bunnies."

She shook her head and shuddered. "Disgusting. Everyone in town loved Mom. It was a disgrace."

She looked my way. "Sorry."

"No, please. Go ahead and talk." Especially if it meant she stopped grilling me. But also, I was curious about her since she didn't seem to mind sharing. "What was your mom like?"

She sighed. "Mom was... She was great, I mean. She loved me. I don't know why she put up with Dad, but they loved each other, I guess. In their way. He was never awesome, but at least when she was alive he *tried*. He never made a secret of the fact he wanted a son. But she had a really hard time getting pregnant with me. There were a lot of miscarriages. It was a miracle she managed to carry me to term, so she always called me her miracle baby. But she had a lot of problems and had to have a hysterectomy a couple years after I was born. Which meant Dad was stuck with just me."

"Parents suck," I offered. And then, because it seemed safe, I shared, "My mom's pretty much a nightmare. Of course I didn't realize it till I was older, but she's a narcissist. So growing up, I was just really confused and hurt a lot of the time by how she was treating me. It sucks."

Ruth looked surprised when she glanced my way again, probably because I'd said anything about my past. I was a little surprised, too, frankly.

"Yeah? So what'd you do when you realized why she was like that?"

I let out a breath. "Well, by that point..." Screw it, I decided to just go ahead and tell her. "Well, when you grow up with a narcissist, the problem is, it can screw up how you relate to people. You end up picking relationships that feel familiar. So of course I was with a guy who was one too."

Ruth's eyebrows went up. "Shit."

"Yeah." Understatement. "Which was so funny because when I graduated high school and went to college, I was thrilled to get out of her house. I didn't know she was a narcissist, but I knew it didn't feel good to live there. I thought, oh, I'm finally free! And then I just went and jumped from the frying pan into the fire..." I trailed off and shook my head, looking out the window.

"What'd you go to college for?"

I rolled my eyes. "Literature. I was so clueless. I couldn't have picked a more useless degree."

Ruth shrugged. "I don't know. I was always shit at English, but I admired the kids who were good at it. I was dyslexic but it wasn't like I had teachers around here who recognized that kind of thing. They just barely passed me. It was my mom who helped me learn to read more than my teachers."

"Wow, that's amazing. Your mom sounds really cool."

Ruth nodded and swallowed. "She was. I miss her. All she wanted out of life was to be a mom and have a big family and instead she got stuck out on this lonely ranch with my dad who barely talked."

"And you. She had you."

"Yeah, I guess," Ruth said. "Just doesn't seem like much of a life."

Now she really had me confused. "But... Then why do you want to stay on the land so bad?"

She frowned. "Because... well, I'm the last of us. Of the Harsh-bargers. It was originally Hirschberger, but they changed the spelling during World War I to make it sound less German. My ancestors came here in the 1840's with a wave of German immigrants. They were badasses seeking a better life. My great *great* grandmother married Hermann Hirschberger after her husband died on the passage over and had three sons, only one of whom survived to adult-hood. They renamed him Hermann Jr when his older brother died and he bought the ranch and built the first farmstead. Each genera-tion fought and *barely* managed to keep hold of it. There were so many tragedies... And then for it all to end like this with *me*. God, it makes me sick."

She was staring straight out the front now, her jaw tight.

"But it wasn't *you*," I said, sitting up in my chair. "It was your dad. There wasn't anything you could do by the time you got control of things, it sounds like."

She shrugged. "Maybe there was some way I couldn't think of to hold onto it. Maybe if I'd been smarter or tried harder, I could've gotten the bank to extend the loan or something..."

I raised my eyebrows. "Well, it sounds like you were pretty tricky in whatever you did to keep hold of the bit of land you did, where the house is. The twins definitely weren't happy about it."

She grinned at that. "Fuck yeah. I'll never forget the look on Jere-miah's face when he realized." She laughed out loud. "Thanks, I needed that. See, I knew we'd be friends. And look! We're here."

We were indeed finally slowing down and I could see buildings ahead instead of more pasture on both sides of the road.

"Welcome to town."

Town was a street, just one street apparently, but to be fair, I did count... two restaurants, a small grocery, and a nail/hair salon in addition to the hardware store/feed shop Ruth pulled the truck into. And there were people out and about, the first I'd seen in weeks other than those on the ranch.

But it also made me slink down in the truck. This was exactly the kind of place I had *not* wanted to land for just this reason.

"Sheesh, what's the population of this town?" I asked, trying to keep my voice light.

Ruth laughed. "You noticed we don't even have a stoplight, did you? I don't know, probably about three hundred give or take."

My heart sank. This was the sort of place where everyone knew everyone. If Jeff ever sniffed me out and came through, all he had to do was flash my picture and all fingers would point to the new girl, number three hundred and one. Dammit, I never should have agreed to come into town.

Ruth shoved open her door.

"Maybe I'll just stay here," I said.

She frowned, "Don't be silly. I know we're hicks, but we don't bite. Besides, I'll need help with the feed."

Dammit, she had me there. I nodded and tried not to let the panic show on my face as I hopped down out of the truck.

Suddenly I really wished I had my old hoodie. Though maybe that would make me look even more out of place. My flannel and jeans were probably the best camouflage. Plus, any photo Jeff had was of the old Penelope. Fully made up, dressed to the nines, glossy blonde hair.

Besides, Jeff wasn't going to find me. I'd covered my tracks. I'd switched buses so many times, been so careful...

I took a deep breath and slouched as I walked with Ruth into the hardware store that looked like it had seen better days. Penelope Chambers had perfect posture. *Charlie* slouched.

The little bell rung as we stepped through the door.

"Hey, Ruth," said an aging man who had to be in his 70's. He stepped out from behind the counter and grinned at Ruth. "What can I do ya for today, Ruthie?"

A big grin spread across Ruth's face. "Heya, Sam. How's Gracie doing? She feeling better after that stomach bug?"

Sam nodded. "You know nothing's gonna keep my Gracie down for long. She's getting all excited about planting spring roses."

Ruth smiled. "Just have her give me a call if she needs any help. You know I always love digging in the dirt with her."

"I'll do that." Sam seemed very pleased by the offer. Then his face got serious. "How you doing out on that ranch? I heard the new owners showed up. They treating you well?"

Ruth laughed. "You gonna come chase them off if they weren't?"

Sam looked completely serious as he moved back to the counter, reached underneath the counter and pulled up the hilt of a shotgun. "Don't think I wouldn't. Ain't nobody gonna hurt our little missy. Especially no outsiders."

"Dear Lord, Sam, put that thing away." But Ruth was laughing, she didn't seem alarmed at seeing the weapon. My heart was pounding. Holy crap, I'd always heard that everyone in Texas was packing, but I was alarmed to find out how true it was.

"Everything's fine. No need to call out the militia just yet. They seem like good guys. We're making it work."

Sam didn't seem so sure and he kept one eyebrow cocked. "Well, you just call me if that changes."

Ruth shook her head and rolled her eyes. "I'm not the little girl Gracie used to babysit anymore. You don't have to worry about me so much. I can take care of myself just fine."

Sam grumbled something under his breath, but Ruth was already moving on.

"Sam, let me introduce you to Charlie. She's a new hire out at the ranch."

I waved. "Nice to meet you."

Sam turned his friendly smile on me. "Lovely to meet you, Miss Charlie. What brings you to our neck of the woods?"

"Oh," I laughed nervously and waved a hand.

Ruth came to my rescue. "Not much time to chat today, I'm afraid, Sam. I'm here to pick up some cake for the cows, and some sheetrock if you've got any in. If not, we'll need to put some on order. The brothers who are managing the ranch are finally fixing up the bunkhouse."

A beep sounded from Ruth's pocket and she pulled out her phone. Her eyebrows went up. "And as many fence posts as you've got, apparently."

"Something wrong?" Sam asked, obviously noting her expression like I had.

Ruth frowned but shook her head as she quickly typed a text message back and then shoved it back in her pocket. "I'm sure it's nothing. They've just been having trouble with the fencing. So, what do ya got for me?"

"Well, you're in luck," Sam said. "Just got in a shipment of sheetrock so you've got your pick. And we always got posts. Just up to how much space you got in the bed of your truck."

Ruth smiled. "Oh, I can get creative. I brought plenty of rope."

"You always were crazy with your loads, girl." Sam shook his head. "You know my policy. After you buy it and it leaves my store, no returns, no matter what fool thing you do to it after it leaves my shop door. Don't matter you're as close as family. I gotta make a living too."

Ruth threw a hand to her chest dramatically. "I would never," she said, making Sam chuckle.

"Better not," was all he said, before leading us to the back.

We'd just reached the section in the large back of the shop that was more like a big, covered garage when I saw him—the obnoxious guy who'd stopped by in the big truck that first day after I'd arrived. He stood by the wheelbarrows on the other side of the small garage.

Ruth saw him at the same time and her step hitched.

It was too late, though, because he'd seen us too.

He smirked and immediately started strutting toward us. "Well, if it ain't Ruthie and her new little girlfriend."

I just tilted my head and stared at him.

Ruth went tense beside me. Then she looked back to Sam and

gave him a smile that was obviously tight. "We'll take five of the big sheetrock panels, thanks, Sam. A half pallet of cake and ten of the fence posts. Is Carlos around? Could he help us load the truck?"

"Come on, Ruthie, don't be like that," said the asshole from across the room.

God, the man was obnoxious.

There were a few others milling around this back area of the store, and they were alternately openly staring or obviously trying *not* to stare, but still looking out the side of their eye at Ruth and Fuckface. What was his name again? I didn't bother too hard at registering idiot's names.

"For the hundredth time, my name is Ruth, not Ruthie. I'm not a child or a dog. Nicknames are only for people I *like*." She grinned daggers at him. "And we both know that's not you, Trent."

Anger flashed across his face. "How many times have I told you not to get uppity. Look what happened to your uppity dad. They would have thrown him in jail if he hadn't gone and died. You should be happy he didn't have the chance to disgrace the family like that. I mean, after all, you do a good job of that all on your own."

"And you do such a good job of showing off what complete *tools* your parents must be to have raised an entitled, whiny, little bitchboy like you."

Okay, I was officially becoming more and more of a fan of Ruth Harshbarger with each passing day I knew her.

I intentionally stayed out of it this time, though, because I did not need to get involved with something that was not my business.

Trent's face got red and he leaned in, having stalked towards us so that he was now only a couple of feet away. He sneered at Ruth. "That's not what you said when we dated and you begged me to fuck you hard. You thought I was plenty man, then, huh, little Ruthie? Remember how slick you used to get for me?"

"You're a pig." Ruth said in disgust, shoving him in the chest when he took another step closer.

"Enough of that, young man," Sam said, stepping between them and glaring Trent down.

Trent looked incredulous. "Did you see that? *She* shoved me!" He looked around the garage. "You all saw. You're witnesses!"

Sam growled at him. "I witnessed you being a jackass, that's all I saw. Now get the hell outta my shop."

Trent scoffed at him. "Please, old man. You wouldn't survive without me and my dad's money keeping this place afloat. But you're in luck." He held up his hands. "I happen to be done shopping for the day."

He shoved a dollar disrespectfully in the shirt pocket of Sam's flannel, then grabbed a beef jerky off the wall, opened it, and bit into it while he laughed and walked out of the open garage.

"Charmer," I remarked dryly as soon as he was gone.

Ruth let out a frustrated breath. "Pain in my ass is more like." She looked to Sam, her eyes remorseful. "I'm sorry, Sam. I know you don't need trouble from him or his dad blowing back on you."

He just patted her on the shoulder. "Ain't your fault that boy came out wrong, honey. And don't worry about me." He smiled. "I been around since long before that boy was just a gleam in his papa's eye. He don't scare me none. Now, come on and I'll get you checked out."

Ruth smiled and followed him back to the front of the store.

———

TWENTY MINUTES later we'd stopped by *Juniper's Hair and Nails* and picked up Ruth's friend Olivia, along with Ruth introducing me to every *single* woman in the shop. This included Juniper herself, an older woman with snow-white corkscrew curly hair down to her shoulders that went out in all directions. She wore a bright turquoise tunic-dress and sandals.

Juniper had taken one look at my hair and declared that I just *had* to come in for a cut and color.

I'd thanked her and looked to Ruth for rescue. She'd obliged and gotten us out of there, which had still taken another ten minutes between all the women saying extended goodbyes.

Now we were in one of the two restaurants in town—Alejandro's

Bar and Grill, and Ruth was treating us to fajitas and she and Olivia were downing big pink margaritas like they were water.

"You shoulda seen him," Ruth cackled. "Trent was all, you can't survive without my daddy's money. And Sam was like, fuck off, little boy."

"He did not!" Olivia slammed the table, pink margarita sloshing over the edge of her glass and onto her bright, sparkly jeweled nails. "Oh shit," she laughed and sucked the margarita slushy mix off.

Olivia had definitely embraced the colorful spirit of her mentor, Juniper. She had bright pink hair and a peacock tattoo that took up the entirety of her left arm. She would have fit right in back in San Francisco. In the middle of Central Texas? Not so much. From my whole ten minutes of exposure to her, she seemed fabulous. Bubbly and expressive in a way I'd only ever dreamed of being.

"Okay, okay, he didn't exactly say it like that," Ruth admitted. "But he still put that little bastard in his place and it was classic. And you know the gossip mill in this town. Mariah Jones was in there, so you know the story will be everywhere by Sunday afternoon after church."

Olivia's eyes went wide, then she laughed even harder. "Oh damn, Mariah was there. That's hilarious. Her sister was always so jealous of you, remember?"

"Dear God, don't remind me."

"I can't believe you actually *dated* that douche bag."

"I said don't remind me, I'm trying to eat here!" Ruth said as she shoveled fajita mixings into a tortilla.

"How did that even happen? Was he a lot different back in high school?" I asked. They both looked at me, like they were shocked I'd actually said something. Which made me feel like maybe I shouldn't have. I was an outsider, and just because they were talking so freely in front of me, God, it was stupid to think that they—

"Sorry," I said, grabbing for my water. "I didn't mean to pry. You don't have to say." I waved my hand and took a big drink, wanting to disappear. I hadn't been out with actual humans in society in a long while and I was terrible at this.

But Ruth reached out and put a hand on my arm as if she could feel my embarrassment. "No, it's cool. It's just weird for someone not to know my entire history from the time I was a baby. Refreshing, actually."

"Seriously, you don't have to say. Forget I said anything."

"Stop it," she said. "It's a totally valid question. Especially since no, Trent was always an asshole."

"I tried to tell her at the time," Olivia cut in, shoving a big, messy bite of fajita in her mouth.

Ruth rolled her eyes. "Yeah, yeah, and I didn't listen. I was really naïve and wanted to believe the best about everybody. I was like, just because he's the town's football star quarterback doesn't automatically mean he's gonna be a douchebag—"

"Except when it does," Olivia coughed into her hand.

"Yeah, yeah. I mean, this town is really cliché Texas. You'll see in the fall. They treat the football team like they're gods."

It was on the tip of my tongue to say I wouldn't still be here in the fall, but I kept quiet so she could keep telling her story.

"We almost went to state in our division the year Trent was a junior and the town *still* talks about it. And his dad and my dad owned two of the biggest ranches in the county, and they share a border too. So almost as soon as we were born within a few months of each other, the whole town had talked about how we'd grow up and get married and unite the two ranches into one mega-ranch."

"That's so messed up," I said.

She laughed. "Exactly. I was totally outraged by the idea as a little girl. *I* was gonna grow up and run my daddy's ranch, not some boy, so I totally ignored him. But then the older I got Dad kept talking about how I'd need to get married so he could have another man around to work the ranch after he was gone."

"So fucked uuuu-ppp," Olivia sing-songed, reaching for her margarita glass and sucking loudly on the neon green straw.

Ruth narrowed her eyes at her friend. "I'm sorry, what were your aspirations in high school? Pretty sure all you wanted to do was be a roadie for your college boyfriend, what was his name? Spike?"

Olivia sighed and sat back against the booth. "Spike. God, I haven't thought about him in forever. I wonder what the hell he's up to these days."

"Dear God, save us all," Ruth muttered. "Where was I?"

"Your dad was talking bullshit about you getting married so you could have access to your own inheritance like you're back in Jane Austen's time," I supplied.

Olivia pointed at me. "I like her."

Ruth grinned. "Right? She cussed out Trent the first time she met him. She's good people."

Okay, I was glowing a little inside. I hadn't had friends in... well, a really long time.

"Anyway, when we first started dating, Trent seemed like a good guy. Not a great guy or anything, but nice enough."

"Except all he wanted was to get in your pants."

Ruth shrugged. "I'd never had a boyfriend before. I thought that's what all boys wanted."

"Well..." Olivia said.

Ruth shook her head though. "No, there *are* good guys out there, I believe it still. They just don't live around here."

I bit my lip, thinking about Reece. Was *he* a good guy? He hadn't pressed to 'get in my pants' since that first time, and even then, I was the one doing most of the pressing.

"Anyway, then Mom died and Dad went off the rails, and Trent was... *there*. Dad liked Trent and he'd always hated guys I brought around before. I didn't find out till later that he was already getting in debt and he'd hoped Trent's dad would buy us out. So I started sleeping with Trent and trying to pretend everything was fine." Her lips twisted and she took a long drink of her margarita.

"Until?" I asked, because obviously there was an *until* coming.

Olivia finished for her. "Until we learned what an asshole he was behind that façade of his. He was cheating on her almost from the beginning. And when she found out, he tried to blame *her*."

"He asked what he was supposed to do," Ruth said with a bitter scoff, "since I wouldn't put out for two months when we'd started dating. What about after that? I asked. When we *did* start having sex? Why had he kept up sleeping around? Not just with one girl, either. He'd slept with a bunch of them. And everyone knew but me."

"I didn't know either," Olivia said. "And I told you as soon as I learned."

"You did, babe. You're the best." She leaned over the table and hugged Olivia, only just nearly missing getting a shirtful of fajita, sour cream, and guacamole. I pulled the platter out of the way just in time. "Always looking out for me."

"Sisters for life. Always."

Looking at the two of them, my chest squeezed. I'd always wanted that kind of friendship. Family. People, I'd always just wanted *people* who'd be there for me.

Maybe when I got to Austin. Maybe I could finally start to build a little tribe for myself. Found family, that was what they called it, right? Or was that just another dream, something other people were able to have, but not me. Maybe I just wasn't built for it.

When Ruth pulled back, she looked at me. "Even then, that bastard still tried to turn it around on me. He said I had unrealistic expectations and that this was what all guys were really like and it was better I get used to it now."

She huffed out a laugh. "It just never even occurred to him with his giant ego that I wouldn't be okay with that and that I'd break up with him."

"Yeah, no," I murmured. "Guys like that don't do well with rejection."

"Oh, so you know the type?"

I nodded. "Really well, actually. They're fine until you challenge them, then all hell breaks loose."

She nodded, frowning. "Yeah, exactly like that."

"Well, here's to cutting all the douchebags out of our lives, ladies!" Olivia raised her almost-empty margarita glass. "Huzzah!"

"Down with the douchebags!" Ruth lifted her glass.

I didn't have anything else, so I lifted my water glass and said, "Don't let the bastards get you down!"

We all clinked our glasses together and laughed, Olivia letting out a whoop for emphasis.

---

I DROVE HOME since Ruth and Olivia had both ordered second margaritas. I hadn't laughed so much in... well, *years*.

It felt good. Really, really good.

But as soon as I saw Jeremiah and Reece waiting for us in the driveway, both with their arms crossed over their chests and identical frowns on their identical faces, I knew something was wrong.

And I felt immediately stupid for not being on alert. Because anytime things were going too well, didn't I know that meant everything was about to turn to shit?

My hands started to shake, old feelings rising up as I put the truck in park. Ruth obviously saw what I saw because she said, "Oh Jesus, what now?"

She jumped down from the truck and walked up to the boys. I followed, a little more hesitantly. I sensed a confrontation coming—I had a Spidey sense for these sorts of things now. I could feel it in the air.

I wanted to grab Ruth and tell her to get back in the truck. But it was too late. She just kept barreling ahead.

"What's wrong?" she asked.

Jeremiah took an angry step forward and I flinched back. Reece's eyes came to me and his brow furrowed, as if he was concerned by my reaction. He definitely noticed.

But I was too concerned by what was happening between his brother and my new friend.

"What's wrong," Jeremiah seethed, "is that you're trying to sabotage us. I should have known from the beginning this situation was fucked up. There's no reason for you to still be here. This ranch isn't yours anymore, and if you think you can run us off and get the land back, lady, I've got news for you. I've called the sheriff, and he's—"

"The sheriff?" I squeaked, feeling lightheaded.

Who knew how far Jeff had circulated wanted posters of his 'missing' wife? Or what story he'd told about my disappearance?

When I'd run away before and gotten as far as Portland, he'd gotten the cops involved—claiming I was mentally disturbed and had threatened to kill *him*. I didn't know if he'd paid them off or if they'd genuinely believed his story. They certainly hadn't helped *me* when I'd begged them not to let him take me back.

Ruth held up a hand, looking irritated to the point of pissed. "Whoa, whoa, whoa, buddy, would you slow down with the accusations for a second and tell me what the hell happened?"

Jeremiah sneered. "As if you don't know. Don't try to play the helpless, innocent female with me. I know you're cunning."

Ruth arched an eyebrow at him. "Damn straight I am. I still have no idea what the hell you're talking about."

Ruth turned to Reece, ignoring Jeremiah. "Would you tell me what your ignorant brother here is so worked up over?"

Would it sound really out of place to hold up my hand and ask, *so um, about the sheriff—what time are they showing up?* I looked at the road behind us. I didn't hear or see another car coming up the drive, but God, it could be any second. I felt sweat breaking out all over my body. And like I was going to be sick. The fajita that had been so delicious only an hour ago was suddenly churning in my stomach.

"Someone's been intentionally taking down the fence posts and letting out the cattle," Reece offered cautiously, obviously still wary of the situation. "But they haven't been stealing the cows."

My eyebrows rose, distracted by Reece's words. Whoa. Damn. I didn't know much about cattle or ranching yet, but that seemed like a big deal. For a second I forgot about the sheriff and zoomed back into the drama.

"Son of a *bitch*," Ruth said, hands on her waist as she started pacing back and forth.

Jeremiah rolled his eyes. "What? You're saying it's not you? Who then?"

Ruth laughed bitterly as she looked back his direction. "My father was *not* popular by the end of his time on this earth. It wasn't just the bank he was in debt up to his eyeballs to."

"But didn't you clear all those debts when you sold this place?" Reece asked, far more kindly than I imagined his brother would have.

Ruth nodded frowning, and then her mouth dropped open and she twisted, looking at me. "Fuckface."

My eyes widened. "Of course," I said. I'd told her and Olivia about my internal nickname for Trent, to their great amusement.

"Of course, *what*?" Jeremiah butted in, sounding annoyed but also curious. "*Who*?"

"The guy from that day," I said, looking between him and Reece. "The one who came over in the pickup truck who was so rude. We ran into him in town again today and he was really nasty. He and Ruth's family have a past. He thinks this ranch should be his." I felt my cheeks warm with anger just thinking about that asshole.

"Oh," Jeremiah said, his eyebrows furrowing.

"Yeah," Ruth said. "Oh. Maybe you should wait and get all the facts next time before you go around accusing people of shit."

His eyes narrowed on her. "You aren't off the hook. We don't even know you and I still don't understand your motives for being here."

Ruth threw her arms in the air. "Would everybody shut up about that? I'm tired of people telling me how stupid they think I am to stay. My grandfather was born in a shack on that hill, right there." She pointed to a rise to the left of the barn.

"My dad was a son of a bitch but I loved him and he spent his *life* trying to hold onto the land that his daddy and his daddy before him fought for. I grew up riding horses here and dreaming of raising a family of my own here someday. So I'm *sorry* if me trying to hold onto even a tiny square acre of that legacy is so hard for you to understand."

With that she stormed past Jeremiah and up the stairs of the porch, slamming into the house.

Reece immediately smacked his brother on the arm. "I told you to go about it *delicately*. How was that delicate?"

Jeremiah shrugged off his brother, his face dark as he looked after where Ruth had disappeared into the house.

Reece looked at me, his features gentler than his brother's. They usually were. It was one reason it was so easy to tell the brothers apart in spite of the fact they were otherwise identical.

"Can you tell us a little more about what happened in town? Who is this guy?

"I don't know much more than she told you." I would let Ruth reveal more of her past with Trent if she wanted to. It wasn't my story to tell. "But you should know, he seemed connected around here. He threatened to take his business away from the hardware store like it would make a big impact, as if he and his father are the old man's biggest customers. I guess they have one of the biggest ranches around here."

And given my experience with entitled assholes, I added, "I wouldn't underestimate him." Then, because I felt bad about it, "I probably shouldn't have antagonized him like that when he came here that day."

Reece let out a scoffing noise. "You were awesome. Don't ever let any assholes talk to you that way."

Well, that had my insides warming. I found myself smiling up at Reece in spite of myself.

"It's a clusterfuck any way you look at it," Jeremiah said, then he looked at me. "Pardon my language."

I held up my hands. "Please, not on my account. Besides, you think Ruth wasn't cussing like a sailor the whole way into town and back?"

Jeremiah smiled at that, a little reluctantly, and his eyes went back to the house. If I didn't know better, I'd say he admired her... Or was it more than admiration? They certainly sparked off each other, that was for sure.

The door opened again and I hoped it was Ruth coming back out, but instead it was Buck, the other hand they'd hired a few days ago, stuffing a sandwich in his mouth with one hand and a beer in the other.

"Jesus, Buck," Jeremiah said. "No drinking on the job."

"I'm takin' a lunch break," Buck said. "So I'm not really on the job."

Reece laughed. "He's got a point."

Jeremiah glared at his brother. "Don't encourage him. You know Xavier never let us drink until after work." Jeremiah walked over to Buck and pulled the beer out of his hand, then kept on going to the kitchen. "I'll get you a cold coke instead."

Buck shrugged. "Whatever you say, Boss." He took another huge bite of his sandwich and looked between Reece and me. "What'd I miss?"

Reece shook his head. "Nothing."

Jeremiah popped his head back out. "Don't wander far, Buck. We're gonna have to bring in all the cows from the far pastures to keep them closer to the main house."

"Isn't that the pasture we just rotated them out of?" Reece asked. "There's not enough feed there for them."

"Which is why we'll have to go buy some hay bales and haul them out there later today. While Buck's having lunch, you and Charlotte go check the heifers. Last thing we can afford is to take our eyes off the ladies."

Reece looked surprised, but nodded. "Sure thing."

His eyes came to me and then they dropped down to the ground. Almost like he was self-conscious or something.

My stomach did a weird swoopy thing, and then my breath hitched.

Alarm bells rang in my head at my body's reaction to him.

But I just smiled and nodded at Jeremiah and started walking out to the field behind the barn. Anything to get out of sight when the sheriff showed up.

Poor Ruth. I knew all too well what it was like to have a horrible man try to sabotage what little happiness and future you were trying to carve out for yourself. I hoped they caught the bastard red-handed.

# 11

I stared down at the crème anglaise in horror. It had split, and I didn't have time to remake it.

Shit!

Oh shit, oh shit, oh shit.

I felt panicky sweat break out everywhere as I looked around. The fresh berries were in their pristine white bowls and a peek in the oven showed the filet mignon was cooked to perfection.

"It'll be okay," I whispered to myself. "It'll be okay." I grabbed the split crème and rushed to the sink, furiously trying to clean it and hide the evidence of my failure. It'd be fine. Fine. Fine fine fine. I'd been so perfect lately. I hadn't given him any cause to—

But I was too late. Too late, I heard the sound of keys jingling in the front door.

I poured out the soapy water from the glass mixing dish, threw the dirty mixer beaters in the bowl, then in a rush, grabbed the oven mitts.

Swearing internally and hearing my own heartbeat rushing in my ears, I yanked the filet mignon out of the oven and shoved the still-dirty glass bowl in the stove instead to hide it.

I pushed the door shut and turned off the oven just in time, because the next *second*, Jeff came around the corner into the kitchen.

I grinned my brightest grin at him and greeted, "Hi honey, how was work?"

His eagle eyes took a survey of the kitchen and I was sweating bullets. Had I missed any evidence of the crème anglaise disaster? Would he discover my deception? Dear God, please. Not tonight, not tonight.

I prayed that the bright smile on my face didn't waver.

Jeff narrowed his eyes at me. "That asshole Barry is trying to weasel in on my case, can you believe that?" He yanked at his tie to loosen it and came further into the kitchen, recounting the many ills of his day. The ways he was slighted, not appreciated enough, and how he could run the firm so much better than the senior partners.

It was a similar litany every day.

I nodded and made sympathetic noises. I made to carry the dishes of filet mignon to the dining room when he frowned.

"Where's the crème? You know I prefer crème with fruit for dessert."

I gulped. "I thought it might be nice one night to try without," I said in a rush.

I immediately knew it was the wrong thing to say from the expression on his face.

"You *thought*? But you didn't check with me? You *thought* you'd just ruin one of the few single pleasures I get in my day because, what? You had a fucking *whim*?"

"I'm so sorry," I apologized, knowing from long experience that groveling was the only way to avoid worse consequences. "I'm so sorry, honey. It won't happen again."

He shook his head, snorting. "You know, I expect this kind of disrespect at work. But in my own goddamn *home*? This is supposed to be where I can come home and relax after a long day providing for the both of us. I don't ask for much from you, do I?"

"No," I shook my head vigorously. "You're so good. You don't ask for a thing."

"But the little that I do expect, you can't even fucking do that right."

I flinched as his voice rose and he took a step towards me when all the sudden he paused, frowned, and sniffed. "What's that smell?"

"What?"

"That smell." He looked at me like I was a criminal and then he walked over to the oven and yanked it open.

My anxiety spiked through the roof and I held out a hand uselessly as we both looked at the leftover cream that was now steaming and smelling strange from the residual heat that had been leftover after cooking the filet mignon.

"I can explain," I scrambled. "I know you love the crème anglaise with the fruit, so I tried. I really tried, but it split, and there wasn't time to remake it, so I panicked. I'm so sorry, it was stupid—"

"So you *lied to me*?" he roared, turning to me. "You thought *lying* to me was better than admitting and owning up to your failure?"

He grabbed one of the small ceramic bowls of perfectly selected berries and threw it against the wall. It shattered into pieces and my entire body jolted with the *crash*. Blue and red berries scattered all over the floor.

"I'm sorry, I'm so sorry," I said pathetically. "I'll never do it again!"

But he'd already crossed the room and the next thing I knew, his heavy hand was swinging towards me.

"No!"

I woke up.

I woke up covered in sweat, curled in a ball, my arms over my stomach. As if it would do any good now.

And then I kicked the mattress furiously and threw one of my pillows across the room.

I flopped back on the bed, swiping angrily at the tears springing from my eyes. I stared at the ceiling in the dark room.

That fucking crème anglaise.

How was I ever supposed to move on if—

The aching well of grief opened up inside me, a never-ending abyss. Sometimes, in the light of day, it felt like I could trick myself into believing a new beginning was possible here.

But then all it took was closing my eyes and I was dragged right back to hell.

I felt the dark gulf creeping at the edges of my vision.

How many times had I given in before? Disappearing inside the darkness was so much easier, it almost felt welcome.

It had taken everything in me to climb out this last time, to cling to dreams of something better, to crawl towards the pin-prick of light in the distance.

But always there was this leaden mud threatening to drag me back down. I wore it like a veil, a wedding veil that had wrapped itself around my neck to choke me and drag me backwards.

Some things a person could never forgive themselves for.

*The fucking crème anglaise.*

I turned over and moaned into the pillow still left on the bed, the dense material swallowing the grief-filled noise. I curled in on myself.

But as I laid there, shaking in the dark, I couldn't stand it. I couldn't stand myself. Being in my own skin. It *hurt*. Every second that ticked by on the clock on the nightstand felt like a stab of pain. Being alive *hurt*.

I threw off my covers and stood up. I'd go out of my goddamned mind if I lay there another second.

My entire body shook as I paced around my small room. I scrubbed my hands through my hair, then reached to the bedside table for my water glass. It was empty.

Good, I couldn't stand to be in this tiny room a second longer. It felt too much like a cage and God knew I couldn't stand to be fucking caged for another second of my goddamned life.

I yanked on a pair of leggings, my robe and slippers. Then I eased out of my room and down the stairs, empty glass in hand.

But when I got to the kitchen, and drank a cup-full of water, I still felt like I wanted to crawl out of my own skin. I looked out the kitchen window at the moon, slammed the cup down on the counter and then went to the door. I pulled it open and walked out.

The blast of cold air on my face felt good. Bracing. Like a shock of awakeness.

I was alive.

I was here.

I wasn't *her* anymore. I wasn't. I *wasn't*, dammit.

I looked up at the sky, my nose stinging as I fought back tears and wrapped my arms around myself. The moon wasn't completely full, but it was close. And the sky was full of stars. So many stars it was almost unbelievable. Always a city girl, I'd sort of thought pictures of skies like this were photoshopped, but here it was, right above me.

I gulped the cold air into my hot lungs. It felt like a knife, but in a good way. It made me feel my body, from the insides and the outsides at the same time.

I was here.

I was here, I'd made it.

This was life.

Being alive in this body.

Free.

"I thought I was the only one who liked to stargaze in the middle of the night."

I yelped and jerked backwards.

"Shit, sorry, didn't mean to scare you." Reece waved from about fifteen feet away where he stood, leaned back against the fence with a cigarette in his hand.

My hand went to my heart. "Jesus," I said, breathing hard. "You scared the crap out of me."

"Sorry, I got that." He did sound like he genuinely felt sorry. "I wasn't sure how to let you know I was here. Guess I did that wrong."

I laughed, the sudden build and release of tension making me feel ridiculous. I was like a jumpy cat around these people.

I sniffed and swallowed, blinking back any tears that had built up. "No, it's fine," I said, my voice a little shaky. "I just had a nightmare, so I came out for some fresh air. Guess I'm still a little jumpy." I uncrossed my arms, then recrossed them, looking around. "What time even is it?"

"A little after two in the morning."

"So what's your excuse? What are you doing up at this hour? You have to be up at dawn. And I didn't know you smoked."

"Oh, well. Only sometimes." He looked down at his cigarette. "It's weed."

"Oh!" Then I felt silly for being surprised. Lots of people smoked in California obviously, I just didn't realize it was easy to get in Texas. Or that Reece... I shook my head at myself.

He leaned down and stubbed it out on the ground, his face a little sheepish when he looked back up at me. "Jeremiah doesn't approve, naturally."

"Hence being out here at two a.m.?" I asked.

He shrugged. "And I can't sleep sometimes."

"You?"

"That surprises you?"

I shrugged, feeling a little embarrassed. "I don't know. You just seem so... I don't know. Solid. Unperturbed by life."

He laughed. "That's a new one."

"What? Are you kidding?"

He shook his head. "No way. Jer considers me the fuck up. The one he always has to look out for."

I frowned. "That's nuts. You're great."

"Huh." He sounded surprised. "Well. Thanks." He rubbed a hand on the back of his neck. "So, nightmare? Wanna share?"

I shuddered, holding my arms even tighter. "No. Definitely not."

Though I had to say, being out here with him was a better distraction than I could have hoped to find. I was finally calming down and the shaking had almost stopped.

Reece nodded.

I looked at the cigarette, which I guess could more accurately be called a blunt, that he'd tucked behind his ear. Then I asked, completely on a reckless impulse, "Could I have a hit?"

His eyebrows went up but he nodded. "Sure. Sorry, it was rude of me not to offer."

Reece lit up the joint again, sucking in and hollowing out his cheeks. Then he passed it to me.

I put my lips around it, acutely conscious that his lips had just been in the exact same spot. Then I sucked and breathed in at the same time.

And coughed so hard I almost doubled over.

"Shit," Reece said, reaching for me but pulling back at the last second like he wasn't sure I wanted hands on me.

"I'm fine," I coughed out, laughing at the same time. Tears from the smoke pricked at my eyes but before I could think better of it or Reece could try to take it away, I sucked in another long inhale.

And coughed all over again.

"Jesus, woman," Reece said, snatching for the joint.

But I danced back from him.

"Uh uh," I said in between coughs. "You are not stealing my first," *cough*, "weed experience from me," *cough cough cough*.

"Oh shit, it's your first time?" Reece's eyes went wide. "Then no more. This shit's the good stuff."

I handed it back. I was already laughing, though I doubted the weed could hit that fast. It just felt... ridiculously good to do something reckless. It helped settle me back into *this* life and made the nightmare life feel worlds away. Where it belonged.

I was this new woman. I was Charlie.

I closed my eyes as my body started to feel a little lighter. I held out my arms and dropped my head back, opening my eyes and looking up at the star-filled sky.

"I'm so *serious* all the time." I shook out my arms and then my whole body, then slowly started spinning. The sky above rotated as I spun. "The whole point of leaving was so I could start to *live*," I murmured. My body started to relax, and it felt like relief. Relief to be rid of *her*.

"Looks like you're doing a fine job of living to me," Reece said and he sounded earnest, not like he was laughing at me or making fun.

I looked over at him and his head was leaned back, also looking up at the stars.

"I grew up in the city," he said. "I didn't know so many stars could even be real."

"Shut the front door," I said. "That's just what I was thinking when I came out! Mind-reader."

He smiled my way, that special smile I'd never seen him give to anyone else. "Nah, it's just that great minds think alike."

I grinned, and for the first time in forever, it felt easy. My facial features just sort of *relaxed* into it instead of having to force my lips to curve upwards. Could a person even go from devastation to smiling in such a short time, or was swinging that far on a pendulum just another indication of how fucked up I truly was?

God, in this second I didn't care. I was just grateful for the relief, so I clung to it. The feeling was so foreign. *Is this what... is this what being happy feels like?*

Reece laughed. "I don't know. Is this what being happy feels like? I sure hope so."

*Shit, did I say that out loud?*

He laughed even harder. "Yep, you said it out loud."

I clapped a hand over my mouth, but I was grinning too hard, so I dropped it. "Screw it. Is it really so bad to just say whatever's on my mind?"

Reece shook his head. "I certainly hope not. I do it all the time."

"Does it get you into trouble?"

He nodded. "Fuck yeah, it has."

I laughed. And I mean *laughed*, like doubled over laughing, holding my gut.

"Okay, okay, why don't we get you somewhere you can sit down. I think the weed's hitting."

He came over and put his hand at the small of my back. I leaned into his touch because it felt heavenly. I suddenly wished the robe I had on wasn't so thick.

He led me forward, which meant he was close. I looked up at him. He was looking ahead so I could just stare at his strong jaw in the light from the moon and stars. Before I could fully think it through, my hand was up, and the tips of my fingers traced along his jawline. Stubbly and prickly.

"I'm obsessed with your jaw," I said. "Every time I look at you, all I want to do is this." I ran my thumb back and forth across the bristles and then pressed harder, feeling the shape of the firm bones underneath.

He swallowed hard, and I watched in abject fascination as his Adam's apple bobbed up and down. "Maybe I should get you back inside, Captain."

I licked my lips. "Or maybe we should go into the stables and make out."

He opened his mouth like he was gonna say something else and I moved in front of him, reaching up with both hands to caress his jaw with both hands.

His face was dark, shadowed, but I imagined mine was clear in the moonlight as he looked down at me.

"Don't you want to kiss me?" I asked, and I couldn't help the vulnerability in the question.

He was silent and it hit me that, oh my God, what if I was making a fool out of myself? Yes, we'd slept together once, but he probably did that kind of thing all the time. It didn't mean he wanted a repeat performance, and certainly not with some high, sloppy chick—

"Are you fucking kidding?" He didn't say anything else. He just leaned down and kissed me.

Not hard. Not demanding.

Just perfect. Eager. Like it was something he'd been waiting to do again.

His lips, so wide and thick, covered mine and the wild roar of wanting roared to life inside me. Foreign, but also familiar. Like it was something my body instinctually knew even though I'd never experienced it before meeting Reece's mouth.

He pulled away, then looked around us. I could see his face looked a little dazed as he blinked. "We shouldn't be doing this out here in the open."

I giggled. "Why not? Who's going to catch us?"

He pulled me against his body and I felt his desire for me. He leaned down. "Because I imagine public indecency is still frowned upon even if you're out in the sticks."

Oh. *Oh*. He wanted to have sex with me again.

Yes. Yes, I wanted that, too.

"So let's go to the stables," I said at the same time he said, "So I should probably get you back inside, Cinderella."

His eyes went wide. "The stables?"

I felt self-conscious again. "Unless you don't want to." But the thought of going back in the house... compared to how good it felt to be out here with him. It was a no-brainer which one I wanted.

He coughed. "Are you kidding? I just... It's your first time with weed."

I shrugged and nodded. I decided that being self-conscious was bullshit.

I felt amazing, light and tingly and electric, but not completely out of control. I didn't want to go back to my bedroom. No, no, I did not want to go back there with the ghosts.

Penelope Chambers was my ghost and I wanted to exorcise her. I wanted her gone forever. I wanted this new life. I wanted this feeling, right here. I wanted to reach out and touch Reece's face again. I wanted him to touch my body. *I* wanted to touch my body.

What if an exorcism didn't have to be about hell and damnation, but with, like, baptisms of pleasure instead? Over and over, pleasure, until I was made new. Reincarnating me into my own body but with a new life. That was the kind of rebirth *I* wanted.

I wanted no boundaries, no one telling me *don't touch, don't taste, not for you*. No more constraints.

So to Reece, I said, "Well, I'm going to the stable. To touch myself. You can come if you want."

And then I pulled away from him and walked towards the stables, swaying my hips as I went.

I did smile when I heard footsteps behind me though.

I felt like a teenager as I tried to walk steadily across the yard, past the barn, to the stable. The teenager I should have been, without a mother weighing my food and making me journal my caloric intake. The college kid I should have been, high on weed and seducing the boy *she* wanted, the boy *she* chose. Making reckless but exhilarating choices that were all *mine*.

I was breathless by the time I got to the stable. I didn't turn around once, but I could tell that Reece was still following by the sound of his feet on the dry grass behind me.

The work they'd done so far on restoring the stable was impressive. It was dry and warmer inside than outside. The floor was swept clean, as were the few stalls that had been repaired.

It smelled like wood and hay and *ranch*, but in a good way.

I spun and turned to Reece.

"What if we played pretend?" I asked impetuously.

He frowned, stopped at the doorway. "How do you mean?"

"Like the first night when I went to your cabin. We were strangers, and think how sexy that was. What if we pretended to be strangers again? Just a game of pretend. In the daytime, everything goes on like normal. But maybe for just one night..." I took a step towards him, and ran a hand down his shirt, "you could pretend to be my teacher."

I arched an eyebrow up at him, feeling a wild thrill even as I said the words that I didn't think had anything to do with the weed heightening everything I was feeling, "And I could be your very, very naughty student."

I went up on my tiptoes, one hand still on his chest as I whispered in his ear. "Professor Walker, I know I failed that last exam, but maybe I could convince you to take mercy on me if I promise to be a very good girl from now on?"

"Jesus," Reece swore, wiping a forearm across his brow in spite of the chill. But I could feel how warm he was through his shirt. His skin was burning up, begging to be touched.

Some twisted part of me recognized that this was fucked up. That this was a twisted version of what had *actually* happened to me with Jeff. But at the same time it was different. I was in control this time. I wasn't being manipulated.

And... and maybe this made all the difference... I was with someone I felt I could genuinely *trust*.

So I leaned into the fantasy.

"I see the way you stare at me in class, Professor," I said, dropping my hand down Reece's chest and letting it rest at the waist of his jeans, my fingertips toying just inside where it buttoned.

His chest heaved as he looked down at me. I waited for his decision to see if he would play along or push me away, say that no, we had to be responsible and go back inside the house. I expected it—Reece was like that. He always seemed to do the right thing, and work so hard at everything he did.

But to my surprise and delight, one of his eyebrows lifted and he dropped his head down as his voice came out in a gravelly tone. "Well, it depends, Miss, on how well you do on the pop quiz I've just decided to give you. If you do well, I might be able to bump your grade up to passing."

A shiver of delight passed through my body, landing right in my sex. I'd never really experienced a sensation like it before. I blinked rapidly, then licked my lips, captivated when his eyes zeroed in on the motion. "What kind of quiz is this?" I asked tremulously.

Reece grinned, and he'd never looked more rakish. "Let's call it an oral exam. Now, this is advanced material. I'm not sure you're up for it."

He pulled back from me, making me lose my grip on the waist of his jeans. "No, I am," I said, taking a step after him.

I reached for him but he caught my wrist, his eyes going serious. "I guess you'll have to convince me, then. You might even have to," his voice dropped, "*beg me.*"

Holy shit, that did something to my nether-regions. I swallowed and then backed up into the stable. It was darker inside, but that only added to the illicit heat burning low in my belly. There was a beam of light from the open doorway. It was colder as I opened my robe, exposing my thin camisole and leggings. I shivered, but I didn't stop.

I teased a finger down along the top of my camisole where it plunged dangerously into my cleavage. "Please, Professor Walker.

Please let me make it up to you. I promise I'll do *so* good at oral. I'll give you the best oral you've ever had." Then I opened my mouth and licked around my lips from the bottom to the top. "I've always had something of an oral fixation, it turns out."

I shoved my thumb in my mouth, sucking just the tip of it and then dragging it down between my breasts.

"Oh, really," Reece said, stepping inside the stables with me as I dropped my robe to the ground. I let the straps of my camisole fall down my shoulders, exposing the tops of my breasts.

I shrugged and bit my bottom lip. "When I watch you in class, I always want to suck on something. It's why my grades are so bad. You distract me..."

He stepped forward and grasped me by the waist, pulling me up against him, so close I could feel his erection through his jeans and my slim leggings. He yanked his shirt off over his head and I couldn't help it. My hands were drawn to the lines of his muscled chest, down to his abs... and lower. I traced the V that led into his jeans and swallowed.

"Beg me," he demanded again.

My eyes flicked up towards his and suddenly it wasn't a game. It was me and Reece. This was his natural dominance shining through and it didn't scare me. It electrified me.

"I— I—" I started, then blinked several times. "I want you."

"Baby, that's all you ever have to say."

And then his mouth crashed down on mine and his hands were everywhere, on my ass, slipping underneath my leggings, moving around to my clit.

Before I knew it, he was bearing me down to the ground. But instead of coming over top of me, he'd moved down my body, dragging my leggings with him.

He shouldered my legs open and growled, "God, I've been dying to taste this pretty pussy," and before I could say, wait, no, that wasn't the kind of oral I thought we'd been talking about—

His mouth was on my center.

And. All. Thought. Stopped.

Because dear all things holy—

My hands dug into his hair as my legs fell open wider, and then my thighs clamped around his head as the first spasms of pleasure hit, and then fell open again. Oh God, I'd never had— No one had ever done this to me— I didn't know it could feel so—

I lifted one hand from his head to shove in my own mouth because I could barely hold back the scream of pleasure trying to come out of my throat.

The orgasm hit me before I was ready and it was— Holy *shit*! It was higher and heavenlier than anything I'd known was possible. Between his tongue and the weed, I couldn't—

I was trembling with aftershocks by the time he lifted his head, grinning in satisfaction as he swiped his mouth with his arm. I'd never wanted anyone more.

My legs flopped open but I wasn't done with him. "I'm begging you," I whispered, tears of pleasure coursing down my cheeks. "Please, fuck me now. I need to feel you inside me."

His eyes widened. Maybe he'd thought the one orgasm was all I'd want, but no, I needed to feel him inside me, plus, I— I couldn't have this just be one way. I needed him to—I needed the closeness and reassurance of him with me, I couldn't even explain it to myself.

But when I reached my arms down to him, he didn't deny me.

He climbed up between my open legs, shoved his jeans down, and he was hard, gloriously hard. He reached in the pocket of the jeans and pulled out a wallet, then a condom out of the wallet, sheathed himself, and was finally, gloriously pushing inside my swollen, readied sex.

We both groaned in pleasure at his entrance.

But it was all getting a little too real. Desperate, I needed to take it back to the pretend world, especially when I looked up into Reece's intense, gorgeous eyes.

"Fuck me, Professor, and tell me what a good student I am now."

If there was the briefest flicker of disappointment in his eyes at my words taking us back into the fantasy realm, he hid it quickly.

Instead, he grasped my jaw with his hand and told me, "Clench on my cock, little girl, and show me how badly you want this grade."

The show of dominance did make me cream all over him that much more. "Yes, sir," I gasped, and strained with all my inner muscles to hold onto him as he began to pump in and out of me. I didn't miss the way his eyes flared in satisfaction when I called him *sir*.

"Dig your heels in my ass and ride me back," he ordered.

I arched into him and did as he said. The robe beneath my back made a soft barrier between me and the dirt floor.

"I said to fucking ride me," he commanded, and I did, lifting my hips to meet his punishing ones as he really started getting into fucking me.

It was dirty and rough and sexy as hell.

"Fuck me harder, sir," I begged, loving the way his large, hard cock filled and commanded me in a way Jeff's never could. Reece was all natural confidence borne of his life of genuine hard work, not manipulation. And he fucked like he lived—genuine, hard, earnest.

And it felt so damn *good*.

I dug my nails into his back as he demanded, "Look at me. Fucking look me in the eye as you come."

I did. Dear God help me, I did.

I came, and I came hard as he pumped into me and then stilled. I spasmed around his cock as he pinned me to the barn floor, eyes locked with mine.

## 12

THE NEXT WEEK, ALL I COULD THINK ABOUT WAS THE FILTHY, THRILLING things I'd felt on the barn floor that night with Reece.

I remembered all of it, in delicious detail. Every time I stopped the ATV, I'd feel some twinge in my body that would remind me of where his hands had been. Or his mouth.

Dear Lord, I'd had no idea my body could *feel* those things.

Just like he'd promised, we were still ourselves during the day. Everything was normal between us at the dinner table. Okay, so maybe occasionally there was a lingering look between us... I didn't know about him, but now that I'd opened Pandora's box...all I could think about was continuing to explore.

So when I happened to pull the ATV into the barn after tagging several more newborns and caught Reece washing his hands at the sink, my heart started hammering.

I should head into the house and start getting lunch together. That was absolutely what I *should* do.

But instead, the same recklessness that had driven me to the stables the other night had my feet taking me towards Reece.

He turned, watching me as I came towards him. Was I just imagining it or did his eyes widen and his nostrils flare as I approached?

Maybe it was all just in my head, but it gave me the confidence to go up on tiptoes and whisper, "You want to play pretend again tonight?"

His pupils definitely darkened at this and I was gratified that there was no hesitation before he nodded, a definitive up and down motion.

A rush of adrenaline hit and I felt more awake, more alive than I had all week, since I'd last been in his arms. I took a step back, looking around to double check no one else was nearby. But still, the barn was the center of life on the farm and anyone could come in at any moment.

"Eleven o'clock." I bit my lip, a scenario popping in my head. After another quick peek around to make sure no one else was coming, I leaned up and whispered in his ear the idea I had in mind.

"Fuck," he spit out. "That's hot." He reached for me but I danced back.

I arched an eyebrow. "Don't be late."

He shook his head. "I won't be."

I smiled at him, shoved my hands in my back pockets, then turned and headed in to make lunch.

"What are you grinning like a fool about?" Ruth asked as soon as I stepped inside. She'd come downstairs to help me make sandwiches.

"What? Me?" I shrugged, trying to rearrange my features and stop the admittedly stupid grin I could feel fighting to reemerge on my face. "It's just nice weather out."

"Uh huh," Ruth said, obviously still suspicious.

"Coffee?" I asked, eager to change the subject, reaching for the carafe. She rolled her eyes but then gave in. "Is that even a serious question? Always."

---

IT WAS ridiculous to get so excited about my "appointment" that night. I mean, I was exhausted as always after the strenuous day of work, and part of me wondered if Reece would even show. He'd looked tired during the evening meal, and there was no chance to get him alone again all day to double check that we were still on.

And slipping out of the house at ten to eleven wearing what I was wearing—well, I'd feel like a giant idiot if he didn't show.

I hesitated at the doorway, wondering if I should just go back upstairs and forget the entire thing.

I mean, yes, I had belabored over what I would wear for hours until figuring out that if I folded in the top of one of my skimpy camisoles and shimmied it down over my hips it made for a fabulous little miniskirt.

And yes, I was wearing the siren-red lipstick that Ruth had given me a few weeks ago— saying it was a shame for a woman to not have even an ounce of makeup. Considering the scenario we were playing out, I hadn't been shy when applying it. I'd even rubbed some on my cheeks for rouge, an old trick my grandma had shown me.

Granted, I still had just my boots instead of pumps, but I thought I was pulling off the whole *prostitute* vibe pretty well. Especially with just my lacy black bra up top, though while still in sight of the house, I was all covered up with my thick terrycloth robe.

I bit the inside of my cheek, then opened the door and rushed out. No more overthinking. I wanted to feel how I'd felt the other night.

And to be honest, I wanted Reece's body against mine. I wanted to be someone else tonight and the freedom that came with that.

So I shut the door *ever so carefully* behind myself so that it barely made a sound, then rushed down the stairs into the cool, crisp spring air. I hurried past the vehicles in the yard to the road and continued down it for about a quarter of a mile, over the first little hill so that any headlights wouldn't be visible to the house.

Then I threw off the robe and I waited.

And immediately felt ten kinds of foolish. And cold. I crossed my arms over my chest. Was I really standing here alone in the dark, when only weeks ago I'd hitchhiked and been in *real* danger—

What the fuck was wrong with me anyway? Choosing these situations that were a little too close to my real life for comfort?

But just then, headlights split the darkness. For a moment I panicked, but I fought back with logic and reason. The headlights had come from the direction of the ranch. It wasn't a scary trucker come to hunt me down. Maybe that was part of why my subconscious had been drawn to this in the first place.

I was going to put down my demons one by one, dammit.

So I stood up straighter, jutted out my hip, and leaned my breasts out as the truck slowed down.

And when the driver's side window rolled down and Reece leaned out, his hair disheveled as if he'd been running his hand through it, I felt a zing of exhilaration like nothing I could describe.

"Well, hello there," I said, walking up to the car and leaning on the door with my elbows, bending over and enjoying the way my breasts swung between us in my lacy bra. "You looking for a date, honey?"

Reece swallowed hard, his eyes briefly dropping to my chest before he dragged them up to my face. He cleared his throat. "Yes. Yes, I am."

"What are you lookin' for tonight? Hand job? Blow job? Full deal's gonna cost ya." I arched an eyebrow at him. "But I promise I'm worth it. I can take you places you never been."

He sucked in a deep breath and nodded. "I have no doubt about that. What's your most expensive package?"

I told him. He didn't bat an eye. "That."

I grinned. "Well, I guess we'll have some fun tonight, then." I held out my hand. "Payment first."

He pulled out his wallet and handed over actual cash. I was surprised. I'd give it back at the end, but I appreciated the realistic props. I took the money and stuffed it in my bra.

"All right, cowboy. Get ready to get rode hard and put away wet." I winked, getting a laugh out of him while I walked around the front of the cab and climbed in.

"Where to?" he asked once I was inside. It was warm, even a little stifling after the cold of the outside.

I leaned in and slid a hand up his thigh. "Hotels don't usually like my kind," I whispered, "So why don't we just drive a little further up the road? I've had a lot of johns but I've never done it in the back of a truck before."

I ghosted my hand over his crotch and felt his enthusiasm for my idea.

He immediately threw the truck in gear and then we were spitting gravel as we drove a few more minutes down the road while I continued massaging his thigh, teasing higher and higher.

"Fuck, this is gonna have to be good enough," he said, slowing down and throwing the truck in park again. "'Cause I can't wait any longer."

He turned to me and pulled me to him, so quick and so strong that he all but pulled me up into his lap.

*Yes.* God, it felt good to be in his arms again. His mouth was powerful and commanding on mine and it made me go so light-headed, for a moment I almost forgot myself. It felt just like Reece and me stealing away in the night to make out in his truck.

A dangerous part of me wanted to throw my arms around his neck, straddle him, and let him fuck me right here like this—anything to get him inside me and cement our connection. At the same time, a panic alarm went off at the thought of that. So I pulled back.

"Ah ah ah," I said. "You ordered the full package and the full package is what you'll get, sir."

I climbed back off him and before he could utter a single word, I'd hopped out of the truck and was walking around to the back of the truck. Where I found a couple of sleeping bags laid out.

I raised an eyebrow at Reece when he joined me, coming around the other side of the truck. I smirked at him. "Why do I have the feeling that this is *not* your first rodeo bringing a woman out in the dark to seduce in the back of your truck?"

It was too dark to see if he was blushing, but by the way he ducked his head, I had the feeling I was right. That was good. Somehow it made me feel more in control if he was a little embarrassed. And it reminded me that this was a night out of time.

Control. Yes. That was what I wanted. What I needed, even.

"Sit with your back against the cab," I said. "You paid to be pleasured, and that is my job and my only desire, sir." I walked up close to him, running a hand down his chest. "I want to make you come harder than you've ever come before. All the things that are too dirty to ask the little woman to do, you can do with me."

I reached down and grasped his cock roughly, making his breath hitch. I squeezed his balls as I leaned in and kissed him, biting at his bottom lip and sucking it hard. When I let go with a lingering *pop*, he swore.

"Actually, I have a better idea," I said. "Something I've always wanted to try with a client but I never dared." I blinked my eyelashes up at Reece. "Are you daring enough to try it with me?"

He sucked in a breath but nodded. "I paid for the full package. I can handle it if you can."

I grinned. "Good. That's what I like to hear. Do exactly what I say," I crooned, "and I promise, I'll make you feel good."

He opened the back of the truck and I climbed up, making sure to swing my barely covered ass in his face. I laid down and then wiggled a finger at him to join me. "Jeans off," I said. "Then climb over my face."

He adjusted his stiff cock, then nodded. The moon wasn't full anymore, but three-quarters was still enough to see how wide his eyes were and to be able to follow his motion as he shoved his jeans down, and toed off his boots. He climbed up into the truck bed, his heavy cock swinging between his legs.

I reached out for it, shocked by my hunger to get my hands on it. It jumped with eagerness the second my palm closed around it.

"That's right," I said as he climbed up on top of me. I urged him up higher until he was straddling my shoulders, his cock hanging right in front of me.

I brought it to my mouth, ghosting it across my lips like I was applying lipstick. Then I peeked my tongue out to lick just the tip, where his slit peeked out. His entire body reacted at the contact. I grinned and began to toy with his tip while I jacked him up and down with my hand.

Damn, but he was long and well-built. He was the girth of my entire hand. "Big boy," I whispered, then dipped him into my mouth, sucked hard, bobbing him in and out past my lips.

I did that for several minutes until I finally pulled him out again, lazily licking at the head, stroking him the whole time.

"Now, I'm going to touch you and you're going to let me because you trust me to bring you pleasure. You paid for it and I'm going to give you everything," I said as I started massaging his balls with my free hand.

"Okay," he said, his voice tight, no doubt from everything I was doing to him.

"Hold off on coming for as long as you can. Don't give in, no matter how much you want to."

"Not a problem, darlin," he said, and I could hear the humor in his voice.

I smiled. Oh, just you wait, cowboy. I tugged him forward so that his cock was in my mouth again, and then with my other hand I opened the little quarter-sized container of petroleum jelly I'd bought at the store this week. It wasn't ideal but would work in a pinch for what I needed.

I dug my finger in, lubed it up, then reached around Reece and slipped my finger towards his ass.

He'd been mostly passively accepting everything I'd done until this point, but he straight up jolted the second I began to probe his ass.

I gave him the space to pull away, but when he didn't, I went for it. I made the plunge, doing what I'd only dreamed about in my naughtiest fantasies long before I'd ever met Jeff. I used to have kinky fantasies and right now, I wanted to make Reece feel like no other woman had ever made him feel. I wanted to blow his head off with pleasure.

So I slipped my finger up his ass and felt around for his prostate. I'd researched this long ago and knew it wasn't very far in. I curved my finger and could tell when I'd found it because of how Reece responded.

His cock which already felt huge suddenly grew to bursting in my mouth. And whereas before he'd simply been on his knees allowing me to guide the blow job—now he was moving his hips, actively thrusting into my mouth.

"Yes," I cried around him, wanting that. I wanted him to lose control with me. I wanted him out of his fucking mind.

And as soon as I gave the signal it was okay he seemed to give into it, fucking my mouth as I stimulated his prostate.

Words started spilling out of his mouth into the night air. "Jesus fuckin' Christ. Never felt so good. Fuck, your mouth feels like fuckin' heaven. So fucking hard. Gonna come. Jesus, I'm gonna blow. Fuck, oh fuck, oh fuckin' *fuuuuuuck*—"

I added a second finger to the first in his ass, really massaging hard against his prostate and then he lost it, fucking my face until all I could do was hold his hip with one hand, keep pressure on his prostate, and accept his cock in my mouth, down my throat while he lost his goddamn mind.

When he came, he blew like a goddamn freight train, so much cum exploding down my throat. I swallowed and then swallowed more, but still his creamy cum spilled out the sides of my mouth.

Still I didn't let up, continuing pressure against his prostate until he was crying out incoherently and fucking my mouth.

When it seemed like he had nothing else and his voice was a mere whine against the night, I finally released him. He collapsed to the side of me.

I continued holding his cock, licking and lathing at the spilled cum until every single droplet was licked clean.

## 13

Two nights later, I collapsed onto Reece's chest, having just finished playing a round of seduce-the-ranch-hand.

We were back in the stables, lying on a sleeping bag Reece had thoughtfully prepared ahead of time. My entire body felt liquid and melty from the multiple orgasms Reece had just pulled from me. I curled my arm around his wide torso as I laid my head on his chest, both of us still breathing hard from our exertions.

Neither of us spoke. We usually didn't in the aftermath. What was there to say when you'd just had your brains fucked out in the best sex of your life? Well, it was certainly the best sex of *my* life; I couldn't speak for him. But if the way he kept coming back for more said anything, he was enjoying himself plenty.

I liked hugging the warmth of him and hearing his heart pound away through his chest underneath my ear. I liked being connected to another human being like this. It was completely novel to me. Touching someone like this and feeling... *safe*.

My eyes dropped shut as I cozied up closer to him. Just a few minutes. I'd allow myself just a few more minutes of this heaven and then we'd pull ourselves together and go back inside...

"WHAT THE FUCK?"

I frowned and snuggled instinctively against the warmth. But then everything was shifting, jerking, and—

"Jer. It's not what you think."

My eyes popped all the way open as Reece shifted out from underneath me and I realized. The stable. We'd fallen asleep in the stable.

Shit.

I scrambled to sit up and pull the thick robe around myself that Reece had draped across us like a blanket at some point last night.

Only to look up and see Reece's face mirrored on his twin's—except unlike Reece's, Jeremiah's face was twisted in a way I'd never seen. Disappointment. Disgust, maybe even. Anger, definitely.

I pulled my knees up against my chest and Reece moved in front of me as a shield. Oh shit, I was naked, and Jeremiah had just caught us—

"We can talk about this later. Just let me get Charlie inside."

"Oh, so now you're a gentleman?" Jeremiah scoffed, then looked at the floor, where a blunt had fallen out of Reece's pocket in the night. He hadn't even smoked it last night, but I knew he carried them with him sometimes.

Jeremiah reached down and picked it up, then shook his head, taking just a quick glance my way before glaring back at his brother. "I should have fucking known. If there's a vulnerable woman within ten miles of you, you're gonna find a way to get your dick involved. This is Peg all over again."

Reece launched himself to his feet. At least he had his jeans on. "Shut your goddamn mouth before both of us regret it."

"Or you're gonna do what, little brother? Hit me? Screw up another opportunity for us and set us back to square one, for what, the hundredth time? Sexual harassment and drug possession—great, real great. Jesus, you just can't help yourself. Except wait, you *can*, because you're a grown man. Or at least supposed to be."

"Stop it," I yelled, yanking the robe around me for modesty's sake. "Both of you, stop it."

Last night felt like something out of a dream. Every night with Reece did. But here, with everything exposed in the daylight, I felt unsteady. Off-kilter. Everything that had seemed so clear last night suddenly evaporated with the dawn and this horrible argument.

I hated to see them argue. I hated to be the cause of the arguing.

The scent of burnt crème anglaise from my nightmares was filling the air. Landing hard on the ground beside shattered glass shards, my cheek on fire. *Why do you ruin EVERYTHING, you stupid bitch?*

I stood up and shoved my feet into my slippers. All these nights trying to be something else, to be some*one* else... God, it was all just self-delusion. I was still *her* and I always would be.

"And look," I whisked the robe around my shoulders. "There's no problem anymore, 'cause I quit, okay? I was never gonna stay around here long anyway. Just give me my pay for the work I've done till now and I'm gone."

I stomped out of the stable, my nose burning and hot tears scalding my eyes.

"Wait, Charlie—"

Reece tried to follow me, but his brother stopped him. Good. A clean break would be the best.

I shook my head, feeling *stupid*. I knew it. I knew everything had been going too good. I knew it was all about to crash down around me.

Well, good. I swiped at a tear as soon as it fell. Now it had happened. Better now than later. I'd gotten it out of the way.

This whole place was just... None of it had ever been real. It was a waystation. Just a strange stop along the way to my real life.

And I'd learned lessons. Good lessons. Don't let people in so quick. What the hell had I been thinking doing everything I had been with Reece lately? Letting down so many guards. If it was all just pretend, then why did I hold him so tightly all night long like that? How could I have let myself trust *any* man enough to fall asleep in their arms?

I covered my face with my hands remembering it, mortified.

Except it hadn't been mortifying then. It had been... well, it had been wonderful, amazing, *beyond*. Every time.

Gah, I just needed to scrub it all out of my mind. None of it mattered. There were far bigger tragedies in my past to be recovering from to be wasting any tears over a few-nights stand.

So what if he'd held me so close to his body all night I'd fallen asleep to the sound of his heartbeat? So what if for the first time in I couldn't remember when, I hadn't had nightmares? It was so chilly out there, at least fifty degrees overnight, and yet I'd slept like a baby tucked against his big body.

I shook my head roughly to expel the memories.

It. Didn't. Matter.

There were things that mattered, and things that didn't matter, and guess what? One night tucked up against a warm, gentle giant, was in the big ol' fat column of things that didn't matter.

So it was nice. I'm sure in my life ahead I'd find lots of things that were nice. I'd meet lots of nice people. Jesus, the last thing I needed to be doing right now was tangling with a man, anyway. Seriously, the absolute last thing.

It was sooooo much better that I was leaving now.

I stomped up the stairs, past where Ruth was brewing coffee and staring at me with wide eyes as I tromped right past her.

"Where've you been?" she asked after me.

"Can you drive me to Austin?" I asked, not really listening for her response because I didn't want to answer her questions. "I'm leaving today."

I kept going up the stairs.

But I should have known Ruth.

She was immediately on my heels. "Whoa, what happened? And were you out doing morning chores dressed like that in just your robe?"

I stubbornly kept looking ahead. Could I get to my room and shut the door before she lobbed any more questions at me?

"Oh my God, is this a walk of *shame*! You dirty bird! Which of them was it?!"

I felt my cheeks flame. How had we fallen asleep out there? I'd just meant to shut my eyes for a moment. I'd thought for sure I wouldn't fall asleep because, hello, we were outside. On the ground. It was cold. And we were in a *stable*.

I spun and faced her. "I don't want to talk about it. I just need to get out of here. You said you'd drive me to Austin. Is that offer still good?"

"Holy shit." Her eyes were wide. "You're serious."

Was she kidding? I clenched my fists together and bit the insides of my cheeks in an effort to hold back all the emotion I was feeling.

Staying as long as I had and getting close to any of them had been a mistake in the first place. I'd had a plan. Disappear in a big city. Don't make friends, don't make waves. Just disappear for a while. Cocoon myself away. Maybe forever if that was what I needed. I wasn't... *fit* to be around people.

Some people were meant to be like Ruth and her friend Olivia— the kind of people who just put themselves out there and lived out loud. But that wasn't me. That couldn't be me.

Every time I tried, I just made things worse, so much worse. I'd tried to escape my mom's house and landed in Jeff's lap. Then in escaping Jeff, I'd come here and screwed things up between Reece and his brother.

Why do you ruin *everything*? It was Jeff's voice in my head, but just because the man was a narcissistic monster didn't mean he was always wrong.

I was the common denominator in my shitty life.

He'd been attracted to me in the first place for a reason. Broken called to broken, like two grotesque pieces of a puzzle. I couldn't even see what he was, I'd been so blinded. I just let him pull me right into his web, absolutely desperate for love and attention.

And hadn't I done the same thing here? Wanting Reece and then grasping for him, not caring about the consequences for anyone involved?

"Can I keep a couple of the jeans and shirts you've lent me?" I asked Ruth, both of us still facing each other in a stand-off in the hallway outside my room.

"Jesus, Charlie, the clothes are yours, but you can't leave!"

"I can and I will," I said. Better now before things got any worse.

Ruth crossed her arms over her chest. "What happened? Did one of those assholes do something to you? Tell me right now. I'll rip their balls off."

"What?" I was appalled. "Of course not!" I finally turned and headed for my room. I was officially over this conversation. I just needed to pack my things and get on the road. "It's just me. I screw shit up. It's time to go. I gotta get outta here."

I pushed into my bedroom but Ruth just followed right behind me.

"Is that what happened wherever you were last? Things got a little complicated and you just took off?"

My mouth dropped open as I spun back to her. "You have no idea what the hell you're talking about."

She threw her hands out. "That's because you don't talk to anyone! You haven't let any of us *in*. So maybe you did last night. Did you sleep with one of the guys? With Reece? Or... Buck?"

And in that moment, I realized the name she had conspicuously not mentioned. "Oh my God, you like Jeremiah, don't you?"

"What?" she laughed, but it was fake. "Don't be ridiculous." But then her facial features transformed from indifference to suddenly looking freaked out. "Why? Did you sleep with Jeremiah?"

Then, as if hearing herself, she shrugged. "Not like it would make any difference to me if you did. I'm just curious. And so I can figure out which asshole I need to go straighten out so we can get you to stay."

But I was shaking my head. "Yeah right, I see right through you. You like Jeremiah. As in, *like* him." Even as I said it, I felt a little junior high-ish. But at the same time, I knew I was right.

Ruth's mouth dropped open and her eyes widened. She looked at the door to my bedroom. And then she hurriedly shut it. Then she went and sat down on my bed, looking a little freaked out.

"I mean," she blinked. "Maybe I... *do*? A little? He's a stubborn ass, but he is really cute, and he's a good guy, and sometimes I do want to rip all of his clothes off when we're arguing."

Then she shook her head. "But I'm just sex-starved and we'd be a disaster in real life. It's ridiculous. And I can't believe you even distracted me like that, witch. We're talking about *you*."

Well, she'd knocked the wind out of my sails with her honesty so I sat down on the bed beside her.

"I slept with Reece," I admitted quietly.

"I knew it!" she said, all but jumping up and down on the bed beside me. "Was last night the first time?"

I felt the blush rise on my cheeks before dropping my head and shaking my head no. "It's just casual sex," I continued hurriedly. "No strings or anything, we both agreed. But then last night we just sort of... fell asleep together and he held me all night."

Her hand went to her chest. "Oh my God, that's so sweet, shut *up*! Except don't. Tell me everything."

So I told her a little more, skipping over the most intimate details about our *play* but getting to the part where Jeremiah found us this morning. And the less than generous conclusions he'd come to, along with the things he'd said.

"I'm gonna stab his eyeballs out." Ruth jumped to her feet. "How dare he go in guns blazing, judging you or his brother like that?"

I reached out a hand and grabbed her arm before she could go storming out of the room. "He was just surprised. And I hate that I put either of them in that position. They usually get along so well. It's better if I just remove myself from the equation and let everything go back to the way it was."

"That's bullshit," Ruth exclaimed emphatically. "They're brothers. I'm sure they fight all the time."

"I've never seen them fight."

She rolled her eyes. "We've known them for what? All of three weeks? And from what you described, whatever boiled over this morning has been something contentious between them that's probably been under the surface for a while. And I'm sure it's not the first time it's bubbled over. You just had a front seat for it this time, and that was shitty of Jeremiah. But from what I've seen, I suspect that's who these guys are. They don't mask what they're thinking or feeling. It's just all right there, hanging out for better or worse."

I sat with that for a second, absorbing what she'd said. I couldn't imagine... Just *saying* and *showing* what you thought and felt instead of covering it over and hiding it to stay safe.

Because everybody on this ranch knew deep down it was safe to say whatever the hell they wanted. To show whatever emotion they were having.

As if... as if it was normal to just have a conflict without it turning into disaster. And that was something I could barely even comprehend.

I blinked harder, getting up and walking towards the window, and for the first time since Jeremiah had come in yelling, my heartbeat finally started to slow.

I was safe.

Everything was okay.

I'd just operated on a fight or flight instinct the second I felt those old feelings. I lifted a trembling hand to my forehead, wiping away the cold sweat.

I closed my eyes and leaned it against the cold glass. It felt nice against my flushed skin.

"I'm a complete mess," I whispered.

"Oh, honey." I felt Ruth's hand at my back. "Welcome to the club."

"I made a fool out of myself."

"I doubt it. I would have been mortified if anyone had found me like that and said those things. Difference between us is, I would have gotten pissed and wanted to start throwing fists. But you're a sweet girl who takes the whole world on your shoulders, it seems like."

I laughed. "You're fight, I'm flight."

Then my smile faded. "I always thought it would be more heroic to stand and fight."

Sometimes I felt like such a wimp for being Jeff's *victim*. The whole thought of it made me want to crawl out of my skin. But I knew if I ever tried fighting back, it would just go twice as bad. It was futile.

Ruth shook her head and made a face. "No way. It's a terrible idea. As someone who got in my share of actual fights all growing up, I can tell you, it doesn't solve much. It feels good for about three seconds to lash out. But then someone's usually hitting you back. And that sucks."

"You can say that again."

Her eyebrow went up at that, and I wished I could take it back. Luckily, she went on talking. "Even the fights I managed to *win*, and there were a couple, it's not like anything good happened. I was suspended for two weeks the last time, ostracized as the girl with the temper. Then boys were even more of jerks trying to get a rise out of me after I got back."

I shook my head. "Kids are ruthless. It's a miracle any of us survive to adulthood."

"Right?" She knocked my shoulder with hers. "But look. Both of us made it."

I scoffed. "I don't know about you, but I'm not exactly the paradigm of mental health and stability. Until I get that paycheck, I still only *actually* have a single pair of clothes to my name. I'm twenty-nine years old and starting completely over again from scratch with nothing. And I have no idea what the hell I'm doing most of the time."

Ruth's left eyebrow rose. "Then it sounds to me that you shouldn't be running away from the few friends you've managed to actually find. Maybe good friends and situations are a dime a dozen wherever it is you come from, but around here—"

"They aren't," I said quickly. "I promise you, they aren't. I've never —" I shook my head. "I mean, I can't even remember the last time I had a conversation like this with someone who was just, totally real and nonjudgmental. It feels amazing. And refreshing. And, yeah, amazing."

Ruth nodded. "Exactly, besides Olivia, I haven't had anyone else either till you and the boys came along."

"You call what you and Jeremiah do having genuine conversations?"

She grinned. "Arguing is the best kind of genuine conversation. I can be my most ornery, crotchety, opinionated self and he's not intimidated. He just gives back as good as I give. In a good argument, there's a level of respect, else why bother?"

"And Jeremiah's a good arguer?" I asked, not getting it as anything *I* would ever want but trying to understand it for her sake.

She grinned. "He's the best I've come across. And he actually listens to what I have to say. That's a new one."

Then she wagged her finger at me. "I see you trying to get the conversation back on me. Back to the point. So you're staying, right? That's where this conversation has been circling round to. We're worth it, trust me."

"It's not that," I sighed. "It was never that. I know you're worth it."

"So why leave then?" she cut in, eyebrows raised like she knew she had me in a checkmate.

And the truth was, she had me stumped. Because if I started trying to go into how the problem was *me*, how I was broken and not fit to be around good people, how I was too selfish, a disease that seemed to infect every situation I was a part of...

Well, of course I knew what she would say. That I was being ridiculous. Of course I wasn't a disease. It was what *I* would say to any friend who told me those things.

...so why couldn't I say them to myself?

I'd left, hadn't I?

I believed I was worth more. I knew there was more. And I'd felt that more-ness almost every day since I'd been here.

I felt it when I stepped out the door on the crisp, cold mornings and looked at the rolling hills bathed in the morning sunlight, wide eternal sky overhead.

I felt it when I fed the newborn calves who sucked so eagerly at the bottles and then ran rambunctiously around the yard together, playing and rollicking from the simple joy of being *alive*.

I felt it when I looked around the kitchen table and Reece and Jeremiah made jokes at each other's expenses and laughter was easy and common.

I felt it when I rode the ATV and felt the wind biting against my face and my muscles burning by the end of the day from doing true, useful work out under the sun instead of being trapped, imprisoned inside all day.

I felt it last night when my body shuddered in orgasm and then I clutched to the warmth of another human being and listened to his heartbeat steady underneath my ear through the hours of the night.

I'd been so brave, and maybe I could be brave just a little longer.

Maybe I could... stay.

I breathed out, long and low. "Okay," I said, peace coming as soon as the decision was made. "I'll stay. A little longer, anyway."

Ruth hugged me and let out a little, "Woo!" and then dragged me to my feet, saying she was starving and it was time for breakfast.

## 14

So I stayed. And a week later, I was still mostly glad about the decision. I'd started taking over the counter sleeping pills again. Okay, yeah, so I took twice the recommended dose. Sometimes with a glass of wine. But I just couldn't handle the nightmares. Maybe that made me a coward, but I didn't care. There was only so much I could deal with at once.

Especially since things between me and Reece were... well, awkward was putting it generously.

Reece wasn't anywhere to be seen when I'd come downstairs that morning after everything happened.

Jeremiah was there instead, and from his tone when he spoke to me, I took it that he'd talked his brother into leaving to do chores.

"I hope you'll stay. You're a good worker. But I don't want to in any way pressure you. If you want to go, I'm happy to give you your pay to date. Again, I apologize for my brother's reckless actions. He'll stay away from you if you decide to stay."

I frowned, wanting to defend Reece. He hadn't done anything wrong. He'd been kind and restrained the night before and I didn't like the way Jeremiah saw his brother, as some kind of screw up. From the way Reece thought about himself, it seemed like it was this very sort of talk from his own brother that had dug deep and made him see himself as lesser or bad in some way. It was wrong. But I didn't think Jeremiah could hear that in this moment. And certainly not from me.

Besides, did I really know either of them? No, no, I didn't. And my track record with men hadn't exactly been stellar. So maybe I was seeing things wrong.

Either way, staying away from Reece seemed like the best idea for everybody involved. I hated to cause strife between him and his brother. That was the last thing I wanted.

I said as much to Jeremiah that morning. "I'd like to stay. But I don't mean to cause any problems."

He waved a hand. "No, it's not you. I'm sorry you got dragged into it. From here on out, things will be strictly professional. I'll see to it."

I frowned a little at that, not sure what he meant, but I was glad for the conflict of the moment to have been smoothed over.

And so life went on. I'd finally got my first paycheck since I'd been here a month, and as I thought, Jeremiah didn't ask questions when I said I needed it in cash, beyond a lingering look. I'd gone with Ruth to a Walmart several towns over and bought some clothes, including new jeans all my own. And I was probably one of the few women who was delighted to find I was two full sizes larger than I used to be back when I lived with Jeff. That was what happened when you were no longer living on a starvation diet. I loved my new body. I loved every bit of transformation I could get that took away reminders of *her*.

So things were going well, except that whatever his brother had said to Reece definitely did something. He didn't seek me out or even talk to me anymore. Which was awkward to say the least, since we all still ate meals together. Things were tense for a few days, the conversation across the dinner table a little stilted with Ruth doing most of the heavy lifting, but eventually it smoothed out to being back to normal. Well, normal*ish*.

I felt a bright warmth in my chest the first time Reece made a joke that including me at dinner the other night—it was the first time he'd addressed me directly since I'd been so warm in his arms that night. Our eyes had caught and I lit up like a damn fire had flamed to life in my chest.

A week later and it was raining, dark clouds overhead bringing on a premature twilight, but I could still remember the warmth in my chest from how it had felt in that moment. Even though he'd been successfully avoiding me since.

I sighed, looking down at Nine and trying to get the bottle back in his mouth. I'd managed to lure him up to the steps of the porch where the roof covered me from the rain for his and Bessie's dinner bottles. She'd finished hers but Nine was being finicky with his.

Ruth was lounging on a rocking chair by the kitchen door, watching me feed and chatting at me about local town gossip. "So then Gracie told me that Mariah, you remember Mariah, the one who was in the garage that day when Trent was being a dick?"

I nodded distractedly. Nine kept turning his head sideways and losing the plot, yanking away from the nipple and staring up at the ceiling where the rain sounded like a barrage of marbles on the tin roof.

"So Missy is telling anyone who will listen that Janice's husband is cheating on her with Brenna. She's a local high school teacher."

Nine pulled away from the nipple again.

"Come on, man," I said to the ornery calf. "I know it's loud, but if you don't finish this bottle soon, my arm is going to fall off. See how good Bessie was?" I gestured with my head to where Bess had already raced off through the rain back to the shelter of the stable.

I shoved the nipple towards his mouth again. "Don't you want to go join your buddy?"

He gave a few sucks again at the nipple but then thunder boomed overhead and he danced backwards, all the way down back into the yard.

Behind me, Ruth busted out laughing.

I turned to look over my shoulder, glared at her and stuck out my tongue.

She held up her hands. "No, no, you're doing an excellent job. Please continue. I haven't been this entertained in days."

"Don't you have something to do? Like look for a job?"

It was her turn to make a face at me. "I'm living rent free essentially, since I own the place and food's cheap. I'm having a quarter-life crisis and taking a break from being a grown up, okay? So leave me be, woman."

A flash lit up the sky and then thunder rumbled, only a few moments behind. That was apparently it for Nine, because he bolted for the stable.

Well, he'd drunk two-thirds of the bottle. Good enough for now since he'd eaten well all day. I wasn't about to go chasing him down anyway.

The door behind us opened and I spun around right in time to come face to face with Reece.

"Oh. Hi," I said, blinking rapidly.

"Hi," he said, then his eyes lowered and he pushed past me. He was wearing a raincoat and I turned, following him with my eyes as he pulled the hood up over his head and jogged right into the pouring rain towards his truck.

*Hi.* That was it. One syllable. That was all I got from him these days.

Ruth was standing and running down the stairs, stopping just short of heading into the rain. "Where are you going? We're going to the bar tonight, I told you at breakfast. Out at Landlubbers, by the lake. You have to come!"

"Sorry, gotta make a run to town," was all he shouted back, barely heard through the rain.

"Meet us there then!" Ruth shouted, almost simultaneously as his truck door slammed shut.

I felt my shoulders slump. "That was weird, wasn't it? It was weird."

Ruth nodded. "Totally fucking weird."

I smacked her on the arm. "You're supposed to *disagree* with me."

She shrugged.

I rolled my eyes at her, just as another car pulled in the driveway. Good timing, because Reece hadn't pulled out yet, and I don't know how he and Olivia's sporty little Honda would have passed one another on the one-lane road into the ranch.

Ruth clapped. "Yes! Now the pre-party can begin!"

"I forgot about going out tonight," I said, looking down at my mud-spattered clothing.

"Go shower and change. Olivia's here to do our hair and makeup."

I looked out at the rain, falling harder than ever. "Won't it be hard to get to town in a storm like this?" Part of me was looking for an excuse to get out of it. More than part of me. I was so tired lately. I wanted to go upstairs with a glass of wine, take a pill, then *sleep*. Sleep and sleep and sleep with no dreams.

Ruth just waved a hand. "It'll probably have stopped by the time you're done with your shower. Besides, I haven't been out dancing in ages and we've all been cooped up in the place for way too long."

I nodded, knowing once Ruth got something in her head there was little chance of changing her mind. And she was right, we had been cooped up here. Maybe that was why I'd been feeling so... off lately.

It was just a little harder to get out of bed in the morning. All the fire and steam that had brought me this far, gotten me out of Jeff's house finally, pushed me through the mad dash across the country, and seen me through the first month here... well, I was running out of steam.

Leaving was supposed to fix everything. It was supposed to be the end of all the bad stuff.

I was supposed to be able to start over as a new person.

I went upstairs and blasted hot water for several long moments, feeling the hot needles punching through the numb cold of my toes, my shoulders, my nose.

How did people do it? How did they keep putting one foot in front of another, day after day, year after year, for an entire lifetime? I slumped against the shower wall. Some days it felt impossible.

The water had started to run lukewarm by the time I finally

washed and rinsed my hair and stepped out. That was selfish of me, in case any of the guys needed to shower. But I'd just sort of blanked out in the enveloping heat. That happened sometimes lately. I'd just kind of drift out...

I shook it off and got dressed, then ran back downstairs. Ruth was right about the storm. It wasn't raining anymore. It was so strange, completely different from California. There when it rained, it rained all day, for weeks at a time sometimes. And there was rarely, if ever, thunder or lightning.

Here it seemed like the storms were determined to live up to the state motto, Don't Mess with Texas. They had to be bigger and better. Louder, flashier. Storms came in with dramatic thunder, even more dramatic lightning.

They could roll in, dump gallons of rain that sometimes caused flash flooding, then be done thirty minutes later. It was completely nuts.

Ruth and Olivia had replaced the noise of thunder with loud music in the kitchen and the TV in the living room blaring some reality TV show. It was no less jarring after the silence and solitude of the shower.

Right as I stepped into the kitchen, the cacophony got even louder as Olivia hit the blender on what looked like a margarita mix.

"I thought we were going out," I said, gesturing at the blender.

"These are the pre-bar drinks. I like to have a buzz before I get there."

I shook my head but Olivia just grinned. "Why do you think I drive over? It's so I don't get stuck being the DD."

Ruth rolled her eyes. Then she looked at me and said quickly, "Not it."

"It's fine with me. I don't mind." And I didn't. After my last experience with the weed, I wasn't in a hurry to lower my inhibitions again anytime soon.

The door to the kitchen and Buck and Jeremiah came in.

"Ooo." Ruth grinned. "Jeremiah can be the designated driver. Then Charlotte can get smashed with us."

Jeremiah grimaced. "What am I getting volunteered for?"

Ruth looked appalled. "We're going to the bar tonight! Don't tell me you forgot." Then she looked over at Buck. "You're invited too, of course, Buck."

Buck nodded, dipping his head as he took off his hat. A small river of water poured off the top of it onto the kitchen floor as he did. "Sounds like a good time."

"Well, I'd be your DD," Jeremiah said, "But I don't think we'll all fit in one vehicle. Gonna have to take two."

"Seriously," I put a hand on Ruth's arm. "I don't mind."

"Okay well, still, take a sip." She held out her margarita to me and obligingly, I took a sip. "Delicious."

Their good moods were infectious and I was feeling a little more in the mood for whatever they had planned tonight. I hadn't been out dancing in... well, *ever*. I mean, I'd been to exactly one party in college before being swallowed up by Jeff, and no one was exactly dancing at the sloppy kegger. Jeff himself hated dancing, so there'd been no opportunity after we were married, not even at our wedding.

Olivia beamed. "Okay, ladies, time to go put on our faces."

Jeremiah rolled his eyes. "I'll never understand women. You all look just fine right now."

Ruth and Olivia exchanged glances and then, at the same time, said in exasperation, "*Men*."

I laughed as the three of us headed upstairs.

---

AN HOUR AND A HALF LATER, we'd arrived at Landlubbers, a bar that was... eclectic to say the least. The largest décor items on the wall were a large, old wooden kayak and oars, not to be outdone by the multiple fully-stuffed deer heads with antlers, along with license plates from all over the country that covered the walls floor to ceiling.

But there was also a large dance floor that was filled with people on a Friday night, and a music system absolutely *blasting* music.

I could barely hear Ruth when she yelled, "All right, baby. Let's get you on the dance floor."

"Oh, I don't know," I said, standing by the bar. "I just ordered—"

But Ruth wasn't having it. She took me by my wrists and pulled me, her walking backwards while she dragged me forwards onto the dance floor, a giant grin on her face.

With her curly hair blown out and wild around her face and makeup on, including loud red lipstick, she looked like a completely different person to the one I usually saw over the kitchen table.

I'd declined Olivia's heavy-handed makeup and curling iron when she'd come my way, opting for just a light mascara and colored lip balm. I'd spent too much of my life buffed and shined to a perfect sheen to ever go back.

"BITCHES!" Olivia screeched, walking towards us with both arms raised up to the sky, a beer in one hand. She'd gone to the other end of the bar to order. We'd taken a divide and conquer approach. "Are you ready to par-tay?"

Ruth dropped my wrists only long enough to give Olivia a big hug, as if she hadn't seen her only ten minutes before. Then again, Ruth had downed two margaritas before we'd left home, so she'd been giggling the entire ride over and had hugged me multiple times as soon as we got inside. She dragged Olivia over towards me.

I was still amazed by how easy these women were with each other. I'd only seen people like this in movies but here they were, in real life, right in front of me.

"Come on, we gotta give Charlie a good night," Ruth said, snatching Olivia's beer and dipping her head back as she chugged it.

"Hey!" Olivia said, grabbing for her bottle as soon as Ruth's head righted.

Ruth handed it back over and then hooked an arm around my neck. "She's been knee-deep in it all calving season."

"Oh honey, then you're the one who really needs this." Olivia shoved the apparently communal beer bottle towards me but I laughed and waved her off. I knew I could have a beer and still be fine to drive, but I hated the taste of it. Jeff loved the stuff and the smell of it on his breath had turned me off it forever.

She shrugged and then repeated Ruth's action, throwing her head back and chugging the beer. I just watched in awe as the liquid in the bottle disappeared inch by inch until it was gone.

"Damn, Liv," Ruth laughed when she was done and let out a surprised little burp. "That kinda week, huh."

Olivia just gave her a *look* and then nodded. "Dear *God*, if I have to listen to *one more* rich middle-aged white lady going on and on and *on* about how the gays are ruining the country—" She raised her finger as a gun to her head and then released her thumb, pulling the trigger. She looked at Ruth. "Didn't we have more in mind than this when we were little kids dreaming about what we wanted to be when we grew up?"

"Oh honey," Ruth laughed from deep in her chest. "I'd drink to that, but you finished off the beer and I want to dance and forget all that bullshit anyway."

She grabbed one of Olivia's hands and one of my hands and then started jumping frantically to the music, mostly on beat.

I laughed, caught up in her joyous, rebellious mood in spite of myself. She might not know what she was doing with her life or what her next move was, but she was enjoying the hell out of this moment, and so could I.

Why had I been so dour lately, anyway? Ruth was right, coming out tonight *had* been a good idea. Getting cooped up at the ranch wasn't good for anybody.

So I leaned into the rhythm with my body and *moved*. My hips hit with the beat, roll and pop, roll and pop, back and sway, with each drum hit. It was a sexy, upbeat Lizzo song. My hands went up over my head as I gave into the energy of the crowd more and more.

In truth, I imagined I probably looked like a goddamned idiot. I only knew how to stand around like a pretty statue and do that fake passing back and forth of rote, petty phrases and conversation that passed for a "party." Often also a fundraiser or work party to network, meant to squeeze or strengthen existing power relationships. Where every conversation was a chess game between the smart players and those on the other side of the power dynamic—prey who devoured.

*Mouse.* Jeff had certainly loved having me around as his personal prey, to spend his anger at whenever he wasn't getting enough respect everywhere else he felt he deserved it. And when he went too far like he did about every other month or so, the other couples in our social circle had been eager to believe his rumors that my occasional disappearances from public life were because of my "mental health condition." That we were "managing" it the best we could, but that sometimes my anxiety crippled me and I went back to old compulsions like my eating disorder.

I'd never had an eating disorder—which was shocking actually, considering my mother. But he convinced them I'd had one since I was a teenager. He'd even convinced my own mother. Sometimes before a party he would limit my food intake, ensuring I was starving before we went. He was a sick, twisted fuck, and it was before I knew what the rumors were.

So of course I stuffed my face once I got there. I mean, I tried to be as surreptitious as I could—only because I knew Jeff would be watching. I'd eat a cucumber sandwich here, a muffin there, a mini-quiche, and then another mini-quiche, and then another. I had no idea he'd use my behavior at the party, which yes, was a bit odd, of course it was!—to then say I had disordered eating. He'd set me up. But that's how it always was with him. He'd back you into a corner so it felt like there was no way to win.

So it wasn't like I could call any of those women up to hang out because I just wanted to *be* with them. Certainly not because we liked each other and could dance and move our bodies and make damn fools of ourselves, and nobody would care because they were doing the same thing.

A country song came on, I had no idea who the singer was, but a cheer rose up in the crowd because they obviously did.

A man came up to Olivia and pulled her into his arms. She laughed and seemed willing enough as he swept her deeper into the center of the dance floor.

"Come on," Ruth said, "two-step with me!"

"I don't know how."

Her mouth dropped open. "You're in Texas now, honey. You gotta know how to two-step."

She proceeded to attempt to teach me how to two-step. I caught on near the end of the song, and either way, we were laughing and giggling enough to have enjoyed the hell out of the dance.

Who said you had to be *good* at dancing to enjoy it? What a liberating thought.

The next song came on was a throwback, the one from the 90's that had, "Jump, jump!" in the chorus. And everyone on the dance floor actually jumped.

It went on like that, a mix of new, old, country, and contemporary dance pop. At one point Ruth disappeared to pull Jeremiah and Buck onto the floor from where they'd been sitting by the bar.

To all of our delight, they had moves. Well, moves inasmuch as tall white dudes could have moves.

Buck was better than Jeremiah, who seemed more reserved. But he was still trying, and he was far less stiff than I would have expected.

I wasn't the only one who noticed. Several local girls were suddenly dancing much closer in our vicinity.

The next time a two-step came around, Jeremiah was swept away by one of the circling locals and Olivia grabbed Buck's hand before anyone else could.

When a friendly-looking guy asked me if we could dance, I figured why the hell not.

It felt a little bizarre to have a stranger's hand on my waist, but it wasn't invasive. He was friendly as I continued bumbling along with the steps and we both clapped when the song was over. He asked if I wanted to dance the next one and I brushed him off with a smile and thanked him for the dance. He didn't make a big deal of it.

When I went back to find the girls, I saw Olivia's hand being taken by another man as a slow song got going, but I didn't see Ruth anywhere. She'd probably moved to another part of the floor during the last dance. It was packed and hard to see much of anything beyond a few feet.

It was as good a time as any to grab a break—and some water. I was parched.

I was heading back to the bar, eyes on the ground to make sure I didn't trip over anybody's feet, when all of the sudden there was a long-legged pair of wranglers in front of me and familiar boots.

I looked up in shock at Reece. "You came."

I'd all but walked right into him. We were only standing about a foot apart, the melee of the crowd moving and swaying all around us.

"Wanna dance?" He had to all but shout it, the music was so loud.

I wanted to ask a hundred things. How come you're here? What about your brother? Why the sudden change of heart?

Instead I just nodded, wide-eyed, and took another little half-step closer to him.

The next thing I knew, he was taking my right hand in his and then pulling me into his body by his other hand on my waist. Like it was the easiest thing in the world. Like that hand had always been meant to fit exactly there.

I blinked a few times as we started swaying to the song. It was still the slow song. He hadn't pulled me flat up against his body or anything, there were still a few inches of space between us.

But it was *nothing* like the dance I'd just had with the other man only minutes before. Everywhere Reece touched me felt alive and electric, that peculiar way his touch always affected me.

I tipped my head back and glanced into his face and whoa— mistake, mistake.

His face was just right there, along with his lips. I immediately looked back down and turned my head sideways, my ear brushing against his shoulder. And tried to regulate my suddenly rapid breathing and speeding heart rate.

It was a slow song for God's sake, and I'd been jumping around for the last half hour. It was ridiculous that this was the dance that had me feeling suddenly overheated and sweaty.

But Reece's body was just so—

It was like he was overloading all my senses at once. And his right arm was snaked around my waist so we were dancing so close, bodies together in a little cocoon of intimacy in the middle of the dance floor as a country singer crooned overhead about never wanting to have missed the dance.

Emotions. I was feeling a lot of emotions at once. I could recognize that even if I couldn't sort out one emotion from another. What the hell *was* this attraction between us?

Reece smelled good. I knew that. I leaned in as we moved, more and more as one. He felt good and he smelled good and when I leaned my head against his chest, it felt like the most natural thing in the world. Natural too that I could hear his heartbeat solid in my ear.

And then his arms curved around my back instead of just a light touch at my waist. I curled into him and closed my eyes. Losing myself in him, in the song, in the security of his strong arms around me, in the magic of this moment surrounded by couples dancing just like us, humans connected and moving and being *alive.*

The fog I'd been sort of existing in faded and everything became sharp clarity. Each moment something to savor, to memorize.

His muscles were so firm under my arms. The way he guided me so solid and sure. His warmth soaked into me.

When the song came to an end, a fast pop track came on afterwards and I clung to Reece for a long moment after it was probably appropriate. I finally let go and pulled back from him, feeling my face heat.

Every time I was near him I felt this irresistible draw, but it was... it didn't change anything. Did it?

So I did the only thing I could—the thing that felt safe but also dangerous at the same time. I reached up, took hold of his shoulders and went up on tiptoe to whisper in his ear, "You wanna play pretend?"

His hand immediately came to my waist. Where he squeezed me possessively as he leaned down. "Where?" he growled in my ear.

I turned my face in towards his, intimate in the crowded bar as my face grazed the five o'clock shadow on his cheek. "The bathroom. We're strangers and you drag me in for a quickie."

I'd barely finished speaking before he'd grabbed my hand and was pulling me towards the back of the club.

The bathrooms were down a long hallway, dark but for a single bulb. My breath hitched in anticipation as Reece walked with purpose. There were a couple women waiting outside the women's bathroom but there wasn't any line for the men's. Reece didn't stop or try to be stealthy. He pulled open the door and tugged me inside with him, shutting the door behind us and flipping the lock.

There was a single toilet and a urinal, no stalls, but I barely had a chance to take in the grungy bathroom before Reece had me pressed up against the door with his body.

"I been watchin' you all night," he whispered low and growly. "You've been drivin' me damn near crazy with this body of yours. Seeing you in this dress..."

He skimmed his hands up my thighs, underneath said dress and my entire body quivered.

"So what are you gonna do about it?" I asked, my breath hitching. "We don't have much time before someone's banging down this door."

He sucked in a breath, his huge chest moving up and down. God, he looked like he was barely keeping himself in control.

"I'm gonna give you what you've been begging for and have you crying out my name in a minute flat is what I'm gonna do. So grab onto something, honey."

And with that, he grabbed my waist and spun me around so I was facing the door. I gasped at the quick motion and my hands flew up to palm the door.

Reece was as good as his word, obviously the one in control tonight. He flipped up my skirt and then, just like that, he had a thick finger inside me. And I was wet and ready for him.

"Good girl," his voice came rough at my ear. "You been wanting this too, huh? You been dreaming about having a big cock inside you? You want it rough and tumble, honey?"

"Yes," I begged, my voice barely above a gasped whisper. I barely knew myself in this moment, but I wanted everything he was about to give me. I arched my back so that my ass stuck out towards him.

"That's right, honey," he said. "That's so fuckin' right. Look at this plump ass of yours."

He gave my ass a quick smack and then he sank inside me, grabbing my hips to hold me in place as he started pumping his huge cock in and out of me.

Oh fuck, but it was dirty and so, so *hot*. I squeezed around him, and when he sank in, he hit a delicious spot. I'd never had sex like this, standing up, but also, I looked to the right and there was the mirror over the sink—

My breath caught at the sight of us. Him in his wranglers shoved down just enough to get the job done, me with the skirt of my dress up, my ass exposed as he thrust into me, over and over—

And the look on his face of absolute raw, rapturous *need*—

Then he reached around and grabbed my pussy from the front, his middle finger finding my clit— I climaxed so hard.

"My name," he demanded. "Say my fuckin' name."

"Reece!" I gasped in a high-pitched whine as I bucked back against him. He fucked me harder and I pressed against the door, wanting more of everything he had to give me. "Reece, oh God, *Reece*."

He thrust one final, rough, exquisite time and then stilled, his forehead falling against my back in between my shoulder blades.

His middle finger kept swirling against my clit and I spasmed several more times. I might have kept going but a hard knocking against the other side of the door had me jerking backwards.

"Give me a second," Reece hollered. He kissed the back of my neck, then behind my ear, then lower, making me shiver as he slowly pulled out of me.

I fell limp against the door as he disposed of the condom in the trash can.

He came back to me and reached back up under my skirt, rearranging my underwear and then zipping his pants back up.

"You ready to go back, honey? Or you need another minute?" His voice was so gentle, different from minutes earlier when he'd been rough and demanding, but both were just different parts of the same, sensual man.

I had the feeling that we hadn't just been playing pretend. That I'd just been with the real Reece. I'd called out his name as I'd climaxed for God's sake. All of this, every time with him felt more real than the last.

The banging at the door came again and I pulled away and nodded, not quite ready for words.

Reece took my hand. "Stay behind me," he said as he unlocked the door and then tugged me along after him as we stepped into the hallway. I kept my eyes down but didn't miss the comments and the one low whistle as we passed by.

But then we were back in the heady mix of the dance floor and, apart from the delicious soreness between my legs, it was as if the last ten minutes hadn't happened.

Except they had. And all I could think about was the feel of Reece pressing against my back, his arm wrapped around me as he brought me to pleasure while fucking me with complete abandon.

My legs felt like jelly and I was glad when Reece led us to the bar. He ordered a beer and I got some water, which I downed, and an apple cider, which I sipped since I was still the designated driver. Feeling completely intoxicated from amazing quickie bathroom sex didn't count, did it?

It was too loud to actually talk, which I was glad for. I sat, sipped my cider, and Reece stood next to me so close our thighs touched, and we watched people dance. It was probably another half hour before Ruth showed back up, Olivia in tow.

They must have been dancing on the other side of the room because she looked plenty flushed by the time she got to us. Good timing too, because the seats beside us just opened up and Olivia and Ruth fell into them, both of them giggling. Reece gave my hand a squeeze and said he was going to look for his brother.

"Oh, don't bother," Ruth said, tapping the bar for a shot. "He said he had to leave when I saw him earlier. I'm supposed to tell you he said he was taking your truck and that you can catch a ride home with us."

Reece's eyebrows went up but he nodded and ordered another beer. After the bartender handed it over, Reece came back to standing by me. Again he stood so close that our thighs brushed even as he followed along with the conversation Ruth and Olivia were having about the merits of whisky shots verses tequila.

I shifted slightly, rubbing my leg experimentally against his. He looked down and gave me a smile that sent shivers down my spine—a smile and a look that told me he was exactly as aware of our contact as I was, and he liked it too.

Holy Jesus. I took another long swig of the cold water. And smiled back at him.

We stayed for another hour and then Ruth wasn't looking so steady on her feet. I said *I* was tired and we called it a night.

Ruth frowned but Olivia and I helped her out to the car.

"I don't feel so good," Ruth said, her facial features souring almost as soon as we hit the parking lot.

"Oh shit, she's gonna blow," Olivia said. "I *told* you you should've had tequila instead of whisky! We had margaritas at home and you don't mix liquors!"

"Don't argue with a dying woman," Ruth wailed as she stumbled to the grass at the edge of the parking lot, dropped to her knees, and vomited in the ditch.

"Oh, honey!" Olivia crooned.

Both she and I leaned over, helping to hold Ruth's hair back and rubbing her back.

"I'm fine, I'm fine," Ruth said, sitting back on her haunches and taking the tissue Olivia produced from her purse to wipe her mouth.

Then she looked over at Olivia, her mascara smeared but smiling weakly in the lights from the bar and parking lot anyway. "Hey look, we got to relive the glory days after all."

Olivia rolled her eyes, then looked at me. "Help me get her up."

We both took a hand and helped Ruth back to her feet.

"The difference is that now I can hold my liquor. And you never could, not then or now."

Ruth collapsed against Olivia with an arm thrown around her. "I'm a lightweight, but you still love me."

Olivia planted a kiss on the top of Ruth's now frizzy-haired head. "Always, boo."

"Keys." I held out my hands.

Ruth fumbled in her jeans and then handed them over.

When we got back to the Jeep, Olivia and Reece helped Ruth climb up and into the back, then Olivia climbed in after her.

Thankfully, the GPS on Reece's phone worked to get us first to Olivia's house to drop her off after much giggling and off-key singing from the backseat, and then I started back home to the ranch.

Ruth fell asleep in the back and then it was just me and Reece up front in the quiet of the back roads at night.

"I really had a good time tonight," he said.

"Me too."

I was glad I was driving and had an excuse not to take my eyes off the road to look at his face.

After dancing so closely all night, it was silly for there to be awkwardness between us now. But I couldn't deny it. And I hated it. I'd hated how awkward it was between us at the ranch lately, too.

So before I could think better of it, I blurted, "Why'd you come tonight? I thought you weren't gonna."

He shrugged. "I—" Then he sighed, eyes still ahead on the road when I took a quick glance his way. "I don't like how it's been lately." His eyes came briefly to look at me. I jerked mine back to the road as he clarified, "Between us."

"Oh." What did that mean? Did...did tonight mean we were going to start up our clandestine night meetings again? Did I want it to mean that? Even when every time we were together, it seemed to be pushing towards something more? I swallowed, not sure if I knew the answer to that question. Everything in my head was such a mess still.

I knew I'd liked being in his arms. I didn't like it when he avoided me around the ranch. That much I knew, but I wasn't sure it clarified anything.

"I know my brother's been an ass. I'll talk to him. Because I really like you, Charlie. Regardless of what's happened in the past, I really want us to be able to be... friends."

Friends.

My shoulders slumped a little in spite of myself. Did friends do the things we had tonight? Did friends feel the way I did about him when I remembered what it had been like to have him slide between my legs? Or think about him when they were supposed to be working, and when they showered, and when they—

I swallowed hard, my fingers tightening on the steering wheel. "Friends," I said tightly, my jaw flexing. "Yes, I'd like that."

And I loosened my grip on the wheel, because the truth was, I *would* like it. Reece as a friend was better than the no-Reece at all of this past week.

I looked at him, flashing what I hoped was an easy, breezy smile. "Sounds good, *friend*."

I couldn't read the expression on his face. It was almost as if he was frowning. But then he nodded, right as I looked back at the road.

"Friends it is," he said.

# 15

THINGS WERE BUSY ON THE RANCH THE NEXT WEEK WITH CALVING season hitting its peak, so even though my mind stayed on Reece, I was genuinely too worn out at the end of every day to do much about it. Or maybe that was just the excuse I told myself to put off making a decision. But no, he'd said we were friends, and friends it was. Friends didn't think about how tight each other's ass was. Friends didn't obsess about wanting to grab each other to whisper about getting together to play kinky sex games in the middle of the night.

I drove the four-wheeler back out for the mid-morning check. I couldn't believe I'd been here for almost the entire duration of calving season. We'd had 87 calves born, with eleven cows and heifers still pregnant. Some days it had just been one or two, but then it had sped up and there'd been one long, exhaustive day right in the middle of it with *nine* born in one day.

I'd been out in rain and cold and sun and mud, so much mud, spending my days more outside than in. Each night I dropped into bed too exhausted to think. I'd even eased up on the pills the past week ever since the dance, taking just the prescribed dose instead of doubling it, and I'd only woken up once drenched in sweat from a nightmare. I was counting that as a win.

And in between the work was the people. Ruth, and Reece, and Jeremiah. And well, Buck was there too, sometimes, though he tended to take his meals in the bunkhouse more often than not. He'd usually grab breakfast at the big house, though.

I thought back to this morning as I rode the four-wheeler over the familiar path out to the far pasture where there'd been a cow in labor this morning that I needed to check on.

Some morning it had been, sheesh. It had started out normal enough. Breakfast had been Ruth doing her usual morning crossword.

"What's a four-letter word for a tall tale? Ends with N?" Ruth had asked this morning from the table where she was bent over the paper.

"Story?" Buck offered before shoving his last bite of his eggs in his mouth and reaching for his mug of coffee, downing it in one gulp.

Ruth rolled her eyes and shot me a what-am-I-gonna-do-with-this-guy? look. He'd been giving similarly useless guesses every time Ruth tossed out a clue for help.

"Maybe a *yarn*?" I offered.

Her eyes lit up. "Yes! You're a genius." She started scribbling in the little squares.

Jeremiah was finishing up his food too. He stood up and grabbed his hat off the hook by the door. "We should start talking about what you wanna do now that calving season's almost over, Charlotte."

I'd looked up, surprised to be singled out by him, and just as surprised at his words. Lately to chase away the doldrums, I'd just been burying myself in my work, taking on extra chores, doing anything I could to keep busy, busy, busy. I helped repaint the bunkhouse, inside and out. I was an extra pair of eyes driving the fence line three times a week to double-check no more of it was downed. I tried to absolutely wear my body out every day to leave no room for maudlin thoughts or dreams.

Especially since I was still trying to respect Jeremiah's wishes and stay away from Reece for the most part. Even though memories of dancing together that night... well, I'd had to fight the impulse more than once to seek him out in the night and have a repeat of the first evening I'd shown up on his bunkhouse door.

But we'd established firm boundaries. Friends. We were just *friends* now.

It didn't stop me from being glad that Buck slept in the bunkhouse now, too. It helped keep the temptation at bay... But it wasn't like I couldn't invite Reece into *my* room. I mean he did sleep there that one night... And maybe if we were suuuuuuuuuper careful and exxxxtra quiet we could—

God, even the fact that I was *thinking* about it as if it was some-thing I was actually considering just showed how I needed to keep busy and stay away from the sexy, gentle, kind, understanding—

Jesus, I was fucked up enough as it was. Adding a man to the mix was a horrible idea. Absolutely horrible.

Friends. We were just *friends*.

All these thoughts went racing through my head, the ones that had been on a circular hamster wheel for weeks, when Jeremiah made that statement this morning.

What genius response came out of my mouth in return to Jeremi-ah's startling suggestion that I should be thinking about leaving soon? "Oh. Right."

"I just mean, we'd only initially talked about you staying on through calving season, and then you'd said you wanted to be moving on."

I don't know why his words felt like a blow to the gut. Except, of course they did.

There was an audible noise as Ruth slapped the newspaper down on the table. "I don't see how that has anything to do with anything. Situations change. People change. She just didn't know us yet. But of course she wants to stay on and keep working here. Don't you?"

I looked to Reece, wanting to hear his opinion, but his gaze was fixed to the floor.

And it struck me—shit, maybe I *was* wearing out my welcome.

They probably did want some burly man as their permanent

ranch hand. Not a woman who was new to the life and had to be taught every little thing. They had the resources to hire a seasoned hand. It had been charity to take me in in the first place, and only at Ruth's insistence.

Then I frowned, for the first time pausing and being like...*wait*. Were those my real thoughts? Or just an echo of the way Jeff would always tell me what a burden I was? Or how my mother would talk to me, calling me useless even though I did most of the housework in addition to keeping up my grades at school?

I frowned, considering the possibility, right as Reece finally spoke up.

"Jer, what the hell?" Reece asked, obviously aggravated. "Of course she can stay. She's a fast learner and this is a good, safe environment for her."

Jeremiah glared at his brother. "What matters is what she wants, not what you want." He directed his attention back to me. "Forgive my brother. It's up to you. You can stay and train as a ranch hand and get some first hand experience. Or I can pay you out here in a week or so, and I'm sure Ruth would help you get set up in Austin if that's still where you're wanting to go. Think on it and let me know."

And with those ominous words he'd just stepped out the door like he hadn't just turned my little world on its head.

"Well, obviously you can't leave," Ruth said as soon as the door closed behind Jeremiah. She scoffed as if it was the most ridiculous thing she'd ever heard. Then she looked at my face closer. I don't know what she saw there, but she jumped up from the table, ran over and threw her arms around my neck. "Oh God, are you going to leave us?"

Over her shoulder, I saw Reece watching me, his forkful of eggs halfway to his mouth, like he was waiting for my answer.

"I- I don't know," I answered honestly.

And that was how I'd left it. I'd gone out to feed Bessie and Nine and looked down at their little faces and eagerly suckling maws and the thought of leaving and not getting to see them grow up...

Which was silly. They'd grow up and just become cattle. Eventually Nine would be sold off as beef. Bessie would be used to breed little calves of her own soon enough.

My sentimentality was silly. Useless.

This had always just been a waystation. A place to do some healing. To reconnect with myself. I'd even called it cocooning. The whole point of a cocoon was so that you could eventually emerge from it, and fly away.

I neared the herd where I'd seen the heifer laboring earlier this morning, before I'd gotten back in and realized the four-wheeler was out of gas, which meant I'd had to take an unplanned trip into town for more—it really had been one of *those* kinds of mornings.

I climbed off the four-wheeler, the back of my hair brushing my neck in a way that tickled in the breeze and I looked out at the land. The huge sky overhead was dotted with puffy white clouds, the now familiar hills of the land sloping into one another, all of it like something out of a movie.

I couldn't imagine not seeing this sight every day.

Just more sentimentality. Of course I felt close to this land, this place. It was the first place I'd felt good feelings and experienced even the slightest bit of happiness after ten years in hell. The first place I'd felt any touches of human kindness. Where I'd learned to reconnect with my body, to trust that I could do difficult things and have *other* people trust me instead of criticize and tear me down all the time.

It had only been six weeks, but it felt like a year, or longer even. After being stagnant and stuck so long, terrified I'd never be free... everything from the last six weeks... I didn't think any of that could ever be *possible* for a woman like me.

And yet here I was. Mud-spattered, wild-haired. No makeup, no masks. No one had kept tabs on me all day and I'd roamed.

Free.

Some days it even felt possible that this could be my life now. That maybe I could keep forging ahead with these new connections I was making, both with these people and this land and with trying to build a new life for myself.

And other days... well, there were mornings it was hard to get out of bed. I couldn't say there wasn't a part of me that thought about how if I left, I could retreat back into myself. Maybe I wasn't ready for all this. Maybe I'd take a break from making close friends like Ruth, someone whose very nature demanded vulnerability and realness.

If I left, I could re-cocoon. Because maybe, in reality... I was terrified of all it meant to fly. Maybe crawling was a perfectly fine mode of travel for people like me...

I frowned, all of it spinning around and around in my head, only confusing me more. I yanked the keys out of the four-wheeler. My eyes searched out the heifer. Her water bag had been expelled at last check two hours ago.

I hopped off the ATV, my boots squelching in the mud. I grabbed the tagging gun and walked closer, expecting to find a baby calf on the ground by the heifer whenever I located her. This would be calf #88. I wouldn't say I was a pro at tagging the little buggers, but I was far more comfortable with the entire process.

But when I got closer, I found the big, pregnant heifer on the ground, small calf hooves sticking out the back end of her.

My stomach sank. Oh no, she'd been in labor too long. The calf should have been born by now.

I blinked, feeling out of my depth all of a sudden, where moments before I'd been all confidence.

I'd been so sure the calf would be born already... because, well, all the births had been going so well lately. But that was stupid. I never should have gotten complacent. I should have been by an hour earlier, but I'd had to go to town for gas.

I had chains on the ATV, but remembering the first night I'd arrived, I didn't dare try to pull the calf myself.

I turned around and ran back to the ATV.

This pasture wasn't too far out, the house was only a ten-minute ride in, but I felt frantic thinking of the mother and calf I'd left behind.

The ride in seemed to take an hour, not ten minutes, and I was terrified of getting stuck in the mud again. Yesterday, Jeremiah'd had to tow me out of an especially slushy pit I'd gotten the four-wheeler stuck in. But finally, finally I made it.

Jeremiah was working on the stables today so I drove the four-wheeler that direction, but on the way there, I saw Reece stepping out of the barn.

"Reece!" I stopped the ATV and jumped off. "One of the heifers is having trouble. I need your help to come and pull the calf."

He immediately stood up straighter. "Do you have chains?"

I nodded, twisting my hands together frantically. "But not the big calf-puller."

He nodded and turned, jogging back into the barn and returning moments later with the big T pole. Without a word we both hurried back to the ATV. He slid the pole through some straps on the back and then climbed on behind me.

I immediately took off, my stomach in knots thinking about the calf stuck in its mother's birth canal. Those little *hooves*.

The ten-minute ride back out to where I'd left them felt so much longer than the ride in, but finally, *finally* we were there. I all but leapt off the ATV, yanking the chains out of the bag before Reece had even climbed off.

I showed him where the heifer was, praying by some miracle she would have delivered the calf by the time we'd returned.

But no, she was exactly as I'd left her, on the ground, occasionally letting out distressed noises and kicking at her stomach with her own hooves.

I looked to Reece and his brows were drawn in concern.

"I'm so sorry. I should have realized we were low on gas earlier. If only I'd looked closer at the gauge last night, I could have gone to town then and I would have been by earlier and we might have caught it when there was still time to—"

"Don't do that." His eyes came to me for a quick second before he took the chains from me and he knelt down behind the heifer. "Don't blame yourself. We were bound to run into a problematic birth sooner or later."

He deftly hooked the chains around the calf's ankles, then the hook to the chains, and he started pulling.

And pulling.

And pulling.

Unlike the first calf I'd watched him pull, this one didn't seem to be budging an inch. Reece shook his head. "It's a big one. Probably too big for the canal. It can happen when we get late in the season like this, especially if it's a bull. Can you get the big calf-puller?"

I nodded and scurried back to the ATV to get the puller with the pole and crank.

Okay, I tried to calm myself. We could still do this. I'd seen it happen before. We were still here in time. There was still time.

It was more awkward with the cow on the ground, but she didn't look like she was moving or getting on her feet any time soon, so we braced the T of the puller against her hind-quarters as best we could and attached the chain.

And then Reece started turning the crank.

It didn't go as smoothly as it had the first time. The puller kept slipping and eventually I had to hold it in place while Reece cranked.

Slowly, slowly, the calf started slipping free of its mother.

"You're getting it!" I cried, laughing.

Except that when the calf finally was pulled all the way out of the heifer and collapsed on the ground...

It was lifeless.

I dropped the pole of the puller and stepped back, stunned.

Reece reached for the calf and did what he'd done the first night. He worked to try to open up its air passages and such, and I had a brief spurt of hope.

But only moments later he pulled back, laying the calf gently back to the ground, where it lay unmoving.

I shook my head. No.

He looked up at me. "It happens this way sometimes."

I shook my head more vigorously.

He wiped his hands on the grass and then shifted to get to his feet.

I could only stare at the calf. Dead. Perfectly formed, but absolutely lifeless.

Reece looked confused and I turned away.

I walked a few feet and gulped air, trying to get ahold of myself. *It's a cow. Just a cow. Get a goddamned grip!* But my entire body was shaking, and then I was bent over, on my knees, hands in the mud, throwing up.

"Charlie!" Reece called and he came close but I held out a hand to keep him back. No, no, I didn't want him close.

The past and present were crushing in against each other again. Collapsing together on me.

I needed to get away from here. From the tragic death and senseless loss. From the mud and the wind and the open sky.

I stood up shakily. Reece tried to offer me an arm but I flinched away from him.

"Can you take me back in?" I asked weakly. "I'm not feeling so well."

He nodded, eyebrows furrowed in concern I saw in the quick glance I cast his way before dropping my eyes back to the ground. I gripped my arms around my stomach as we walked back to the four-wheeler. Anything to turn my back on the sight behind me.

"You drive," I said. I could hear how dull my voice was, but I didn't care. Couldn't care. I wanted to climb in bed and not get out. I squeezed my eyes shut when I thought about how I had a job and responsibilities.

All of a sudden, I felt so *done* with it all. Squeezed dry. Used up like a sponge that had scrubbed too many pots and pans. My edges were worn and nubby, and could I just sleep? Could I just pull a Rip Van Winkle and sleep for a hundred years? Please, dear God, please?

Reece didn't say another word, but his body in front of mine on the four-wheeler seemed tense as he drove us back into the ranch house.

I climbed off and my body felt like it weighed a thousand pounds as I dragged myself up the porch stairs, and then all the way up to the second-story bathroom.

Reece asked me if I was okay before I disappeared into the house and I offered him a lackluster, "I'm sure I just need to sleep it off. I hope it's okay with Jeremiah if I take the rest of the day off."

"Of course!" Reece was quick to assure. "I'll let him know you aren't feeling well."

I'd nodded and continued my arduous climb up the stairs.

I peeled off my mud-soaked clothes and climbed in the shower. Usually I enjoyed my showers at the end of the day, especially lately since it had been raining so much, and I was usually dealing with some level of mud and muck.

But today I just felt... numb.

I went through the motions of washing myself mechanically, and then I climbed into bed and I slept.

---

EXCEPT THAT ALL I'd hoped to escape in my waking life followed me into my dreams. And ten times worse, because it meant reliving it as if I was back there.

I was on the floor.

The smell of burnt crème anglaise. The fucking crème anglaise. If only I hadn't—

The slap across my face hadn't been that bad. But when he got good and angry, it usually didn't stop with a slap. I'd cradled my arms across my stomach.

I didn't care about the pain radiating across my cheek, my split lip. I didn't care. He could break my face and mangle me, just not—

I panicked and did the exact wrong thing.

Like always. If only I'd played it different. Kept the secret instead of blurting it out. Done anything other than what I did. I knew what Jeff was like. He couldn't even stand us having a dog because it drew attention away from him.

He'd taken the dog to the shelter in the middle of the night. He knew how much I loved the dog. He accused me of loving it more than him.

So why the hell did I think it would be different when, lying there on the kitchen floor, burnt crème anglaise in the air, rage in his eyes, I thought it would make things better to hold up a hand and beg, "Wait, please. I'm pregnant! Jeff, please. We're going to have a baby."

I'd smiled through my tears. "A little baby who will look just like you. A son to carry on your name!" I didn't know it was a boy, it wasn't like I'd been able to go to the doctor about it, but I figured he'd tolerate a son much better than a daughter.

Jeff hated children. He kept me on strict birth control.

"You bitch," he said, his voice ice. "Did you skip your pills to try to trap me with a kid?"

"What?" I shook my head vigorously. "It was after you— After I had to go see the doctor last year." When Jeff had thrown me down the stairs of the back deck so hard I'd needed stitches on multiple lacerations. He'd been a hair trigger all last year because it was right after he'd hauled me back from Oregon. I'd just been healing up from the initial broken arm and collarbone when he threw me down the stairs and back to the hospital I went.

"They put me on antibiotics," I tried to explain, "and it must have interfered with the birth control. I didn't know they could do that but I looked it up on the internet—"

"You looked it up on the internet," he said, voice mocking. He reached down and yanked me to my feet by my forearm, his hand a crushing, bruising grip. I yelped but scrambled up to release the pressure.

"I know we didn't expect it," I rushed out, still trying to salvage the situation, "but it's a miracle really, if you think about it—"

"How long have you fucking known and been keeping this a secret from me?" he asked, his voice low and cold.

My mouth went dry and I opened my mouth but no noise came out.

He shook me by his crushing grip on my arm. "HOW LONG?" he bellowed.

"Four months," I cried. Five, it was really five, but four sounded better. "I suspected when I didn't get my period two months in a row. But I didn't know for sure—"

He hit me then, another hard blow across the face.

And I was *glad*. I was glad he'd hit my face and not my stomach. I thought maybe he'd gotten it out of his system. Maybe he'd need to hit me a few more times, but if I could just protect my stomach—

Just that week I'd felt the baby move. A swimmy sensation in the pit of my belly. I had to protect them. I had to—

I woke screaming, my hands scratching at my stomach.

Empty.

Devoid of life.

The image of the dead calf flashed through my head.

I yanked my pillow up, barely getting it to my mouth before letting out a wailing *scream*.

My hand scrambled outwards, reaching for the bottle of pills. Ugh, I was sticky with sweat, my hair matted to my forehead. It was dark out and I had no idea what time it was. I'd slept all day and if I could, I'd sleep all night and then another one and another. I didn't give a damn. I just needed it to stop. All of it, just stop. Stop, *stop*. Dear God, make it stop!

I clicked on the nightstand light to find the pill bottle, then popped two of the sleeping pills into my mouth. I chewed them into a chalky paste and swallowed them down with the tiny bit of water still left in the cup on my nightstand. And then, before I could think better of it, I shook another little blue pill into my hand and tossed it into my mouth too.

There was no water left, though.

I chewed up the pill and tried to swallow anyway, but grimaced. It left a terrible taste in my mouth, sticking to my tongue. It wasn't going to do me any good unless it hit my blood stream. I needed more water.

Groaning, I pulled my robe around me and grabbed my cup. Going to the bathroom on this floor meant walking past Ruth's bedroom though, and the wood was creaky. Safer to head downstairs.

Ruth had stuck her head in my room several times today. I'd pretended to be sleeping even though the sound of the door had woken me at least two of the times, and who knew if she'd checked in more than that.

So I snuck down the stairs. My foot creaked on one step near the bottom and I froze, eyes squeezing shut. I listened, but didn't hear any movement from behind me, breathed out, and continued down to the kitchen.

I filled up the cup and drank a gulp, swishing the water around in my mouth to get rid of the awful pill taste before swallowing.

I was about to turn around when I paused, glancing at the top shelf of the cabinet across from the fridge. The kitchen had been remodeled not long ago, with pretty glass door cabinets. So I could see several bottles of Ruth's favorite cabernet sauvignon winking at me from the top shelf. Ruth wasn't one to bother with the fancy stuff, so it was a generic brand. I'd reimburse her next time I went to town.

I pulled down a bottle and winced at the noise the drawer made when I opened it to find a corkscrew. I finally found it and was just aiming to stab the pointy end into the cork when the outside door off to the porch suddenly opened.

I screeched and jumped backwards, brandishing the corkscrew outwards.

Only to see Reece standing in dim outline in the inside of the door. He flipped the kitchen light on and I jumped again.

"What are doing down here in the dark?" He looked at the clock on the wall. "At two in the morning?" He gestured at the wine. "Popping a bottle of wine?"

"I, uh." I waved my hands. "I just—" I shrugged and my shoulders sagged. "—needed a drink."

Then I crossed my arms over my chest and glared back at him. I was embarrassed at being caught and angry he was stopping me from just going back upstairs. "What are *you* always doing up in the middle of the night anyway. Don't you ever *sleep*?"

He just shrugged and averted eye contact to the fridge. Hmm. Who was being cagey now?

"Then don't make me drink alone?" I said, tilting the wine glass towards him. I wasn't sure if it was generosity on my part or because now that I really thought about it, spending time with him sounded a million times better than climbing back into that bed.

He narrowed his brows at me but still nodded. I grabbed two wine glasses, finally popped the cork, and poured. I filled mine a tad more generously than his, but set the wine glass in between both of us, figuring he could pour more for himself if he wanted more. I wasn't going to pretend I wanted an appropriate amount simply for propriety's sake.

Reece's eyebrows went up when I tilted my glass back and chugged it like Ruth had the beer at the bar.

"Is that something I should be worried about?" he said, gesturing with his glass at mine.

I looked at him surprised. "Of course not. I mean, yes, it's likely concerning, but not something *you* should be worried about."

He let out a startled laugh. "I'm not sure that distinction matters."

I shrugged, then reached for the bottle I'd set between us to refill my glass. Reece put a hand on the long neck to stop me. "Charlie. What's going on? Ruth said you were in bed all day. You didn't seem sick at all before— Before what happened with the heifer. What's wrong?"

I glared at him. "Nothing's wrong. I'm *fine*." I jerked the wine bottle out of his hand and, just to spite him, upended it and chugged from the mouth of the bottle. The wine was a bit bitter, but sweet enough, and I downed what was left in the bottle fairly quickly.

Reece had crossed his arms over his chest. "You done?"

I leaned my hands back on the counter behind me and let my head dip backwards, the world around me growing a little fuzzy. "Yesssssss."

"Okay, Captain. You say you're fine, you're fine. It's just, I got a history of saying I'm fine when that's the last thing I was. Jer and I, we just bottle shit up. We never talk about it or deal with it."

He let out a heavy rush of breath, then looked at me. "You wanna take a walk or sit outside or something? I could use a cigarette."

When I raised an eyebrow at him, he hurriedly added, "Not a blunt. I got rid of my stash after Jer busted my ass last time."

I shook my head. "Too bad. That was—" I felt my cheeks grow warm. Easy to blame on the wine, but the memories of being held in his arms that night were too fresh to deny. "—fun," I finished off in a choked voice.

He grinned at me before ducking his head. "Yeah, well. Jer doesn't have much sense of fun these days."

We walked to the door and he grabbed my coat, holding it out for me. I was a little sluggish on my feet, but not bad. Now I wish I hadn't taken so many of the sleeping pills. Three wasn't enough to be concerned about—Jeff'd had me on so many damn tranquilizers, sleeping pills, you name it, I'd been on it. But in the bright lights of the kitchen, even through my foggy brain I knew it was... not good behavior.

Reece and I stepped out onto the porch. It was chilly, but not like in San Francisco at night. It had been in the 80's lately during the day even though it was only March, and was likely in the 60's now. I hardly needed the coat, but I still clutched it around myself none-theless. I felt fragile, and even though I hated feeling that way... well, it was what it was.

I stumbled as soon as we stepped foot on the porch and Reece steadied me. I looked up into his eyes. "Do you want to play pre—" I started, my voice a little slurred.

He shook his head. "Charlie, you're drunk. Look, I'm not judging, but how about we just sit out here? Cause frankly, I don't think you could make it much past the porch steps."

I yanked away from him but swayed on my feet, not giving much of an argument to my case when he had to grab me to help hold me steady.

"Fine," I said, because all right, my feet did feel clumsy. I collapsed in the chair by the little table on the porch and pulled my legs up to my chest, circling them with my arms as I looked out at the night sky.

He lit the citronella candle in the center of the table with a lighter, then pulled out a pack of cigarettes from his pocket. "You mind?" he asked.

I shook my head.

"I'm trying to quit," he said. "It's an old habit, and a bad one. But sometimes, when I get stressed out..." He shrugged, his face boyish with a little bit of embarrassment that disappeared the second he took a draw on the cigarette.

I certainly wasn't one to look down on vices after my demonstration with the wine bottle inside.

"Look, Orion," I said, pointing up at the sky beyond the porch.

"Always my favorite," Reece said. "It was the only one you could sometimes see in the city. I grew up in the Bay Area, so you could rarely see the stars. That was the only constellation that was bright enough to see."

"No way." I sat up straighter, surprised. "You grew up in the Bay?"

"Lived there my whole life except for the last seven years when we moved east, why?"

I bit my lip, then decided there was no real harm in sharing. "That's where I'm from too."

His eyebrows went up. "Oh, yeah?"

I went quiet, afraid he'd start asking questions now that I'd shared the small tidbit. But he didn't. He just puffed on the cigarette, smoke curling into the air, looking out at the night sky.

Since he wasn't asking questions, I decided to venture one. "Why can't you sleep?" Maybe it wasn't fair to ask since I certainly didn't want him putting the same question to me in reverse, but I was curious. Forever curious about the enigma of a man sitting in front of me.

He shrugged, looking my way and finally stubbing out the cigarette on the bottom of his boot, half-smoked.

"Told you Jer and I have that bad habit of bottling shit up instead of talking about it, right? Well, at night... it all kind of leaks out of the bottle. I try to sleep but my mind just replays shit, over and over and —" He shrugged again. "It makes sleeping hard."

He said it all so casually, and I felt my chest constrict in pain for whatever kept him awake at night. He'd once mentioned he and his brother had been homeless. Living in the Bay Area, I'd seen enough of the homeless kids to know that had to be a terribly tough life.

"Well, maybe..." I ventured slowly. "Maybe you should try another way. If, you know, bottling it up and shoving it down hasn't worked in all this time."

He looked over at me, blinking a few times like he was startled by my words. "Well, okay." He paused for a long moment, then went on. "Like there was this one time I'd gotten really sick. January in San Francisco sucks, especially when you're on the streets."

Oh. Shit, I hadn't meant for him to unbottle it and tell it to *me*, like, right now. I'd meant more that he should try talking to his brother about it. Or a therapist. But I nodded encouragingly anyway. I could be a good listener.

"You know how it is. It doesn't snow, but the winters still get so brutal. The rain goes on for months and months some years, it just won't stop. And always with that bone-chilling cold."

I shivered just thinking about it. He was right. Winters in San Francisco could get cold in a way that wore down beneath the skin and stuck there. I'd liked to take long baths in winter, one of my few reprieves.

But Reece and his brother hadn't even had a roof over their heads, much less hot water. Jesus, I couldn't even imagine.

Reece looked outwards, eyes still to the night sky as he went on. "It was weeks, then months, of being so cold, and never getting all the way dry. I got real, real sick, and Jer and I were in line for a homeless shelter. We'd stand in line for those places all day long but they were always full up. So one day we're standing in line even though it's pouring rain. And when we get to the front door, they only have *one* spot left."

I watched Reece's brow contract in pain as he retold the events. "I was shaking so bad with fever I barely knew what was going on. I was vaguely aware of Jeremiah arguing with the lady that we could share a cot, since we were obviously brothers."

He gave a little shake of his head. "But the lady didn't care and was sick of arguing, and about to give the spot to the man in line behind us when Jeremiah shoved me forwards. Then he took off, yelling that he'd find me in a few days. It was getting dark and he just disappeared and I was getting shuffled inside where it was nice and warm."

Reece shut his eyes, his jaw flexing with the pain the memory obviously still caused him.

"I shoulda gone after him. We had a code. Never separate. No matter what." He shook his head again. "I shoulda gone after him."

"But you were sick," I said, frowning. "You just said you had a fever and barely knew what was going on."

Reece shrugged. "I was young and strong. I would have been fine anyway, most likely."

I frowned harder. "If it had been him who was sick, what would you have done? Would you have wanted him to come after you?"

"Of course not," he said quickly, a deep furrow appearing between his brows as he looked my way.

I raised an eyebrow, and he sank back, eyes going to the sky again. "I guess the what ifs don't really matter. It's not like I can go back and change it."

"What... happened? Obviously, Jeremiah turned out okay."

But by the look on Reece's face, he seemed like he wasn't so sure even though he shrugged and gave a half-nod.

"They got me showered and deloused and then gave me a warm cot with blankets. God, those warm, clean blankets. It felt like heaven after how we'd been living. I slept for two days straight, and on the third day, woke up feeling human again. I ate as much as I could, and stuffed the rest in my pockets for Jer. Then I went out looking for him."

I held my breath.

"And I couldn't find him."

I wanted to reach out to touch him, but I didn't dare. If he'd kept this inside for this long, maybe he just finally needed to let it out.

"The rain had finally let up, but I couldn't find him anywhere. I was so scared he was—" Reece swallowed. "I was sure he was dead. I even checked with hospitals and obituaries and stuff. Every day I hung around the homeless shelter since that was the last place I'd seen him, but I also checked all the other places we'd usually go. He wasn't anywhere and no one had seen him. I couldn't think of *any* reason he wouldn't come for me. We always had each other's back. After awhile I thought, maybe... Maybe he was just finally tired of looking out for me and he'd split just like our mom."

"God. Reece."

I reached for him then, unable not to. I leaned across the table and took his hand. He let me but didn't really grasp back. His hand was limp in mine.

"He didn't show up for another three weeks. And when he finally did, he wouldn't say one goddamn word about where he'd been."

His brow furrowed, still pained. "But he was different after that. He was still the brother I'd always known. He tried, anyway. He couldn't fool me, though. There was this... this seriousness to him. A shadow that separated him from me after that. He had less patience for what he called my *childishness*. As if we weren't both eighteen years old.

"And he had money for the ticket east. He said it was time to stop fucking around. That if we stayed on the streets, we'd end up like all the other street kids, or dead.

"The other street kids... well, a lot of them... They did whatever they could to earn money. They sold drugs. They sold... whatever they could. And it was my fucking fault. I should never have let him go without me, I shouldn't have—"

"Reece, no, you had no idea—"

He looked over at me, alarmed, and pulled his hand away from mine. "Shit, I shouldn't have told you this. Jer would kill me if he knew I ever told—"

"I'll never say a word. I swear. I *swear*. And I'm so sorry both of you went through that." I shook my head. "And I can't believe you were in San Francisco too," I said. "We might have crossed paths and not even known it."

That had him looking my way. "Charlie, what happened to you there? What made you run?"

My first instinct was to shut him down like I did everyone when they started poking too close. But as I sat there in that chair, my mind a little cottony from the pills and the wine, I just wanted to laugh at myself. What good was keeping this precious secret to myself doing?

Bottling his secrets up kept Reece awake at night and mine were slowly eating me up from the inside out.

So I just blurted it out. "I was going to Stanford. I'd grown up in San Jose. My parents weren't really rich or poor. They were kind of the last of the middle class but my mom was never happy with that. God, nothing could make her happy, and certainly not me. Nothing I did was ever good enough." Then I realized complaining about my mom to a man whose mother had abandoned him when he was just a kid was a dick move. At least I'd *had* a mom.

I waved a hand, embarrassed. "Anyway, so I got to Stanford on scholarship, hoping for better things. That was where..." I swallowed and then pushed through. "That was where I met m-my husband."

Reece straightened in his seat, his shoulders turning more towards me. I definitely had all of his attention now, though I had a feeling I always had.

I swallowed, my mouth suddenly tasting sour and dry. I ignored it and continued anyway. This story wouldn't get any easier to tell even if I was well-hydrated. He'd shared and maybe I could too. I wasn't likely to get therapy anytime soon and he was the only ear I could see myself trusting anyway.

I took a deep breath and then jumped in. "I was a freshman and he was everything out of the romance novels I'd read all my life. Confident, smart, handsome. Everybody loved him. When he started paying attention to *me*, little ol' me, I was flabbergasted. And at the beginning, it was something out of a movie. Gifts, constant messages, I felt so adored."

I closed my eyes. "He loved how sweet and innocent I was, he said. All the other college girls were just there to party and sleep around, but I was a serious girl."

I huffed out a bitter laugh. "I thought that meant he really *saw* me. I thought that meant he understood how hard I worked to keep my scholarship, how I didn't take school for granted, that I'd worked hard for everything I'd earned."

I shook my head, so angry for buying up everything he was selling. "They say cults go after people like me too. Vulnerable, love-starved, searching for meaning. Smart, but *stupid* in the ways that count. We're like narcissist catnip. They come in and fill up every hole that's been empty for so long. But it's all a lie. It's just to draw us in. And then, after we're hooked and caught in their web, everything changes."

Reece's hand reached out and his fingers closed back around mine, squeezing. "It's him you're running from, isn't it? He's why you were hitchhiking with nothing but the clothes on your back?"

I nodded, tears squeezing out of my eyes and rolling down my cheek. I swiped them away angrily with the hand Reece wasn't holding.

I could tell in Reece's eyes that the reverse of earlier was happening now. His features knotted in pain. For me.

He leaned down and pressed the gentlest kiss to our hands clasped between us. When his eyes came back to mine, I could still see the pain in them. "I'm so sorry, Charlie." And then, quieter. "Did he hurt you? Hit you?"

I didn't ask how he knew. I just nodded, more tears flooding out. Some into my mouth, salt on my lips. Stupid, useless tears.

His eyes shut, and his grip on my hand became even firmer. He bowed his head into our linked hands. "I'm so sorry that happened to you, Charlie."

"M-my given name is Penelope," I whispered. "But I do feel like Charlie, sometimes anyway. I'm trying to become this new person. But I'm still haunted by my old life. It's the ghost I can't rid of. Right when I think I've got a handle on living again, when I think I could actually make a life..."

I shook my head. "Her memories hit and take me back and then it's like I can barely even *breathe* or stand to be in this skin another second longer."

I yanked my hand back from his and dragged my hands down my face. This was a bad idea. I didn't feel better talking about this. Saying it all out loud made me feel raw and ragged and—

"Because you aren't two different people, Charlie. She *is* you. You can't pretend you didn't go through what you went through and just ignore it."

I dropped my hands and looked at him in shock. "Why not? Isn't that what you just said you try to do?"

"Exactly." He waved a hand. "And look how well it's working out for me. I sleep maybe four hours a night, if I'm lucky!"

I slumped back in my chair, shaking my head. "You don't understand."

"What? What don't I understand? Talk to me, Charlie. From everything you're saying, you got caught by a manipulative abuser who kept you trapped for...how long? How long were you with him?"

"Almost ten years," I said, my voice thick with shame.

"Charlotte. Oh my God." He sounded stunned.

I stood up and turned away from him, unable to look at his face. "See? Not so heroic now. A stronger woman would have found a way to get out so much earlier."

"What? Jesus, no. The fact that you got out at all, especially after so long, is a fucking miracle. It tells me you're an amazingly resilient woman and frankly I'm shocked you've been keeping it together as well as you have. Ten *years*. Jesus Christ."

I turned back around, feeling irrationally angry at him and his readiness to overlook my sins. "You don't understand!" I said furiously. "I burned the crème. I got my baby killed!"

He sat, mouth dropped open, a horrible moment of life stretching out between us.

And then he said, "I'm gonna need a little more than that."

I squeezed my eyes shut, the words coming out in a babble. "I *knew*. I knew what would happen if I stayed. So why the *hell* didn't I leave? I should've left! I don't care that he was having me followed. If it wasn't the stupid fucking crème anglaise it would have been something else. I could have made it to a women's shelter maybe. I could have done anything else but what I did. Staying in that house a second after I found out was a death sentence for my baby. He couldn't even stand me loving the *dog*. Why did I think a baby—"

His arms suddenly closed around me. He hugged me so tight. So tight I could barely breath and I didn't want to. My grief was choking me.

"It's not your fault. God, I know that's cliché—" His arms squeezed even tighter. "I don't know if you'll ever believe me. But it's only *his* fault, whatever happened to your baby."

"He never got a chance to be born. He never even had a *chance*—"

Reece pulled back, hands still gripping my shoulders as he looked into my eyes. "You are *not* responsible for whatever that evil bastard did."

He just didn't understand. "But I could have—"

"You did the best you could with what you knew at the time. Plus from what you just said, you'd *tried* to get away before."

I immediately shook my head. "But if I'd only—"

"Only what? Had the hindsight of 20/20 somehow magically when there was no way you could have? You did the best you could with the information you had at the time. Let go of everything else."

I scoffed, tears burning. "Tell that to yourself. You just told me you can't forgive yourself for not running after your brother even though you were about to drop from fever and couldn't have had any clue what was going to happen to him."

He opened his mouth, and then closed it, and then opened it before closing it one last time. Then he pulled me back into an embrace, looser this time, but no less warm.

His chin notched on the top of my head. His chest rumbled when he spoke. "Look at the pair of us. We both just need to take our own advice. How come we can see the answer so clearly for the other person, but not for ourselves? When I look at your situation, I'm just like, duh, it's nuts not to see how obviously it's not your fault and you need to let go any guilt or shame. You didn't do anything wrong."

I smiled a little wanly, a little off-kilter, both from the wine and because what he was saying...seemed reasonable. "Yeah. Shit. I must be drunk because you're making sense."

He pulled away again, a grin on his face. "I'll remind you that you said that tomorrow, in case you forget. Or try to pretend you didn't just say I'm the king of the world who's always right."

I choked out a laugh, swiping at tears. "That is *so* not what I said."

"Uh, pretty sure that's what I heard."

"You fit through the door with that big head?"

He winked at me. "I got my ways, Captain." Then he looked down at his phone he'd pulled out of his pocket. "Shit, I better be getting you back to bed. It's almost three in the morning."

I nodded. I did feel exhausted. The wine, the pills, plus the emotional unloading we'd just done.

I hesitated, though, still afraid of the nightmares that might await me.

"I suppose it's too much to ask for you to stay the night with me?"

His eyes immediately went round.

"Just like in the barn. Not...doing anything. I know we're just friends now." Then I felt my face flame. I waved a hand. "Forget it. It's stupid. Good night. *Friend*." I gave an awkward wave and tried to turn away but his hand caught mine, his fingers interlacing and locking.

"I'd like that," he said quietly, the levity from moments ago dissolved.

We were quiet, not saying another word as we went back inside, took off our coats, and he trailed me upstairs.

I felt embarrassed for the request I'd made as soon as we both stepped inside my room. But Reece had this way about him that made everything natural, so that within minutes, I wasn't feeling awkward anymore.

I climbed underneath the covers and he kicked off his boots, then laid on top of them beside me. Still, he curled his strong arm around me and spooned me from behind, knees and thighs notching so naturally behind me.

I immediately felt warm, cozy, and safe. I started drowsing almost instantly.

"Charlotte?" Reece whispered.

"Mmm?"

"I'm so glad the wind blew you this direction and you ended up on this ranch that night."

I smiled and snuggled back against his warm, solid body. "Me too," I sighed. "Me too."

## 16

I MANAGED TO PULL MYSELF OUT OF BED THE NEXT DAY BY NOON. I WAS startled when I looked at the clock and saw it was so late. Reece wasn't there, long gone, I imagined. No doubt he'd taken off for morning chores and, if he was smart, been out of my room long before his brother found him in here to avoid a repeat of the stable incident. I hadn't even thought of it in my wine-addled state last night, but he likely had.

I was embarrassed to be so late getting downstairs, but figured that as far as Ruth and Jeremiah knew, I'd been actually sick yesterday. And well, I had genuinely needed a mental health day, even if I hadn't used the healthiest coping mechanisms.

I held a hand to my head, still feeling the effects. I went straight for the coffeemaker. The house was so... quiet. It was strange. Usually when I came down, the place was bustling with noise.

One of the things I loved about Ruth was that she was *not* a quiet person. After a decade of enforced quiet, I loved that she kept the house filled with noise. She always had some story or town gossip to tell, or she was loudly seeking help with her crosswords, or she had music on, or the TV, or she was picking a fight with Jeremiah. I admired her ability to take up *space* in her own world.

I switched on the radio as I poured myself a cup of black coffee and drank down half of it, then refilled my cup. Out the window, I could see the sky was getting dark, those rolling thunderclouds that were still so strange to a California girl like me. It hadn't started raining yet, but occasionally I heard thunder in the distance.

Footsteps on the stairs behind me surprised me. I turned to see Ruth herself tromping down them. Instead of her usual jeans, t-shirt, and ponytail, she wore a skirt, heels, and had her hair blown out.

"I didn't even know you were home. Where you headed off to?" I asked as I sipped the lukewarm coffee. "Hot date?"

"Well hey, sleepyhead. You're looking good. You feeling better today?"

I nodded, looking down into my coffee cup. "Yup. Must've been a 24-hour bug."

"Well, I'm glad to see you up and at 'em. And ha, I wish it was a hot date. I'm just getting lunch with Olivia. Oh my gosh, you should come! I can wait while you get ready—"

I waved her off. "No, no. I feel bad enough about taking yesterday off."

She rolled her eyes. "You work too hard. Believe me, as someone who busted her ass her whole life with nothing to show for it, it won't hurt any dead things to take a day off now and then. Especially if you were sick yesterday, even more reason to take it easy." She lifted her eyebrows several times. "I suggest taking it easy with mimosas at Alejandro's."

I giggled but still shook my head. "You go. Tell Olivia I said hi. I'm gonna get out there and feed Bessie and Nine before that rain hits."

Ruth rolled her eyes. "Fine, fine." She came forward and hugged me, a quick squeeze and release. "Glad you're feeling better, babe."

"Thanks."

Then she was off out the door. I shoved my feet in my boots and followed behind her, heading for the barn.

Fat raindrops hit me on the forehead right as I came close to the open entryway to the barn. I was about to charge right in like always when raised voices stopped me in my tracks.

"Jesus, Reece, I told you to stay away from her."

"Who are you to tell me what to do? I'm trying to be straight with you here."

Oh shit. Jeremiah and Reece were arguing. About me.

I froze, knowing I should back away. Behind me, I heard Olivia's car drive off.

"She's different, Jer. She's a woman I could actually *have* something with."

I blinked, a little stunned. Reece thought... He really thought we could be something... for real? What about being just friends? But didn't I want to be more than just friends?

Jeremiah made a dismissive noise. Good Lord, they had to be standing not far inside the barn at all if I could hear them so well. I should back away now. Carefully, quietly. They never had to know I'd been here.

"What do you even know about this woman?" Jeremiah asked. "Sure she's nice, but she showed up here hitchhiking for Christ's sake."

"What the fuck's that supposed to mean? After the way we grew up, you're really going to give someone shit for—"

"No, no," Jeremiah cut him off. "I'm just saying, what do you even really know about her? Where did she come from? Is she running from some sort of trouble?"

"Not that it's any of your goddamned business, but yeah, she is, okay? She got away from an abusive husband."

My hand went to my mouth. I didn't know why I felt horrified and a wave of shame at Reece sharing my darkest secret so carelessly. But my stomach suddenly churned.

*This is what you get for eavesdropping.*

I stumbled a step back, about to turn and flee back into the house.

The rain started coming down heavier and their voices became a little more muffled.

But I still heard Jeremiah, maybe because he'd raised his voice when he said, "Christ, so this *is* about Peg?"

Peg? It was the second time that name had come up when things were contentious between Reece and his brother.

Again, I was frozen in my tracks.

"This has nothing to do with Peg," Reece said, sounding angry for the first time during the whole conversation.

"Yeah, right. You have a savior complex, little brother, but guess what? It only ends up landing us in shit when you try to be a knight in shining armor. Most people see a woman in need and they want to get them help, sure. But you? No, you start fucking them and think it's love until it all blows up in your face."

My gasp was swallowed by the rain that was now pelting the ground in hard, angry drops that felt like needle stabs all along the skin of my exposed forearms and face.

"You son of a—"

A strong wind blew, catching the barn door and making it bang against the outside of the barn. The storm was coming in fast today.

I couldn't hear the guys arguing anymore, but when I heard a stuttered curse heaved out—I couldn't tell which one of them it was, their voices were so similar—I realized they were fighting.

*Stupid slut. You think anyone but me could love you?*

His voice in my head. My fists went against my temple.

*Look how useless you are.* A vase flung against the wall. *You're such a dumb bitch you can't even dust the nice shit I buy you. There. Now you don't have to dust it, since you seem to be incapable of keeping a nice house.*

I pounded at my head. The rain poured down, drenching me. Get out, get out, damn memories.

Him standing over me, heaving for breath while I curled into a ball in the corner. *Look what you made me do again. Why can't you just be a normal woman? All I wanted was a good, easy life but then I got stuck with you. What a fucking disappointment.*

It was so visceral, the memory of him walking off. Me bawling, useless, clutching my stomach that was completely void. Void of life because I'd failed my little baby.

And now this was my curse, to be stuck with *him* forever. Punishing me forever.

"Stop!" I screamed, charging into the barn. "Stop it!"

I found the two brothers on the floor grappling with each other, but they both froze and looked up at me with twin looks of surprise.

Reece let go of his brother and struggled to get up, one hand raised. "Charlie. Wait. I don't know what you heard, but—"

"Who's Peg?" I asked him.

Jeremiah got to his feet, dusting the dirt and hay off himself, and watching us warily.

"That's not important," Reece said, waving a hand distractedly. "Look, my brother's an asshole—"

"No, why don't you tell her about Peg?" Jeremiah said, and Reece shot him a murderous glare.

"Fine!" Reece finished glaring at his brother and then his face softened with... remorse?... as he looked back to me.

"Peg was the first woman I ever really..."

"Had an affair with," Jeremiah supplied.

My mouth dropped open and Reece swung his head to glare at Jeremiah. "Isn't there somewhere you need to be, *brother*?"

Jeremiah crossed his arms over his chest and didn't look like he was going anywhere, but just then, the barn door slammed again and Buck ran in, startling all of us.

"Whoa, what'd I miss?"

"Not now, Buck," Jeremiah said. "You can wait out the storm in the bunkhouse or take a long lunch if you want."

"It's not that, boss. Just got a call from the sheriff, who said the cows are out on the 284 again."

Jeremiah swore and swung down to grab his hat off the ground, which I assumed he'd lost while fighting Reece. "That's the last goddamn thing we need, especially with the storm, who the hell knows how disoriented they'll get if they start running. Come on, Buck. Let's go see if we can round 'em up."

"In *this*?" Buck said, eyebrows up as he threw a thumb over his shoulder. "Can't we wait it out, then go?"

"Jesus fucking Christ, do I have to do everything myself? You," he pointed a finger at Reece. "Clear this up before I get back." Then he stormed past Buck right out into what was now a deluge.

"Jeez, what crawled up his ass and took a shit?"

"Not now, Buck," Reece said, sounding exactly like his brother as he turned his glare on Buck. "I need to have a private conversation with Charlie."

"Damn." Buck held up his hands. "Don't get your panties in a twist."

When Reece just kept staring at him, Buck shook his head, muttered something under his breath, and then turned and headed back out into the rain.

Leaving just me and Reece in the barn, a dull roar on the tin roof as the rain blew sideways in a torrent.

Reece took a step toward me but I held up a hand. "Don't."

"Charlie—"

"Have I just been some substitute all along? For Peg, whoever she is?"

"God, I'm gonna kill my brother. No. *No*." Again he tried to take a step forward and I took a step back, a warning look on my face that had him stopping in his tracks.

"Peg was a woman I knew when I was barely grown myself. Jer and I were nineteen, we'd just left California. It was the first time we'd worked a ranch. Wayne took us on because we'd accept almost no pay, just eager to learn a trade of any kind and frankly glad to have a roof over our heads. For a while it was great."

He let out a heavy sigh. "Then I'd hear Wayne and his wife fighting. No, I'd just hear Wayne *yelling* at his wife though the windows of the ranch house. I didn't know he beat her, not at first."

I swallowed, but too many emotions were bubbling up so I swallowed again.

"And you fell in love with her?" I managed to get out.

For a moment, Reece looked lost. "I just—" his voice trailed off. "One day after her husband was yelling at her, I heard a crash. Wayne stormed out of the house and drove off. Jer told me not to get involved, that it wasn't my business. But after all the ranch hands went off to our duties for the day, I doubled back to check on her. Which was when I found her on the floor in the kitchen. There were a couple of shattered plates on the floor beside her and her face—"

Reece sucked in a breath and shut his eyes hard, like he was either reliving it or trying to get himself under control.

"I told her she should leave him, but she just said I was a sweet kid. She was fifteen years older than me, and said I didn't understand how the world worked. But we started up a... a friendship, I guess. I was the only person she could talk to who was safe."

I swallowed again, hugging my arms around myself. "And it turned into more?"

Reece hesitated, then nodded. "She liked to have a companion when she rode her horse, so sometimes I'd go with her. We got closer and closer..."

Reece's brow bunched as he looked to the floor. "I loved her and yes, I thought I could save her. She never said she loved me back, but she said her time with me made the rest of her life possible. That she'd thought about slitting her wrists plenty of times until I showed up."

Uneasily, I rubbed my left wrist. I'd kept them perpetually covered here with long sleeved flannels. When it got warmer, I used a thick-banded waterproof watch on my left wrist and a scrunchie on my right, no matter that I had short hair and no use of one. I'd found both in Ruth's bathroom drawers.

I took a step towards Reece, feeling my nose sting with emotion both for him and for the woman. Peg. To have dared to grab at what joy she could in the midst of her own suffering... I couldn't imagine.

But I could totally see how Reece, kind, gentle Reece showing up, an even more earnest and boyish version than the man in front of me, just having survived the streets of San Francisco... I could see how he would have seemed like a miracle. Enough to make a woman reckless.

And I could also see how he could have fallen into the situation, wanting to help her, then developing a close bond with the woman. The intimacy of a secret shared. How that could turn into long afternoons that felt like an escape and also salvation, to both of them after all they'd been through. And how natural feelings would follow, and desperate bodies would meet—

"So what happened?" I asked, almost afraid to know the answer.

"Her husband caught us."

I gasped and took another small step forward.

"It was fucking awful." Reece turned away from me. "Jeremiah's right. I should have tried to get her help earlier. Not—" He shook his head vehemently. "Not... do what I did.

"You were barely just more than a kid yourself. You said you were just what, nineteen? God knows how stupid I was at nineteen. I didn't do anything right." As soon as I said it, I realized just how true it was. And yet it was so much easier to cut Reece the slack I could never seem to give to myself.

But Reece was still just shaking his head. "No, I should have done anything else. Tried to protect her better. Wayne came in and he just started whaling on her. I fought him and told her to run, but I only slowed him down. Like you said, I was nineteen, skinny as a bean pole, barely fed enough after years on the street. He was a full-grown man and more than a match for the both of us."

My heart was in my throat even just hearing about it. "Oh my God, so what happened?"

Reece bowed his head. "My brother. I'll never be able to repay him for all he's done for me, and that day was just another example. He came in and gave Wayne the beating I couldn't. We'd both been in scrapes before, growing up like we did, but it was nothing to Jeremiah that day. Once Wayne was down, the three of us stole his truck and drove to the bus station."

"Holy shit," I said. And here I'd thought Jeremiah was such a straight-laced guy... I could barely imagine him doing the things Reece was describing. And yet, I supposed, for family, one might do anything.

I winced, thinking of my own mother and how she wouldn't listen to me the two times I tried to tell her about what was really going on with Jeff. The second time, when I asked for her help, she called Jeff to tell him she was worried about me, that my mental health was getting worse—he had everyone so snowed. But still, how could she believe *him* over her own daughter? I got the shit beat out of me and learned that what family might be to other people, it wasn't for me.

But Reece and Jeremiah, they had the real thing.

"Did she make it?" I asked, feeling anxious for a woman I didn't even know. "Did her husband find her again and take her back?"

Reece shook his head. "We got on a bus and headed north. I was definitely naïve. I thought I could protect her, that we could settle down somewhere and I'd work construction or something." He smiled, a little sadly. "But we'd played our parts in each other's lives and she was old enough to know it even if I was heartbroken for a while. At the next bus stop, we bought her a bus ticket to her sister's back east. The sister had always hated Wayne and Peg knew she could help her."

I frowned, still feeling worried for the woman. "And she got there and was able to do it? Get free and start over?"

"Honestly," Reece said, "I don't know. That was the last time I ever saw her. But once Jer and I got settled in Wyoming at Mel's Ranch, I did some digging online and found that Wayne was arrested for a couple DUI's and a drunk and disorderly. I don't think he was in any shape to go after Peg, even if he knew where to start."

I breathed out a sigh of relief as thunder rumbled right overhead, so loud it seemed to shake the barn. The wind outside was really picking up too, blowing the rain sideways into the barn.

"Come on," Reece said, frowning at the worsening conditions outside. "Let's get in the house."

I shook my head, gesturing toward the back of the barn and the sink. "I need to feed Bessie and Nine." Though looking around, I wasn't sure where they were. Probably huddled on the other side of the barn wall where it opened to the pasture. I hoped so, at least, so they could stay warm and safe from the weather.

"Not in this you don't," Reece said. Thunder *cracked* overhead, so loud it had both of us jumping. "Come on," he said, holding his arm over my shoulder and blocking my head as much as he could as we headed toward the open barn door.

"Dammit," Reece yelled. It was so dark it was like the day had sped forward to twilight, and the rain hit my back. Except *ow*, that was more than rain. It was hailing.

Gum-ball size chunks of ice spattered the ground all around, and pelted us, too. White ice balls fell from the sky and bounced up from the ground as we ran for the porch.

As soon as we got up the porch stairs and inside the house, Reece took my shoulders, looking me up and down. "Are you okay?"

I nodded, shaken but all right. "I'm fine."

A jarring, insistent alarm came from Reece's pocket. We were both drenched, and rainwater dripped from his hair onto his forehead as he frowned and pulled out his phone.

His eyes immediately went wide at whatever he saw on the screen. "Shit." He stabbed at the phone again and raised it to his ear.

"What?" I asked. "What is it?"

But Reece just waved a hand for me to wait.

Which was when we both heard the tinny noise of a ringtone sounding from the counter, beside the coffee pot.

"Son of a bitch." Reece shoved his phone back in his pocket, his eyes coming to me. "That's Jer's phone. There's a tornado warning and that asshole is out wrestling cows." He dragged a hand through his wet hair and I could tell he was freaking out.

"Well, that's not such a big deal, right?" I tried to reason. "That just means it's a bad storm. Tornados don't actually, I mean, they're not really a *thing* that happens."

Reece just looked at me like I was nuts. "Tornado watch means conditions are ripe for a tornado, but a *warning* means some have actually been sighted in the area."

That had me gulping. And it had Reece heading back for the door, even as the wind started to howl louder outside. The hail hadn't stopped either. Oh my gosh, Ruth was out in this, too. Town was a good fifteen minutes away. It had maybe been ten since she'd left.

I jumped forward and grabbed Reece's arm. "How is you going

out in this gonna help anything? Surely your brother will come back in with the weather this bad?"

Reece hesitated, and I could tell he was considering what I'd said. But then his eyes went back to the window and both of us watched as the barn door, which we hadn't shut in our quick escape, was battered by the wind. So hard that it came free and flew across the yard.

That apparently decided it for Reece. He pulled free of my hold and crossed the last few feet to the kitchen door. He yanked on a coat and grabbed the keys from the hook by the door.

"Reece!"

He turned, face down, but then he looked at me, features tense. "I've told you how many times my brother's had my back. He doesn't know how bad it could be out there. I have to go. Go to the bathroom closet and close yourself inside. You should be safe in the center of the house."

My mouth dropped open. "Isn't there a storm shelter or something?"

"Not in Texas, they're too hard to dig. Look, I'm sure this will all die down and be nothing, just like you said. I've seen plenty of bad storms. I just wanna be safe, okay? Okay?" he demanded again when I didn't answer quick enough.

I nodded. "Okay."

"Good." And then he opened the door, the howling wind and battering rain ten times louder when he did.

I wanted to cover my ears. I wanted to go grab him and jerk him back inside. I wanted to scream at the sky for it to stop, to shut up, to *stop.*

But the next moment, Reece was gone, and I was left alone in the house, the sky and wind and rain roaring around me on all sides.

I knew I needed to do what Reece said, but I couldn't help running to the kitchen window. The rain was falling in such thick sheets I could only just make out Reece's figure as he ran to his truck, got inside, and took off down the dirt road.

It was moments like this I really wished I believed God was anything more than a fairy tale.

"Please, please protect him," I whispered anyway. I turned around, then back to the window, then, when I knew I positively couldn't see any speck of the truck's back lights, I finally took a deep breath and started to head towards the inner bathroom closet.

Except that halfway there, the doorbell rang.

The doorbell! In a storm like this! Who on earth?

I hurried through the part of the house I rarely spent much time in, just to occasionally watch a movie with Ruth.

Maybe Buck was stranded out there on the wrong side of the house and had gotten locked out. I hurried faster. I needed to get him inside. He wasn't my favorite person in the world, but frankly I wouldn't mind some company to ride out this storm. Yeah, we had earthquakes in California, but a few minutes, tops, of shaking and it was over. Nothing like this roaring, thundering terror. How had I thought this was majestic? It was official, I hated Texas storms.

I yanked the front door open, ready to usher Buck in the house.

Except it wasn't Buck.

It was my husband.

And he took advantage of my surprise, shoving the door open into me, and knocking me backwards off my feet before I could even scream.

He slammed the door behind him and looked down at me where I lay on the rug, shocked, astonished and about to piss myself I was so terrified. Lightning flashed up the windows behind him so that he looked like a demon straight from hell.

"Finally they've all left and I can get some alone time with my own fucking *wife*."

# 17

---

I SHOOK MY HEAD, REFUSING TO BELIEVE HE WAS HERE EVEN THOUGH the pain in my backside told me of course he was, of course he'd found me.

Still, I stupidly asked, "How are you here?" even as I scrambled backwards.

I had to get to my feet. I knew from so many past encounters with him that if he cornered me on the ground, it was all over for the night. And this wasn't just any night.

He advanced on me and the second I tried to get up he kicked me in the ribs, knocking me back down.

"How did I find you? That's all you have to say to me?"

Another kick and God—

I doubled over with the familiar explosion of pain. Except a part of me had forgotten. Had actually *believed* that this part of my life was behind me. Stupid, stupid.

In the past, this is where I'd start apologizing, groveling, playing the insipid wife begging for scraps, trying to soothe his ego, anything to get him to let up sooner.

But I couldn't muster her up. I just couldn't. All that had been an act while the fury burned inside, with every blow I'd planned escape. That was how I'd borne it. But now— But now—

I'd never go back. I'd sworn it. I couldn't.

I *wouldn't*.

He stood over me, waiting for it, waiting for the simpering. Instead, I looked up at him and snarled, "I'd rather fucking die than go back with you, you crazy, evil fucking bastard."

I saw his haze of rage and I tried to get up and run. I tried to grab for a chair to throw at him, but I'd barely gotten my hand around the bottom rung of the back of it before his next blow was landing.

It was a serious one, his fury unleashed. I'd known it was coming. I'd known there was no real escape even as, for once, it felt good to give into the fight response, to not just lay there and *take it*.

I looked up at him and laughed, tasting blood between my teeth. Thunder shook the house and as I looked up at my murderer, I laughed, feeling liberated for the first time in my entire goddamned life. "When you get to hell, I hope the devils roast you over an open spit."

His next blow made the world go black.

# 18

I woke up to pain. My shoulders were wrenched above my head. Rain hit my face so hard I coughed and sputtered against it.

Only to realize Jeff was dragging me across the front yard on my back, a dead weight, by my wrists.

Ow, fuck, ow. It *hurt*. And my face. Pain, God, fucking ow— Everywhere, it was blinding. My back scraped across rocks as he dragged me through the yard.

Did he know I was conscious? Would he have cared?

He yanked harder at my wrists, heaving me step by step even as the storm raged overhead. It made the yard slick and muddy, but with each wrenching step it was like he was trying to pull my shoulders out of their sockets. Maybe he was.

I'd hoped he'd finish it off in the house. That he'd go into such a rage...

God, I just wanted the pain to end.

But if he was trying to take me *back*...

An entirely new horror hit me. Oh God, if he got me back in that house...

I blinked up at the sky, through the rain. Or tried. The storm wasn't quieting, only getting worse. It felt like the world around me was churning, growling, roaring to echo my own fury and grief.

The wind howled around us and bits of tree branches and other debris flew around the yard. I tipped my head back and saw Jeff was having to bend his body into the wind, his hair flattened against his head.

But he didn't stop, his face was still mottled with that anger I knew so well, and there was his car, parked behind a stack of hay bales to the right of the property.

I could try to pull away, a stupid instinct for self-preservation fighting its way to the forefront in spite of what I knew was reality. Jeff, mad as a bull, would never let me go. Come hell or high water. Or roaring storm.

I went lightheaded, my eyes shut against the rain, bright spots dancing.

Pain.

Bright lights.

Drift away.

Reece's face, smiling at me as dawn light filtered through the window. A gentle caress of his finger tracing down my cheek.

Pain splintering my shoulders.

Blackness.

Wet.

Rain.

Mud squelching in my hair.

Shackles around my wrists. The devil had hold of me. He'd never let me go.

Hands on my body.

I was being lifted.

My head hit something hard. A car roof? A shouted curse, Jeff's voice, screamed into a screaming sky.

No one heard. No one cared.

My body tumbled onto something softer than ground. Leather in my nose.

I blinked against the muddle, trying to swim back to the surface.

Swollen eyes, couldn't open them.

Everything was spinning. Pain. It all hurt. I needed to throw up.

Drifting back down while hands on my legs shoved more of me wherever I was being shoved.

Back seat.

It was a back seat.

Wake up. Danger. I needed to wake—

The roaring howl outside was loud, louder, so loud.

I rolled against the back of the seat as the car started forward.

Car. I was in a car.

Jeff's car.

He was driving away.

Away from the ranch. Away from Reece and Ruth, and—

I blinked again, against the pain of my swelling right eye, against all the pain. It was so loud, so loud I wanted to cover my ears.

Jeff was shouting curses.

Close my eyes, drift away, let him take me. Find a way to die later.

That would be easiest.

I couldn't fight anymore. Nothing was left. I was too broken. I'd tried, I'd tried and look, *look*, here I was again.

Give in. Go to sleep. Fly away from the pain, from all of it. Give up, give in. You always do, you always will. There never really was any escape, you knew it all along.

But the sunsets.

The wind in my face and my hair as I rode the four-wheeler, day after day. Free.

Laughing at Bessie and Nine, at their joy and curiosity at simply being *alive*.

I'd been alive, too. Shining moments of life, flowing through me, the sky in my soul, expanding me.

The roar of a train thundered by outside the car.

A train?

I blinked in confusion. There weren't any trains or tracks near the ranch.

How far had we gone? Had I blacked out?

I struggled to hold onto consciousness. I fought my way to the surface and blinked my eyes open, holding them even though my right eye was just a slit against the swelling.

A car, I was in a car.

Jeff was in the front seat. He swerved the wheel and my body jostled, almost falling off the seat. My hand shot out to brace myself and I came more into awareness. My head pounded and my shoulders and ribs hurt, they hurt bad, but I sat up, and looked through the window, and—

My eyes widened in spite of the pain.

It wasn't a train.

Not a train, no, not a train.

The ground beside the tiny dirt road Jeff was speeding down was being ripped apart by a funnel that reached from the dark sky above to the ground, so wide I couldn't see the other side of it.

And Jeff was still just *driving*, even though the twister was barely half a field away and swerving back and forth.

"Jeff, get off the road!" I screamed.

He looked back at me, swerving the car again dangerously as he did. "Shut the fuck up!" he screamed. "I know what I'm doing."

No, no he didn't. He had no clue. I didn't know much about tornados but I knew that thing was huge and could cross the road in front of us at any moment.

Terror suddenly pumped fresh adrenaline that had me more awake than I would have thought possible.

Jeff wouldn't stop. He'd never listen to me. He wouldn't stop.

I reached for the back door of the car to push it open, but it was locked. The bastard had put on the child safety locks. Of course he had.

I turned to look in horror at the huge tornado. Only Jeff thought he could fight a tornado and win.

And I wasn't laughing, even though I was again looking at my death.

It was ridiculous, and stupid, and useless, and still I wanted to live. I wanted to fucking live, goddammit, and see a thousand more sunsets.

So I didn't think. For once, I didn't think, I didn't plan.

I reached forward with my right hand, ignoring the wrenching pain in my shoulder, and found the release lever to let the front seat lean back. I got hold of it, pulled, then yanked on the top of the chair.

Jeff screamed at me, he reached for me, of course he did.

But I was single minded.

Get the fuck OUT of the car.

No hesitation or he'd have me again. So I scrambled over the seat, reached for the side passenger seat door, opened it, and threw myself out.

The ground hit me hard. Or I hit it. And rolled, my body tumbling end over end.

The train was louder than ever and I looked up, the funnel twisting towards the road. I dragged myself to standing even as the car came to a stop fifty feet ahead.

I screamed as I stood, my right arm lancing with a pain that I knew meant it was broken. Wind lashed all around me.

Debris flew in the radius of the funnel cloud and I fought against the wind, clutching my broken arm to my side with the other as I stumbled toward the open pasture on the opposite side of the twister. Futile, probably, to try to outrun an act of God. But I was done giving in. I'd fight till my last breath.

I fought the wind, leaning my head and then my whole body against the furious gusts pulling me backwards.

I lost my footing and rolled backwards, pulled by the wind, until I was crawling against it. I scrabbled on the ground like an animal, clutching at roots with my good hand, grass, anything.

And losing the battle.

I was being dragged backwards. I dug my feet in and kept trying, finally managing to make it to a slight divot in the ground, a ditch beside the road that was full of water. I didn't care. I thought I'd heard someone talk once about ditches being a last resort if you found yourself caught in a tornado, so I laid my body out and tried to dig my good hand into the mud and muck as deeply as I could to hold on.

The train howl continued and I closed my eyes and prayed to a God I wasn't sure I believed in and thought—if this was my last moment on this earth, at least I'd gone my way. It wouldn't be at *his* hands.

*God take my soul and let me be as free in death as I found in these brief last months of my life.*

I squeezed my eyes shut and I prayed. I prayed for myself and I prayed Reece and Jeremiah and Ruth were safe.

I screamed my prayers into the wind and spit out water and clutched onto mud for life.

And the train roared on as God reached down from the sky and spent his rage upon the earth.

# 19

---

REECE SPED BACK DOWN THE DIRT ROAD TOWARDS THE RANCH HOUSE faster than was wise. The roads were mud, but Christ, the funnel cloud had been huge, and it had torn straight down the middle of the ranch.

He and Jer had watched in horror from the cab of his truck after he'd pulled his brother off the road and inside to tell him about the tornado warning right as the funnel cloud had touched down about a mile off.

Right on the ranch.

There wasn't much to do at that point except drive in the opposite direction and then stop the truck and watch on in horror from a safe distance a few more miles off.

When everything in him had wanted to drive straight back.

Charlotte.

He'd left her there. He'd just *left* her there. What the fuck had he been thinking?

The house should be safe. That was what he'd been thinking. From most storms, yeah.

But that thing... dear God. He'd chosen wrong, again. Thinking to save his brother, he'd just left her there...

He pushed the gas pedal harder.

"Slow down!" Jeremiah yelled from beside him. "You ending up in the ditch isn't going to do anybody any damn good."

Reece did slow down, but only because ahead he saw the road itself was torn up.

"Jesus Christ," he swore.

"It came across the road," Jeremiah said, stating the obvious.

Reece slowed down, navigating around debris of all kinds that was covering the torn-up road. A kid's bike, tree branches, fence posts, a car tire, all sorts of shit.

The path seemed to be almost 500 yards wide, the earth completely flattened and decimated. Before it had crossed into the road, it had run beside it, and the path headed back towards the house.

Reece navigated past the debris and once the road cleared again, he slammed his foot on the gas.

It wasn't much further to the house, maybe half a mile.

Except when he pulled up over the last hill when he should have been able to see the gable of the two-story structure... there was nothing there.

"No," he said. No, no, no. His brain refused to process even as the truck pulled up to the pile of bricks and wood and roof that had, just thirty minutes before, been a standing house.

With Charlotte inside.

He slammed the truck into park and was out in a flash, running up to the absolutely *demolished* house.

He just kept shaking his head, his brain refusing to process. No, no this wasn't— The house was safe. He'd gone to get Jeremiah who was out where it *wasn't* safe. This was the safe place. He'd left Charlotte in the *safe place*—

"Charlotte!" he screamed at the top of his lungs, running forward towards the ruin. "Charlie!"

His brother was in front of him, grabbing his chest and stopping him. "What are you doing? You can't! It's not stable."

Not stable, was he kidding?

"Charlie's in there!" Reece screamed at him, yanking to pull away from him.

"If she was then she's dead," his brother shouted back at him. "And there's nothing you can do."

Reece threw him off, knocking him backwards to the ground. Reece didn't care. Jer would be fine.

"Charlie!" Reece screamed again, running up to the rubble. It was unrecognizable as a house. He climbed up some boards that he thought might have once belonged to the porch. They shifted underneath his feet and he almost fell, but he righted himself at the last moment, trying to climb further into the rubble.

"I don't think she's in there, man."

"What?" Reece swerved to look behind him to see Buck, standing beside his brother and helping him up off the ground. "What do you mean?"

"I was watching out my window and I saw a car drive off right before the storm hit."

Reece scrambled back off the unsteady wreckage to solid ground. "What do you mean? What car?"

Buck shrugged. "Don't know. Never seen it before. Just saw the taillights booking it down the road. Then the sky got green and that noise started up like the sky was screamin' and I hunkered down in the bathtub."

Reece looked past him to see the bunkhouse, still fully intact. "And you saw Charlotte get in the car?"

Buck shrugged again. "Just saw the taillights, like I said."

"It had to be her," Jeremiah said. "Who else?"

Reece looked back at the wreckage. Who the hell would have shown up on the ranch during a storm like that? And would Charlotte really have gotten in a car with them? Had they seen the funnel touch down and realized they needed to get the hell out of there, whoever *they* were?

"Call the sheriff," Reece said.

"Already on it," Jer said, and when Reece looked over, he saw that yeah, Jer already had his phone at his ear.

Reece paced back and forth, dragging his hands through his hair, still feeling like he should be digging through the rubble. That he should be doing *something*. What if Charlotte *was* still in there, trapped? *Suffocating*? And he was just standing here like a dumb bastard, doing nothing while she choked to death? Or slowly bled out?

He imagined her dying a hundred different ways in the time it took a deputy to arrive. Twice more he'd tried to go searching for her in the collapsed house and twice, Jer had held him back and talked him down.

When he heard the sirens, he jumped up from the ground where he was crouched with his hands on his head.

The deputy let out a low whistle when he stepped out of his cruiser, and immediately pulled the radio from his shoulder and started speaking into it.

Reece ran over to him and started explaining there might be a woman inside. His words were spilling over themselves when the deputy frowned and held up a hand.

"Wait, wait, wait, you don't happen to mean a small woman, about yay tall with short, dark hair?" He held up his hand about the height of Reece's shoulder.

"Yes. Yes!" Reece grasped the deputy's shirt and dragged him closer. "That's her. What do you know?"

The deputy looked alarmed, but answered. "She's back up the road." He hitched a thumb over his shoulder. "Maybe half a mile where the road's all tore up. She was crawling out of a ditch when me and the ambulance were coming and flagged us down."

"The ditch!" Reece yanked the deputy into a hug, then let him go, looking at Jeremiah. "The ditch!"

Holy shit, did that mean they'd driven right past her earlier? And how the hell had she ended up in the ditch? But thank God. Thank God she wasn't in the house.

"Where?" Reece asked, already heading for his truck. "Half a mile back you said? Was she okay? Jesus, you said she flagged you down?"

But Reece barely waited for an answer, he was already almost to his truck.

"Yes," the deputy said. "The ambulance stopped to treat her."

Reece shouted his thanks and then he was peeling out down the road.

The half mile felt like it took half an hour even though it was only minutes. He came upon the ambulance which, thank Jesus, was still there. He got out of the car and threw the door shut, sprinting towards the back end of the ambulance.

And there she was, looking dazed as the paramedic helped put her arm in a sling, but intact. Intact! Alive!

"Charlie!" he shouted, and her head jerked his direction, right before a grin lit her face. And it was like a rainbow scattering all the clouds of the world.

Charlotte was safe and she was smiling at him.

He didn't care about any other goddamned thing in the whole goddamned world.

He rushed toward her, ignoring the paramedic and shoving him out of the way with the sheer force of his size and will.

And he wrapped himself around as much of Charlotte as he could. She winced and he yanked back.

"Sorry. Shit, sorry! How'd you know to run? Thank God, thank God. The house is demolished. I was so afraid. I was so scared—"

He grabbed her cheeks in his hands and kissed her hard, just to make sure she was there, she was solid and not an apparition. And then he kissed her gentle and slow and indeed, she didn't disappear again like so much ethereal dust.

She was safe even though he hadn't been there to save her. Maybe the whole world wasn't on his shoulders after all, but he was damn glad she was the kind of woman strong enough to catch herself and pick herself back up when she fell down.

Or, ya know, when a damn *twister* was tearing shit up nearby. That was the kind of person he wanted on his team.

## 20

RUTH AND I RENTED A PLACE IN AUSTIN SINCE THE RANCH HOUSE WAS torn to shreds. It was ironic in one of those messed up Alanis Morissette ways that I finally got to Austin, just not exactly like I ever imagined. And Ruth had certainly never intended on being there with me, though at the end of the day, she, like Reece, was just glad I was in one piece.

And as we moved in, both of us with just the clothes on our backs this time, she was waxing philosophical. "Well, nothing was going to get me off that land except an act of God and—" She threw her hands up in the air, "There we have it!"

"So you're actually doing it? Selling the rest to Reece and Jeremiah's boss?"

Ruth nodded and collapsed on a couch that had seen better days. We'd rented an already furnished apartment since it wasn't like either of us had furniture. The furniture here was...well-loved was a good term for it.

I liked it because it was so different from where I'd lived for most of my adult life. It was eclectic and fit the hippie vibe I'd dreamed of.

Ruth hated it.

She looked over at me as I sat down beside her. "Promise me we're just here for six months? Then we'll get some place better and decorate it to be cute and modern, okay?"

I shrugged. "Sure, as long as we both get jobs where we can magically afford that. We were lucky to get this."

"Ugh, I know! And I want to go back to school, so I'll be a poor student!"

I laughed and threw a throw pillow with a faded sunshine cross-stitched on it at her.

She grabbed it mid-air and stared at it, obvious distaste on her face. "What even *is* this? How did anyone think this was good décor?" She made an appalled noise and threw it to the floor.

I giggled. "You just crushed the eternal spirit of someone who spent *hours* on that labor of love."

Ruth snorted. "Well, thank fuck for women's lib so we don't have to sit around cross-stitching." She perked up, sitting up straight. "That reminds me. I went shopping." She got to her feet and picked up a grocery bag. All I could hear was clinking as soon as she lifted it. As she started to unpack it, I could see why.

First one wine bottle, then another, then a big bottle of Tito's vodka, the kind that was so big it had a *handle*.

"Jesus, Ruth, do we need to have an intervention?"

She waved a hand. "I invited the guys over. A house-warming party. I told them I'd provide the booze if they brought food. I didn't want to deal with snacks."

I shot to my feet. "Holy shit, you invited Reece? Why didn't you tell me?"

"I'm telling you now," she grinned. "Plus, I'm enjoying this reaction."

"Witch." I ran my hands through my hair and looked down at myself. It was better than when I lived on the ranch and was perpetually covered in mud, but still. "When are they coming over?"

The doorbell rang. I felt my eyes widen. "I'm going to murder you," I hissed at Ruth.

I'd only seen Reece once since everything happened last week. They hadn't let him ride in the ambulance with me since he wasn't family, but he'd visited in the hospital where they'd taken me for observation. I'd been with Ruth pretty much solidly since then, but every time I had seen him he'd immediately grabbed my hand and held it the whole time. I wasn't sure what to make of it and was trying not to make *too much* of anything. He was just concerned for me. Anybody would be, considering I'd all but knocked elbows with an F3 tornado.

Ruth answered the door while I slipped a tinged lip gloss out of my pocket and ran it over my lips.

Which was when I heard a voice that was decidedly *not* Reece or Jeremiah.

"Where is she? Penelope? Penelope, I know you're in there. Get out here right now before I call the cops!"

My blood went cold in my veins at Buchanan's demanding, entitled voice shouting for me.

Apparently Ruth didn't like it either. "Hey, fuckface, I don't know who the hell you think you are, but you need to step back off my doorstep—

"I'm not leaving till you show your face, Penelope. I know you killed him and I can prove it—"

I wondered if Buchanan had identified Jeff's body. I'd certainly been reading local coverage of the tornado. When I came across the story of a Tesla that had been found over two miles away, and about the mangled dead body inside, I'd curiously felt... very little other than powerful relief.

I came out from around the corner, hands on my hips. "Oh, so now you can prove that I have the power to call a tornado down from the sky? Please, Bruce, tell me how I managed to do that one."

Ruth just looked over her shoulder at me, blocking Buchanan from me with her body.

"You killed him first." He pushed easily past Ruth since he was twice her size and came towards me, finger pointed in my face. "Then parked the car in the path of the twister so it picked him up."

I just stood there, for once not cowed by the big oaf. "Wow. Do you even hear yourself? Did the cops buy that ridiculous theory? Is that why they're right behind you?" I pointed to the empty hallway.

"I'm certainly calling them," Ruth said, phone at her ear. "Yes, I'd like to report an intruder."

Buchanan grabbed me by my shoulders. "He was coming out here to get you and then he ends up dead? I know you killed him, you little slut. And I'll prove it."

"How did he even find me?" I asked. It was the one part of the puzzle that never fit. "Did you help him?"

"It's called facial recognition software, you dumb bitch. It can scrape public social media feeds and he saw you. He saw you." He shook me so hard my head rattled. "Out dancing with another man and breaking your marital vows."

"Hey, let go of her, you bastard!" Ruth cried. "Now he's assaulting my roommate," she said into the phone, turning it around and taking video.

Buchanan was getting more and more pissed, but he was also an attorney. He let go of me and turned towards Ruth. "I'm a private citizen. You have no right to take video of me. Turn that off. This business is between me and my best friend's wife."

"Oh," Ruth said. "Your best friend who used to beat his wife regularly? Is that the best friend you're defending right now?"

Buchanan reached for the phone but Ruth danced back away from him. "I'm livestreaming buddy," she said. "So this is already going straight to the cloud. But please, assault me as well. That'll do great things for your case, friend of a man who liked to assault women."

Buchanan looked murderous, and I knew well from hearing him and Jeff talk in the past that there was nothing they hated more than...well, *women*. But especially a woman like Ruth who wasn't going to take any shit.

I officially loved her in this moment.

Buchanan backed out the door, but that finger of his still wasn't done pointing at me. "You better watch out. I can make things very difficult for you."

"And how's that?"

That voice came from behind Buchanan. At first I thought it was Reece, but no, as they got closer I realized it was Jeremiah. "That sounded like a threat to me. Did that sound like a threat, Reece?"

"Sure did, brother," Reece said, dark eyes glaring at Buchanan.

"Don't know who you are, sir," Jeremiah said, clapping a firm hand on Buchanan from behind and dragging him back from the threshold of our doorstep several steps. "But you better rethink going around and threatening folks I consider family. It's unwise and frankly, ungentlemanly. Good day to you. Let's never see each other again."

"Aww," Ruth called out, holding out her phone. "You're trending. Where does he work again, Charlie? I bet they'd *love* to see one of their employees treating a woman with such disrespect."

Buchanan looked briefly panicked and I stepped up to the door. "Get the hell out of here and I never want to see your face again." I straightened my shoulders. "Jeff died of a *tornado* that he did not treat with enough respect. And I'm no longer the meek, unprotected woman the two of you could push around. So leave me the *hell* alone. Or I'll ruin you and take pleasure doing it."

Buchanan stormed off without another word. I imagined that him letting me have the last word was preferable only to actually having to agree with me.

I felt like a thousand bucks as his back disappeared. Not only had I told him off, but for the first time in my life, I had people behind me. Friends who would support me. Jeremiah of all people had called me family.

"Shit, Charlie, are you okay? That asshole had no right—" Ruth started.

But I just pulled her into a hug.

"Group hug!" Ruth called, reaching out for Jer and Reece. And as their arms closed around me, I felt truly loved for the first time in my life. I had people in my corner who would actually back me up and take my side.

I laughed and cried, and when we pulled apart, I finally told them all the whole story. Of Jeff and me. Of how I'd escaped two months ago and then how he'd come for me. I told them how I ended up in the ditch and how Jeff... how Jeff was finally gone forever.

I didn't know if God had finally heard my prayer or if Reece was right, and it was just karma finally catching up with Jeff, but either way, I was going to live the hell out of the life that was now mine, free and clear.

And afterwards, while Ruth and Jeremiah were in the kitchen getting drinks, Reece sidled up beside me. "So, I know everything's been nuts, but I was wondering... Would you want to go on a date sometime?"

I grinned up at him. "I'd like that a lot."

# EPILOGUE

BUCK STARED OUT AT THE RUINED RANCH HOUSE THAT HAD FINALLY driven that bitch off the land, chewing on his tobacco and then spitting into the grass.

It wasn't as satisfying as if *he'd* been the one to drive Ruth off, but at least the slut was finally gone.

But she wasn't ruined. To hear Jeremiah tell it, she was getting insurance money for the house, plus money for finally selling the last plot of land to the brothers' boss.

Buck shook his head in disgust.

Wasn't right.

That money should be *his*.

He spit again, feeling the hate rise up like bile in his gut.

This whole fucking ranch should be *his* by rights. It was stolen from him, pure and simple.

Pulling up fence posts now and again and letting out the cows— that had always been thinking small. It had taken a damn tornado to get her off the land, but Buck shook his head and spit out another long stream of tobacco juice.

Ruth hadn't even been *in* the house.

She hadn't suffered.

Now Buck, he'd suffered. His whole damn life had been suffering, and all because of *her*. And what, she just got to ride off into the sunset with all *his* money? With everything that shoulda been *his*?

That wasn't right. That wasn't fair.

And Buck was fucking tired of shit that wasn't fair.

If he couldn't get back what was due him in this life, then by God he could make sure that he'd make them that made his life this way *pay*.

Starting with that uppity bitch Ruth Harshbarger. She mighta quit this land finally, but she wasn't nearly done payin' her debts.

And Buck, well, Buck was here to fuckin' *collect*.

---

WANT MORE DARK ROMANCE FROM STASIA?
Keep reading for a sneak peek at Without Remorse: A Mafia Romance...

# WITHOUT REMORSE

CHAPTER ONE
Sloane

"Thank you, BJLover69." Sloane giggled and turned over on the mattress so that her butt was to the camera. Her laptop was positioned on a stool at the foot of her bed.

"Almost there. One hundred more tokens and I'll give myself ten spanks."

She wiggled her hips back and forth to make her booty jiggle. Butt shots were always a good go-to. "Anyone? Who wants to see this ass turn pink? Come on. You know you do." She rubbed her butt, teasing her hand toward her thong covered center.

A soft *cha-ching* noise sounded from her computer. She looked over her shoulder and saw someone in the chat room had tipped the hundred tokens she'd requested. Score.

She grinned wide. "Thank you, LadiesMansManXL. You've just made everyone in the room very happy." She shook her booty at the camera again before picking up the small paddle on her nightstand.

She looked back at the computer again when she heard another *cha-ching*.

BigDaddy288: *Say DADDY while you spank yourself*

"You got it, Daddy," she said, smiling wide. Over the past three years she'd been a cam girl, she'd learned early on that the biggest way to make bank was to smile. Always. If you dropped your smile for even a minute, guys would quit the room in droves.

And really, it wasn't hard to smile. She basically had the best job in the world. She got to chat guys up all day and occasionally get herself off—all the while making wicked bank off it.

She didn't have to deal with managers or bosses or office politics. She could make her own schedule and work as little as fifteen hours a week if she wanted.

So okay, she usually worked thirty to forty but that was because she got bored and she was saving for retirement. Her tits and ass weren't going to be this taut and bouncy forever, after all.

Speaking of.

She rubbed the paddle against the flesh of her butt cheek and then pulled back and smacked it once with a resounding spank.

"Ooo, that was a good one. Daddy, I need another."

She smacked herself again and then cried out. "Daddy!" She arched her back. "Another." She wriggled her butt back and forth in front of the camera and then gave herself three, four, and five in quick succession.

She smiled even as she breathed hard and squirmed on the bed. "Daddy, I've been a *bad* girl," she said in a high-pitched whine. She looked over her shoulder and bit her lip, the edges of her mouth still up. "I think Daddy needs to punish me more. What do you guys think?"

Several responses popped up in chat, all of them affirmative. Sloane laughed and then proceeded to give herself the rest of the five spankings. She squealed and squirmed at the sting of the last few.

She turned around and sat on the bed facing the camera.

She got up on her knees on the bed and swayed sensuously back and forth. She teased the strings of her thong. "I love hanging out with you guys. But I'm sorry to say our time is almost up. How should we end out the night? Are we gonna have a *show*? The tips have to get up to fifteen-thousand tokens if we are."

Fifteen thousand tokens equaled seven hundred and fifty bucks. Not bad for a day's work if she did say so herself.

She rubbed her thumb over her panties and cried out, biting her bottom lip. Then she rubbed up her body and grabbed her chest. Carefully though because she had nipple clamps on. They'd gotten that when the pot had reached eight thousand.

Several token tip deposit sounds came in quick succession and Sloane read through the messages.

She shook her head, a smile still on her lips. "Oh so that's how it's gonna be? Looks like we've got a bunch of orgasm deniers in the room tonight. MichaelAlmighty and Penguin_Rogue want to leave me unsatisfied. What do the rest of you think?"

Another ping sounded. "You too, MrMoneyBagz?" She gave a dramatic sigh. "Well, alright. I'm a slave to my adoring public. Just three hundred more and it'll be show time."

She dipped her thumbs into the side of her thong and teased it down her thighs. She exposed the top of her sex for just a second before covering it up again.

"Who's going to be the hero tonight and get us that last three hundred?" she asked, swaying her hips and teasing the thong again.

The tip noise sounded as a user named SuckMyPeter deposited the last three hundred and wrote: *show us that pretty cunny.*

She grinned. "Thank you, Peter. Your wish is my command." This time when she edged her thong down, she kept going until it was at her knees. She sat back onto her bottom, scrunching up her face to let her audience know her ass still stung, and slipped her thong all the way off.

Then she opened her legs wide in front of the camera.

"I'm already wet, you guys," she said breathlessly, reaching down and playing with herself. "This is what you do to me."

Okay, so really she'd lubed herself up a little before she'd gotten on cam but what they didn't know wouldn't hurt them.

Otherwise, she did always try to give her clients what they paid for. It was how she'd built up her business from being a nobody three years ago to being in the top fifty cam girls on the site.

"What should I think about to get myself excited?" she asked the chat room. "Tell me your fantasies."

Answers started popping up almost immediately. The room was feeling filthy tonight. Then again it was a Friday, and the men who could afford her fees were often feisty on Friday nights.

"Ooo, some of you are naughty, naughty boys, aren't you? But wow," she sucked her bottom lip into her mouth, "thinking about all your suggestions..."

She laid down on the bed and tipped her face back to look at the camera. The position thrust her breasts out, always a plus. Her hand never strayed from her sex. She reached down and unclipped the camera from the top of the laptop. For some shows she used multiple cameras, but ones like this, her 'clients' usually liked the intimacy of a single lens.

She continued with her show, bringing herself to the climax they'd all been looking for. She thought about the sexy bad boy hero in the motorcycle club romance novel she'd been reading earlier to get herself there.

The guys who joined her chat weren't exactly her type, though they proclaimed they loved her often enough. She always let them down easy. It was against company policy to take clients off the platform, but she knew some girls did it anyway.

Not her. She was quick to cut off anyone who didn't take her boundaries seriously.

"My time's almost up guys," she said, putting regret into her voice. She'd been working for five hours straight and she was ready for a break. Still, she always tried to keep her shows energetic.

Guys came to her for escape from their own daily grinds. One of the first rules of camming was to be yourself—she did it too many hours a day, every day, for it to be a character she played—but still. She tried to keep her moody days to a minimum.

She continued for another ten minutes, switching between the self-torture of orgasm denial and chatting with the guys in the room.

After she logged off, Sloane collapsed back on the bed, eyes closed. She clenched her teeth as she released first one nipple clamp and then the other. Her breath hiccupped as sensation rushed back in. Usually she did it on cam but the time had run out before she could.

She grabbed her sore breasts and massaged them. She barely had a second to breathe out in relief before an alarm went off on her computer. She groaned as she rolled up to a sitting position. Right. She knew she'd put a time limit on the show for a reason—her 'date' with Oliver, or Olly, as he liked her to call him.

"No rest for the wicked," she murmured, pulling her silk robe off the floor from beside the bed and slipping it on. It was only long enough to skim the tops of her thighs. That was how Olly liked it.

He'd been her client for over a year now and it was good to have regulars like him. She went to her walk-in closet and found a pair of red lace panties—another Olly favorite—and slipped them on. Then she grabbed her laptop, phone and bluetooth headset, then headed for the kitchen.

She shouldn't bitch, though. Oliver was a low-key client.

She set everything down on the little dining table she had set up in the middle of the kitchen. Then she made sure her robe was opened so her breasts were visible, her nipples just peeking out.

She clicked through the windows on her computer until she came to the one that linked the system of cameras placed throughout her house. She turned on the three kitchen cameras. One was a circular fish-eyed lens in the ceiling that looked like just another smoke detector, another was right behind the sink, and the third was the webcam attached to the top of her laptop.

Along with the bathroom cams and bedroom cams, this made up the voyeur-cam network that brought in a hefty chunk of her income. All the cameras were linked to her laptop at all times, and she could choose which cameras to have active during whatever hours she chose. It was still a somewhat novel idea—the equipment alone had cost a pretty penny. But the startup costs had been worth it. They'd paid for themselves within three months.

Which was good because she'd been *extremely* cash strapped after her great aunt Trish died and left her this place. She didn't have any other marketable skills and due to her condition... well, suffice to say, her options were limited. After four months of the mortgage going unpaid, the bank was threatening foreclosure.

That was when Sloane discovered camming. It was entirely by accident. She was looking on Craigslist for jobs a person could do from home when she came across an ad that claimed employees could make five-thousand dollars a *week*. It sounded too good to be true. Especially when she looked into it and the job requirements were extremely vague. All it said was something like, *Wanted: attractive friendly and personable female applicants who are self-motivated and good conversationalists*. She called and it eventually came out that the company was an agency looking for cam girls.

She hung up with the guy as soon as she realized what it was about.

But then she got another foreclosure notice and, out of options, she started researching it on her own. Turned out that a lot of women were making a good living as cam girls.

And you didn't need an agent to do it. Whether you were old, young, small, large—camming was for women of all shapes and sizes. The way the girls talked and wrote on forums about it, it was empowering. They got to make the rules and take home the money. Work their own hours and not be a slave to a boss or work schedule. They were mothers, college students, grandmothers.

So one night, Sloane downed more than a few shots of tequila and started broadcasting. She made three hundred dollars that first night.

Not every night was that easy. Far from it. They put new models at the top of the list and she had to fight hard to get the kind of visibility she enjoyed today. It took hard work, determination, and a never-give-up attitude. But she made enough that first month to start paying the mortgage again and to stop the foreclosure process.

Granted, she didn't eat much more than beans and ramen for a while, but she kept her house.

She shuddered even remembering that time in her life. She'd suffered almost daily panic attacks, only pulling it together for the hours she'd been on camera.

She shook her head. She'd never be in a situation like that again, she swore it to herself.

Even though she was rolling in the dough now, relatively speaking, she still lived spare. Things could change on a dime and she'd be prepared this time. Who knew how long she'd be able to cam? Yeah it was working for now, but what if guys stopped showing up to her room? She had to be smart. She invested a third of what she made each month in long term IRAs. Another third went into shorter term savings, and the last third she spent on monthly expenses.

So even though she was tired, she bucked up, slapped on a smile, and turned on her headset. She dialed Oliver's number.

"Hello?" came the familiar timid voice she'd been talking to for almost a year now.

"Hey babe," she said, walking over to the computer. "How ya doin' this week?"

"Chrissy." She could hear the confidence and pleasure infusing his tone as he said her cam pseudonym.

"Hi Olly. You ready for our date?"

"Of course. Always."

"Fabulous." Sloane clicked to connect their chat session so he could watch her on the cameras. He liked the intimacy of being on the phone with her at the same time he watched the feeds.

"Hi beautiful," he said. "You don't know how good it is to see you."

"Rough week?" she asked, moving around the kitchen to the sink. She turned on the water and started washing her bowl from breakfast. Oliver liked watching her do things like this—the mundane little daily tasks were his favorite. And even though he always requested she be naked—he liked when she worked her way up to it throughout the call—that was as far as he ever took it. All he ever wanted to do was talk.

As far as Sloane could tell, he was just a lonely guy longing for connection.

"You have no idea. But I have to thank you. I took your advice and moved out of my parents' house."

Sloane couldn't hide her surprise. She leaned her hip against the counter and looked back at the laptop camera. "That's amazing, Olly. Congratulations." She smiled wide. "I know you were struggling with that decision for a long time. How does it feel?"

He laughed a little, like he was embarrassed. "Good. It feels really good."

"Did your mom make a big scene when you left?" Sloane was genuinely curious. She'd been talking to Oliver for almost a year now and his weekly drama with his mother had been a long saga of code-pendence and dysfunction, from what Sloane could tell.

Like she was one to talk about mental health. Ha.

Still, sometimes she felt like a therapist. Wasn't listening what therapists spent most of their time doing? From all the hours she'd spent listening to guys unload, she ought to have some sort of counseling license ten times over.

"It wasn't pretty," Oliver admitted. "She wasn't happy. She threatened she'd hurt herself if I didn't stay."

God, that sounded horrible. Was it any wonder this guy had trouble making connections in the real world? "I'm so sorry, Olly. You know those are just her manipulation tactics though, right? She's the only person responsible for her own happiness. She has her path and you have yours. You aren't responsible for anyone else's journey but your own." It was something Sloane told herself often enough.

"I know. It took me so long to see her for what she really is. And you were the one who helped me with that. I can't thank you enough, Chrissy."

"You're welcome, Olly. I'm so glad you're in a better place now. Have you found a place to stay?"

"I'm working on it. But I mean it, Chrissy. None of it would have been possible without you. And I've been wanting to tell you something for a while now."

His loud intake of breath came across the line. "You're so beautiful and perfect and I just— You're perfect and—"

He broke off again until he finally finished in a rush, "—and I love you. I know I've said it before. But I really mean it this time. Like for real. I really love you."

Sloane turned back to the sink and turned on the faucet to rinse out her bowl. Oliver had been saying he loved her more and more lately. Ignoring him seemed to be the best way to deal with it.

Clients confessing their love was fairly common. All the other cam-girl friends Sloane had made online said the same thing happened to them. Sometimes it was the guys shouting it out right before they climaxed but more often it was the talkers like Oliver.

"Did you catch the latest episode of—"

"Did you hear me?" Oliver interrupted her. "I said I love you. I know you must hear that all the time, but I mean it. This is different. I want to meet you. In real life. We could move in together."

Sloane paused, warm water rushing over her hand holding the clean bowl. She pursed her lips and then turned off the water, setting the bowl in the drying rack.

"We've talked about this before, Oliver."

"Olly," he admonished. "You know I like it when you call me Olly."

She turned from the sink and sat down at the table, trying to think of how to put what she needed to say. Oliver was a good client. He booked hour-long sessions and sometimes, if their conversations were going well, he'd push it for another half-hour block. It was easy money.

She listened to him complain about his mother or they talked about TV he liked. She watched his shows so she could discuss them with him. But if he kept pushing this see-her-in-real-life-thing, she'd have to drop him as a client. She'd only had to do it twice before in her three years on the job and it was never a fun prospect.

She looked into the camera. "We've talked about this before. Boundaries are important to me. I need to—"

"At least tell me what state you live in. I just want to know how close I am to you."

Sloane shook her head. "You know I live in Florida—"

"That's just what you put on your profile." He was right. She lived in Oklahoma.

His normally soft, easy tone went hard. "I know it's not where you really live." Then he turned wheedling again. "Please, Chrissy. Give me something."

Sloane sighed. "Oliver, I—"

"*Olly.*"

"Olly. I like what we have now. It's good as is. I'd hate to lose it." She looked in the camera then, hoping he'd pick up on what she meant without her having to say it explicitly.

"What's your real name?"

She sighed and stood up. He was determined to be difficult.

"Oli—"

"The first letter."

She shook her head. "It's important for me to keep my personal and my professional life sep—" There was a click and Sloane frowned. "Oliver? Olly?" She walked over to her phone on the counter and saw he'd ended the call.

One glance over at the computer showed he was still connected to the feed though. The little token counter in the corner still rose every ten seconds.

Olly still had the hour, so as long as he stayed and paid, she wasn't going to complain. Though she had a feeling it was just putting off the inevitable.

He was a sweet guy, and lonely. He didn't sound like he got out much and yeah, she might have let that cloud her judgement a little, occasionally letting down the wall of strict separation between professional and personal.

Plenty of guys paid for the privilege of watching her go about her regular life—while she was naked. She had cameras set up all over the house. Well, not upstairs, but she never went up there anyway, so that didn't really count.

But even though she was still officially on-cam, she was good about forgetting the voyeur feed and going about her life as she normally would.

So as far as she was concerned, Oliver hanging up before his session was done meant happy hour had come early. Sure she had a shower show scheduled later and maybe a couple of privates, but those were cake.

She poured herself a glass of wine and grabbed her phone. Tipping her glass back, she took a deep swallow and switched on her end of day playlist. It started with Kesha's *Woman*. Oh yeah.

"Wanna come dance, roomie?" she asked, going to open the door between the kitchen and the living room—it was an old house, each space very segmented—and opening it.

She was met by excited meowing as Ramona scampered into the room. Ramona was an anomaly when it came to cats, as far as Sloane understood. Ramona *loved* being underfoot wherever people were— well, at least wherever *Sloane* was. There never were any other people around to see if it was people in general her kitty loved, or just Sloane.

Sloane loved her gray short-haired bestie back, more than anyone else in the world.

Sloane scooped Ramona up. "You gonna rock out to some Kesha with me?" Sloane asked, grabbing Ramona's little kitty paw and swinging with her around the kitchen.

Mona just nuzzled her face into Sloane's neck and tried to crawl up onto her shoulders. Sloane giggled and continued dancing, balancing her kitty as Mona used her as a climbing gym, meowing loudly in her ear while her tail curled around Sloane's neck. It tickled and Sloane shrieked, lifting Mona and putting her back on the floor.

"Okay, okay, I get it. Dinner first, dancing after."

Ramona meowed and nudged at Sloane's legs.

"Don't tell me," Sloane rolled her eyes. "The only thing you heard in that sentence was *dinner*."

Ramona crawled between her legs in a figure-eight pattern, continuously meowing.

"Fine, fine. God, I'm such a pushover." Going to the cabinet, she pulled out a can of Fancy Feast. Ramona made excited cat noises that got louder and louder as Sloane opened the can and upended it on a plate.

"Must be nice to be so single-focused," Sloane said wryly. She held the bowl of food in the air over Ramona's head. "Sit. *Sit.*"

Ramona's tail swished furiously and she dug her nose into Sloane's shins again.

"Sit, Ramona. Show Mama what a good girl you can be. *Sit.*"

Ramona's tail flicked back and forth for another few seconds.

"Good enough," Sloane laughed, setting the bowl down on the little mat where Ramona immediately dug in.

"What I think you mean to say is, *thank you, Mom.*"

Sloane shook her head at her but couldn't help the ridiculous smile on her face. She'd never been allowed any pets growing up. Her mom thought she was too nervous to have them, but Dr. Noah thought a pet would be a good idea. He was right, getting Mona had been the best idea ever.

Did Sloane spoil her cat and buy her tiny little best-roommate-in-the-world sweaters in addition to ridiculously expensive food, cat toys, and treats?

Yes, yes she did.

Was it ludicrous to give a cat an entire room of the house for her own?

Yes, probably, it was.

Did Sloane give a shit about what anybody thought? No. It also helped there was no one else around to judge her.

Besides, it was more like Sloane had converted the den into Ramona's room, and if you thought about it, the den was the domain of most pets. So what if she'd entirely redesigned her house space around her pet? The den was an exciting vista of climbing spaces and enough toys to delight any cat for hours at a time.

Normal people did that.

Right?

Sloane took another deep drink of wine. Who was she kidding? She'd abandoned normal a loooooooooong time ago.

And fuck it, her life was great. Just as it was. *Fabulous,* even.

She was living the dream.

She was her own boss. Sure she lived on a budget, but really, she had everything she could ever want. With all the apps and services out there now, she could have almost anything she wanted at the tip of her fingertips within two delivery days.

She kept in shape, ate three square meals a day, and ran a successful small business. Most days, her job was even kinda fun. And if she wasn't feelin' it on a particular day, screw it, she just didn't login. No harm no foul.

She was living the damn *dream*.

She restarted the Kesha song.

"I'm a motherfuckin' *woman*," she sang along at the top of her lungs, bouncing on her feet as she finished washing her dishes. She slapped the last cup down into the drying rack and then spun on her toes.

Spontaneous dance break time.

She swung her hips and lifted her arms up. She threw her head back and danced the fuck out of the rest of the song.

Fuck *yeah*.

She finished the dance with a wonder woman power pose.

She held it for a few long seconds before collapsing in a fit of laughter. Ramona meowed, busy licking her bowl since she'd finished all the food.

"It's not going to magically produce more food, babe," Sloane laughed. She picked up the laser pointer from the counter and started pointing it at the wall. Ramona abandoned the bowl of food and started jumping excitedly after the moving red dot.

"If only everyone was as easy to please as you. All right, enough with the fun and games," she said, even though she continued to point the laser to different spots as she heated up a burrito for herself.

Sloane bopped her head along to another Kesha song as Mona kept leaping for the light dot. Once the microwave *pinged*, she carried her plate into the den/Ramona's room where she had her big office desk set up by the front window.

Time to continue the business of growing her empire. Okay, okay, so maybe she was just one little measly cam girl. But some girls out there had used camming as a platform to launch whole businesses. They marketed videos, photographs, swag, had huge followings on OnlyFans—some even sold 3D silicone replicas of their vaginas. It was a brave new frickin' world. While Sloane didn't think she'd go so far as to sell pocket pussies of her vag, she was game for other creative ways to bring in income.

She clicked on her email. Oh, good. Her groceries had been delivered. She glanced toward the front door. She'd turned off the doorbell while she worked but it was below freezing out there, so it wasn't like anything would spoil. She'd go get them in a minute.

She printed out yesterday's paystub from her cam site—she was paid bimonthly—and then clicked over to her bank's website.

She loved this time of the month. She liked to pay all her bills early, then split the rest of her paycheck into neat little columns on her spreadsheet. Forty percent went into savings. Twenty percent went into long term investment accounts and ten percent she put back into the business. Buying new toys or camera equipment or lingerie. It was always good to keep it fresh and change things up.

The last twenty percent she allowed herself to spend however she wanted. She'd been saving up for a new elliptical. Her old one had started up with an unholy creaking noise that was so loud it almost drowned out her workout music.

She signed into her bank, still humming along to Kesha. She had a couple hours until her shower show was scheduled. She thought about the elliptical again. Technically, she *could* argue it was a work expense. If she—

"What the fuck?" She jerked upright in her office chair

Her checking balance was in the red. -$13.48.

She clicked on it to look at the detailed balance sheet. What was going on?

Her eyes skipped across the screen in disbelief as she saw the line that said Wire Transfer made this morning for $-7,467.

Sloane couldn't breathe. Literally. Her mouth kept opening and closing, but no air was getting in. Her hand shook as she went to click back to the main page. She went to her Savings account and coughed like she'd just been smashed in the chest with a baseball bat.

Available Balance...........$0.00

Sloane shook her head back and forth. No. *No.* There was some sort of mistake. She had thirty thousand dollars saved up. Thirty *thousand* dollars.

She stood up, shoving the chair back and stumbling over her feet. She fell hard on one knee but barely even let it slow her down, scrambling back to her feet and racing for her cell phone in the kitchen.

Phone, phone, fuck, where'd she put her stupid phone?

*There.* It was by the microwave. She ran over, snatched it up and then ran back to the computer. She clicked around furiously until she found the *Contact Us* button. She ended the session with Oliver, too. Being frantic was not a good on-camera look and she couldn't keep her cool while she tried to figure out where all her money had gone!

"Oh thank God," she breathed out when she saw the twenty-four hour 1-800 number. She dialed the number and put the phone to her ear, pacing anxiously back and forth.

"Come on, come on, come on," she murmured, waving her hand as the automated voice went through all the *this call may be recorded for quality and training purposes* yada yada.

"Hello, this is Mason, how can I help you?" a real voice finally came over the line.

She explained what happened and he asked for her name and account number. She gave them to him.

Then he asked her for the password associated with the account. She gave it to him.

"I'm sorry. That password is incorrect."

"What?" The word came out so high-pitched it was almost a screech.

"Yes, it looks like you called in to change it three days ago."

"I never called! That wasn't me."

"I'm sorry, ma'am, but I can't discuss your account details unless I have the password."

"What the fuck is wrong with you? Someone obviously hacked my account. They stole *thirty thousand* dollars from me and you're going to sit there and tell me you can't do anything about it?"

"Ma'am, there's no need for profanity. I can transfer you to the fraud and consumer protections department."

"Yes." She nodded her head vehemently. "Do that. Transfer me there."

Forty-five minutes later, she'd been transferred three more times and told that the best way for her to clear up her identity was to just "come in person to a local branch location," she wanted to scream.

When she'd tried to explain she couldn't do that and they started asking questions that had her chest tightening, she could tell that they'd all suspected *she* was the fraud. Fucking infuriating.

At least the last lady had good advice—she said Sloane should run a credit check on herself and freeze her credit while she was at it.

Which was when Sloane found out that her credit score was at an insane low of 323. Tens of thousands of dollars in credit cards had been taken out in her name. All within the past month.

She finally just had to hang up the phone when she started feeling the beginnings of a panic attack.

It was the first she'd had in months. She glanced toward the stairs and shuddered, then leaned over and put her hands on her knees, head between her legs.

"Breathe," she whispered hoarsely to herself. Shit. Why hadn't she paid better attention back when her grandma was still dragging her to therapy back in California. She'd learned methods for calming herself down when the panic attacks hit, but right now, her mind went blank except for the terrifying thought—no money, no safety net. It was all gone. *Gone.*

Sloane's breath just hiccupped and the next second she clawed at her throat, feeling like she was going to die if she didn't get another breath.

Awesome. If she died right here, then it wouldn't matter that she didn't have a penny to her name.

A hysterical laugh burst out of her and with it, a much needed gasp of air.

Okay. Okay. She shook her head, standing up and pacing again. Everything would be okay. People had their identity stolen all the time. There was probably a process to follow. Orderly steps she could take.

She just needed to calm down and find out what they were.

She bunched her clammy hands into fists and tried to breathe. Oh shit, she couldn't breathe. Couldn't breathe—

All right, screw calming down. Plan B. She'd distract herself until she could think more rationally.

The groceries! She could bring the groceries and put them away. Organizing things always made her feel better.

She managed a deep gulp of breath and headed for the front door. She did *not* look toward the stairs. She was trying to calm herself down, after all.

Flinging the door open, she was immediately hit by a blast of freezing air. Damn, it was cold out there. The large box of groceries was waiting on her stoop as expected. Sloane pulled her flimsy silk kimono tighter around her as another gust of freezing wind smacked her in the face. Brrrrrrrrr. Frickin' freezing.

On the bright side, it was bracing enough to distract her and she was breathing a little more regularly.

See? She'd get past this. Just like always.

Life threw shit at her, she maneuvered her way around it. Shit-ducker. That was her M.O.

She glanced around the dark yard as she bent over to grab the box. In the little bit of light from the house, she could make out icy patches all over the ground where the early snow from a couple days ago had melted and then refrozen. And it was snowing again.

She'd have to start calling Tom to shovel soon. Otherwise the UPS man wouldn't be able to get to her front door. It was only mid-November but come January and February, the snow could get up to a couple feet high. Plus, it looked like winter was coming early this year.

Sloane shivered. She hated winter.

She grabbed the furthest edge of the box of groceries and started pulling it in across the threshold of the doorway. Or trying to, anyway. Damn, it was heavy today. What had she ordered? Barbells? She thought for a second. Potatoes, actually. It was probably the potatoes.

With a huff of frustration, she leaned over and yanked on the box with one big pull. It slid suddenly over the threshold, knocking her off her feet. She landed hard on her ass. She slumped back on the floor and banged the back of her head against the ground. The perfect end to a perfect day.

Excited meowing had her lifting her head and looking up. Then her eyes widened.

"No, Ramona, don't!"

But Sloane didn't scramble to her feet quickly enough. Ramona was heading straight for the open door.

"Stop. Ramona!"

But the box of groceries was between Sloane and the doorway and by the time she stumbled around it, Ramona had already bolted through the door.

"Ramona!" Sloane shouted, grabbing the doorframe with one hand and reaching out uselessly with the other. "No. Come back!"

Ramona streaked across the yard and up a tree. Sloane could only watch in horror as Ramona's swinging tail disappeared into the darkness of the tree branches.

Sloane's hand frantically searched for the switch to the outside light. She finally got it flipped on just in time to see the midsize dogwood tree in her front yard start to shake. Ramona let out an ungodly cat screech, and the branches shook more, snow tufting down.

"Mona!" Sloane screeched. "Get back in here right now!" Sloane called. Ramona didn't respond to the authority she tried to put in her voice. Maybe because even the cat could tell Sloane was more terrified than authoritative. Or she was too busy with whatever was making her continue to howl and rustle the tree.

"Ramona!"

Oh God.

Sloane needed to go out there. She needed to stop whatever was happening. She had to get Mona back.

"Ramona!" Sloane yelled, louder. It was snowing and that meant it was freezing. More like ten below, taking the wind chill into consideration. Stupid cat, why had she run out there in the first place?

Ramona let out another terrified screech that had Sloane's heart in her throat. She clutched the doorframe, her nails digging into the wood. Shit, no, she didn't mean it. Ramona wasn't stupid, she was amazing.

Sloane was the stupid one. She usually made sure Ramona was shut away before she opened the front door. Ramona was too curious for her own good. Why had Sloane forgotten this time? Stupid, *stupid*.

Another yeowl, and the tree shook so much that larger and larger snow tufts fell to the ground. Ramona and some other animal in the tree were making a real racket.

Sloane put her hand over her eyes as if that would help her see into the dark night to see what the hell was going on in the top of the tree, but of course it didn't help.

Shit. *SHIT*.

Sloane just needed to go outside and bring Ramona back.

It was that simple.

Simple.

Okay.

Her fingers were already white-knuckled from her grip on the doorframe.

Because going outside was the one thing she hadn't been able to bring herself to do in the last six years.

*Agoraphobia*. That's what the shrinks called it.

Sloane preferred to just think of herself as an extreme homebody. It wasn't a big deal. Her life was great. She never felt disabled.

Until it came to something like this. She loved Ramona. And it wasn't safe out there for her. She could get lost. If she was out too long in this weather, she'd get frostbite on her ears. Not to mention that whatever was in that damn tree didn't sound friendly.

Was Sloane really going to let her suffer just because she was afraid of having a panic attack?

She squeezed her eyes shut and moved one foot to step onto the small stoop outside her front door.

"You can do this," she whispered to herself. "It's just your front yard."

She bit her lip hard, clung even harder to the doorframe, and moved her front toe out into the space beyond the front door. Her chest immediately cinched up tight.

It was the first step that was the hardest, right?

God, the wind was so icy. Sloane *hated* winter. There were enough things to be afraid of in the world without *nature* trying to kill you too.

"I'm coming, Ramona," she said confidently. She *felt* confident.

She could do this.

Of course she could. She always told herself she could go out if she ever *really* needed to. There just hadn't been any incentive.

But here it was. A reason. The best reason. To help her best friend.

She lifted her right foot into the air and shoved it out the door.

"Okay," she whispered to herself. "Now step."

She blinked and stared at her raised foot. "Step down." She held onto the door frame, feeling ridiculous with her foot lifted. "Oh my God, just take the freaking step!"

But then an insidious little voice asked, *remember what happened last time?*

The last time she'd tried to leave the house was three years ago, right after her great aunt Trish died. Sloane had made it as far as the front porch before a panic attack had her curled in a ball on the ground and crawling back to the safety of the house like a dog.

Her chest went tight again at the memory. Like her lungs were being squeezed and she couldn't get any new air in.

Shit. If she didn't get air in, it meant she wasn't breathing. If she wasn't breathing, it meant she'd die.

"Fuck!" she yelled, yanking her foot back inside and finally taking a gulping breath. She put her hands on her knees and sucked in another huge breath. Dammit, she felt lightheaded.

As soon as spots stopped dancing in her vision, she went back to the door.

"Ramona," she shouted again, her voice disappeared into the freezing wind. Maybe she'd come back on her own after she got over her curiosity?

A horrible high-pitched cat squeal of pain cut through the air.

"Ramona!" Sloane screamed, leaning out the door from where she gripped the frame.

The squealing continued. Sloane had never heard Ramona make that noise before.

It was a sound of awful pain. Or terror. What was happening? Ramona needed her.

Now.

Sloane lifted her foot again.

Ramona's screeching yeowls continued.

And *still*, she couldn't.

Shame choked Sloane as she pulled her foot back in again. She couldn't. She just *couldn't*.

She slammed her fist against the door frame. This was so *stupid*. She took a huge breath and stuck her foot out the door again.

Her heart began pounding so loud she could hear it in her ears. It was racing. She put a hand to her chest. Oh God. She was going to have a heart attack. Ramona was out there, caught by some animal, suffering, and Sloane couldn't breathe, she couldn't breathe—

Sloane crashed to her knees and bowed her head, sobbing.

And all that shit she'd been thinking earlier about how perfect her life was—what a crock of shit. First with the identity theft and now this.

She was a freak who couldn't leave her own house. She hadn't been outside for over six years and even then... God, Aunt Trish had to sedate her in order to bring her from California up here to the ranch after her grandparents washed their hands of her when she turned eighteen.

Ramona was suffering and she couldn't even—

*Please*, she prayed to a God she wasn't sure she believed in, *help!*

"Hello?" called a voice from the darkness. "Do you need some help?"

---

**The moment I saw her, I knew I was going to break all the rules.**

I grew up fighting for every scrap I had.

I earned my place in the Brotherhood through my fists and through blood.

Proving my loyalty, year after year.

And in all that time, I never asked for anything.

Until I meet *her* on a job.

She's supposed to just be collateral damage.

But for once in my life, I'm breaking the rules.

**I'm taking her for *myself*.**

**One-click Without Remorse now so you don't miss a thing!**
https://geni.us/WiRe-EN-n

# ALSO BY STASIA BLACK

DARK CONTEMPORARY ROMANCES

VASILIEV BRATVA SERIES

Without Remorse [https://geni.us/WiRe-EN-w]

Without Forgiveness [https://geni.us/WiFo-EN-w]

Without Mercy

DARK CONTEMPORARY ROMANCES

BREAKING BELLES SERIES

Elegant Sins [https://geni.us/ElSi-EN-w]

Beautiful Lies [https://geni.us/BeLi-EN-w]

Opulent Obsession [https://geni.us/OpOb-EN-w]

Inherited Malice [https://geni.us/InMa-EN-w]

Delicate Revenge

Lavish Corruption

DARK MAFIA SERIES

Innocence [https://geni.us/Innocence-EN-w]

Awakening [https://geni.us/Awakening-EN-w]

Queen of the Underworld [https://geni.us/QuOfThUn-EN-w]

Innocence Boxset [https://geni.us/InBx-EN-w]

BEAUTY AND THE ROSE SERIES

Beauty's Beast [https://geni.us/BeBe-EN-w]

Beauty and the Thorns [https://geni.us/BeNThTh-EN-w]

Beauty and the Rose [https://geni.us/BeNThRo-EN-w]

Billionaire's Captive [https://geni.us/BiCa-EN-w]

## Love So Dark Duology

Cut So Deep [https://geni.us/CuSDe-EN-w]

Break So Soft [https://geni.us/BrSSo-EN-w]

Love So Dark [https://geni.us/LoSDa-EN-w]

## Stud Ranch Series

The Virgin and the Beast [https://geni.us/ThViNThBe-EN-w]

Hunter [https://geni.us/Hunter-EN-w]

The Virgin Next Door [https://geni.us/ThViNeDo-EN-w]

## Taboo Series

Daddy's Sweet Girl [https://geni.us/DaSwGi-EN-w]

Hurt So Good [https://geni.us/HuSGo-EN-w]

Taboo: a Dark Romance Boxset Collection [https://geni.us/Taboo_Bx-EN-w]

## Freebie

Indecent: A Taboo Proposal [https://geni.us/SBA-nw-cont-w]

## Sci-fi Romances

## Draci Alien Series

My Alien's Obsession [https://geni.us/MyAlOb-EN-w]

My Alien's Baby [https://geni.us/MyAlBa-EN-w]

My Alien's Beast [https://geni.us/MyAlBe-EN-w]

## Marriage Raffle Series

Theirs To Protect [https://geni.us/Th2Pr-EN-w]

Theirs To Pleasure [https://geni.us/Th2Pl-EN-w]

Theirs To Wed [https://geni.us/Th2We-EN-w]

Theirs To Defy [https://geni.us/Th2De-EN-w]

Theirs To Ransom [https://geni.us/Th2Ra-EN-w]

Marriage Raffle Boxset [https://geni.us/MaRaBx-EN-w]

Freebie

Their Honeymoon [https://BookHip.com/QHCQDM]

# ABOUT THE AUTHOR

**STASIA BLACK** grew up in Texas, recently spent a freezing five-year stint in Minnesota, and now is happily planted in sunny California, which she will never, ever leave.

She loves writing, reading, listening to podcasts, and has recently taken up biking after a twenty-year sabbatical (and has the bumps and bruises to prove it). She lives with her own personal cheerleader, aka, her handsome husband, and their teenage son. Wow. Typing that makes her feel old. And writing about herself in the third person makes her feel a little like a nutjob, but ahem! Where were we?

Stasia's drawn to romantic stories that don't take the easy way out. She wants to see beneath people's veneer and poke into their dark places, their twisted motives, and their deepest desires. Basically, she wants to create characters that make readers alternately laugh, cry ugly tears, want to toss their kindles across the room, and then declare they have a new FBB (forever book boyfriend).

---

Join Stasia's Facebook Group for Readers for access to deleted scenes, to chat with me and other fans and also get access to exclusive giveaways:

Stasia's Facebook Reader Group: https://www.facebook.com/groups/1047415562052038/

Want to read an EXCLUSIVE, FREE novella, Indecent: a Taboo Proposal, that is available ONLY to my newsletter subscribers, along with news about upcoming releases, sales, exclusive giveaways, and more?

*Get Indecent: a Taboo Proposal:*
https://geni.us/SBA-nw-cont

When Mia's boyfriend takes her out to her favorite restaurant on their six-year anniversary, she's expecting one kind of proposal. What she didn't expect was her boyfriend's longtime rival, Vaughn McBride, to show up and make a completely different sort of offer: all her boyfriend's debts will be wiped clear. The price?

One night with her.

---

Website: stasiablack.com
Facebook: facebook.com/StasiaBlackAuthor
Twitter: twitter.com/stasiawritesmut
Instagram: instagram.com/stasiablackauthor
Goodreads: goodreads.com/stasiablack
BookBub: bookbub.com/authors/stasia-black

facebook.com/StasiaBlackAuthor
twitter.com/stasiawritesmut
instagram.com/stasiablackauthor
amazon.com/Stasia-Black/e/B01MY5PIUH
bookbub.com/authors/stasia-black
goodreads.com/stasiablack

Printed in Great Britain
by Amazon

23605531R00155